Craig A. Lewis is a former advertising executive who is presently a reporter in the Los Angeles Bureau of the National Enquirer. He is the author of *Blood Evidence*, a nonfiction account of a sensational murder. His research into the case, and in particular the drama of the trial, inspired him to write his first novel, *Testimony* – 'A great courtroom thriller. Completely engrossing' *Manchester Evening News*. He lives in Los Angeles.

Also by Craig A. Lewis

Testimony

High Profile

Craig A. Lewis

First published in Great Britain in 1995
by HEADLINE BOOK PUBLISHING

First published in paperback in 1996
by HEADLINE BOOK PUBLISHING

A HEADLINE FEATURE paperback

10 9 8 7 6 5 4 3 2 1

ISBN 0 7472 4820 6

Typeset by Keyboard Services, Luton, Beds

Printed and bound in Great Britain by
Mackays of Chatham PLC, Chatham, Kent

HEADLINE BOOK PUBLISHING
A division of Hodder Headline PLC
338 Euston Road
London NW1 3BH

For my beautiful daughter, Courtney,
who makes me proud.

Acknowledgement

I would like to thank my friend and mentor, Harold King, for his generous help in writing this story.

Had I a hundred tongues, a hundred mouths, a voice of iron and a chest of brass, I could not tell all the forms of crime, could not name all the types of punishment.

Virgil, 70–19 BC

Prologue

She turned the hot water faucet off with her toes and slowly ran her foot across the top of the steamy bath. The gentle splashing was sensual, and for a moment, she wished she were twenty again.

She took her time shaving her legs, making short, decisive moves with the pink ladies' razor. She inspected each thigh for new deposits of cellulite, and frowned that she had to put up with it at all.

This bathroom was her favorite place in the whole world. She had spent hours with the contractors and plumbers and decorators, making sure every detail was just so.

The tub itself was on a raised platform, three steps up, made from a single, expensive piece of black and white Italian marble. The hardware was deliciously gaudy, and the built-in whirlpool came in three speeds – simmer, cook, and hard boil.

The bathroom was huge by conventional standards, ten feet wide and almost twenty feet long. Best of all, the ladies' half took up over two-thirds. The large marble tub butted against one wall half-way along the room, surrounded by built-in shelves and bronze towel racks. The room displayed its decorator influence, but it was she who had made it homey by adding dozens of small, personal items.

In the shelves around the tub were at least thirty giraffes, the smallest no more than an inch tall, the largest a ceramic piece she had brought back from Africa. The largest giraffe was craning its neck sideways, as if it had been startled while feeding from a tree. It stood four feet tall and kept watch at the bottom of the bathtub's steps.

A type drawer filled with tiny figurines was on the wall next to a shower stall, and fresh cut flowers were placed at strategic places in large, crystal vases around the room.

She was careful not to slip when she got out of the tub. Her favorite pink chenille robe was hanging in a familiar place near the tub's platform. She smiled knowingly, dried off and put it on. Alan hated this robe. He must have bought her a dozen or more silk and fancy replacements, but she always came back to her terry cloth friend.

The steam from the bath had fogged her mirror, so she opened the bathroom door to allow in fresh air from the master bedroom. She sat at the vanity in front of the mirror and began her nightly regimen. L'Ambrigue Firming Gel was first, to return radiance and luster to her skin. European Eye Cream came next, to relieve puffiness around the eyes, the label promised.

She had just finished working the eye cream into her lids when her peripheral vision detected movement from the open bathroom door.

The figure at the door was a man. The cream had blurred her vision, and she had to force her eyes open wide in order to see. It was her last moment of consciousness.

HIGH PROFILE

The gun blast was deafening in the enclosed room. The .357 magnum tore a large hole through her skull and propelled her backwards in a half cartwheel against the Italian marble tub.

She fell hard, the profile of her killer reflecting in the glassy stillness of her hazel eyes.

1

Garth Stakeman parked on the front row of the penitentiary's visitor parking lot, several spaces away from a shiny, white van. He frowned when he noticed the small antennae and the KPRC-TV logo painted on the side of the van.

It was the middle of the week, 3 p.m., and the parking lot that was packed and jumping on Saturdays was now almost empty. Garth turned off the engine and stared straight ahead. The cracked concrete pavement had been warped by years of relentless Texas sun, and was little more than a merciless minefield of weeds and grass, fighting to push up between the crevices.

From the parking lot Garth could see the penitentiary's two lighthouse-shaped guard towers. The rest of the prison was hidden behind a small rise, a man-made levee that effectively discouraged curiosity seekers and helped the locals forget that there were bad guys nearby.

Encircling the facility was a twenty-foot-tall, heavy-duty metal fence, lined at the top with shiny new razor ribbon. Signs warned that the fence was electrified, and Garth wondered if the current was enough to kill or merely maim.

Garth Stakeman hated this place. He hated the smell, the drab concrete and steel buildings, the fake manners, and the suspicious, condescending way the guards treated him. Garth had hated it just about every Saturday for the last fifteen years. A hundred-mile drive, an hour-and-a-half with his dad, another hundred back.

He'd done it so many times it had become routine. He'd long ago stopped wondering what normal people did on the weekends, and on the rare Saturday when he didn't make the trip, he felt guilty. It had been years since anyone else had bothered to visit his father, and Garth knew that their ninety minutes together was the only connection Dad had with anyone in the real world.

But today was it – this was the last time he'd have to come out here.

Garth got out of the car and strolled toward the walk-up entrance. He glanced up at the guard towers and imagined two pairs of eyes looking down at him.

The young guard at the entrance looked barely old enough to vote, much less be responsible for the sizable pistol strapped to his leg. He gave Garth a nod and feigned interest.

'He's getting his papers today?' the guard asked.

Garth shaded his eyes from the morning sun. 'That's right.'

'Probably already in the General's office. Want me to call up there for you?'

'Yes, please.'

Garth's mouth was dry. He'd been nervous on the drive down. *What if there's a mistake, and they decide to keep him? What if there's some kind of paperwork foul-up, and I have to come back?*

The South Texas Correctional Institute was more modern than most prison facilities. Located south of Houston in the middle of nowhere, it was laid out like a formation of flying saucers, with five pie-shaped buildings, each connected to a larger, centralized area that housed the main security section. A soccer field was off to one side, with rickety stands and small flags for the goals, the grass worn flat by use.

About fifty inmates were housed in each of the buildings, and prisoners were segregated into groups based upon their time remaining and propensity for violence. From where he was standing Garth could only see the very tip of Building C, which had been his father's home since Garth was a teenager.

The guard hung up the telephone. 'They're ready for you. Go on up.'

Garth nodded and passed through the visitors' entrance. He didn't know why but he felt nervous, and he had to continuously wipe the sweat off his palms.

Garth Stakeman was a good looking man, dark blond, well groomed and trim, in his early thirties, with the willowy build of an Armani model. He wore stylish wire-framed glasses over green eyes, and combed his short, wavy hair back on the sides and up in front. He was clean shaven and soft spoken.

Garth took care of his health religiously. Every morning he did two hundred sit-ups and fifty push-ups, every night he jogged four miles around the neighborhood. Today, even though it was the middle of the week, he wore his favorite weekend attire – a forest green Polo shirt and tan slacks with deck shoes. Garth didn't own a pair of jeans and wouldn't be caught dead in a T-shirt.

Fifteen years, Garth thought, *one hellaciously long time to be in jail*. Fifteen years of seeing this same beige walkway (with occasional graffiti), of listening to his footsteps echo down the stone tile path, of hearing the endless banging of steel cell doors. The prison might have come between him and his father – it had with others – but Garth had been determined not to let the physical separation create emotional distance.

The first year of confinement had been the most difficult. Garth had to get used to seeing his dad dressed in prison gray, in the midst of hard timers, multiple offenders. Initially, his dad had been assigned to Maximum Security, in a bank of cells housing thirteen of the state's cruelest killers.

Over time, the system came to recognize what an asset a man like Alan Stakeman could be. In a facility of over five hundred men, many of whom didn't have even the most basic reading skills, someone of his education and background was a unique asset. For the last seven years his father had taught a literacy class twice a week.

Passing through the final check point, Garth waited quietly while the remote controlled gate opened briefly, then began to close. As he walked toward the central offices, Garth admired the landscaping around the individual buildings. It was mid-April and the flowers were in full bloom. An overnight thunderstorm had left a glossy sheen.

The walkways and bushes were all perfectly trimmed, and the morning air had the clean smell of fresh cut grass.

And he wasn't going to miss it one goddamned bit.

2

[illegible] to
[illegible]

[illegible] been a POW [illegible] prison psychol[illegible] [illegible] after his release [illegible] where he could [illegible] and there [illegible] the Third [illegible] words of the [illegible] [illegible] regard Alan [illegible] touch[illegible]

[illegible] from the Hall [illegible] and he [illegible] up to that stereotype. The general poured two cups of [illegible] tea into his matched set of [illegible] china. "I wish I could offer you [illegible] nothing, but [illegible] [illegible] with the [illegible]"

[illegible] "Good advice."

Alan [illegible] was short and [illegible]

2

They didn't call him by his name, nor did anyone refer to him as Warden. It had always been simply the General.

The General was an English transplant who had himself been a POW in Korea. He had a unique perspective of prison psychology and dedicated his career to that end after his release. In the late fifties he was offered a position where he could put his experience and theories to work in the Texas Department of Corrections. He had been the warden of the South Texas Correctional Institute for the past twenty-seven years. During that time he had come to regard Alan Stakeman as his own personal triumph; a model prisoner.

The General knew Americans expected certain manners from the British, and he worked hard to live up to that stereotype. The General poured two cups of hot tea into his matched set of Wedgwood china. 'I wish I could offer you something with a bit more of a sting, but the wife won't let me drink anymore. Said a man my age has no business letting liquor interfere with his constitution.'

Stakeman nodded. 'Good advice.'

Alan Stakeman was shorter and thicker than his son,

with white hair he kept swept back from his receding hair line. He was clean-shaven, with intense black eyes that were alert and knowing. During the last year, he had worked to get in shape by volunteering to do yard work and other manual labor. Hours outdoors had given him a tan, but try as he may, he couldn't quite get rid of the paunch around the middle.

Alan Stakeman had perfect, brilliant white teeth. His resonant voice, honed by years as a public speaker, carried only a barest hint of his southern heritage. Even in this humblest of settings, he carried himself like a member of the ruling class. Other inmates looked up to him, and made sure he wasn't bothered.

The General lit his pipe and blew out the match. 'So, Alan, have you given much thought to what you'll do out there?'

'My son has that all worked out. He wants me to get back into politics. It's the only thing I know anything about. Garth keeps talking about us going into business together.' Alan sipped his tea. 'Big plans. Maybe too big. I've been in here so long, it's hard to imagine living back in the real world.'

The General pushed back from the desk and walked over to his picture window. A speech was coming, Alan guessed. It was why he was here, the farewell address.

'Alan, let me get serious for a moment. Fifteen years is a long time. It's a long time to have the same job, live in the same house, or even be married to the same woman. It's probably hard for you to remember much about your life before you came here. But from what I can tell, at one time you had it all. And you earned your success – no one gave you anything. It wasn't luck that put you on top, it was intellect and charm and tenacity. As I've watched you for all these years – I've grown quite fond of you, you know – I feel that you and I are men alike. Driven, focused, disciplined, and destined for greatness. I have no doubt you can do it again, build yourself up from the bottom, place yourself up at the top. You can do it.'

Alan shrugged. 'A fifty-eight-year-old political consultant, fresh from prison with a murder conviction under his belt? You're more optimistic than I am. Don't get me wrong, I am very ready to get out of here. But I'd be a liar if I didn't admit to wondering about how I'm going to deal with life on the outside.'

'That's perfectly natural. When you're here all you can think about is getting out. When it's time to leave, you worry about life out there. Just give it time.'

'I will.'

'One more thing. Your freedom is stirring up quite a controversy. Take a look at the Houston papers – front-page stories on both. There might be news vans out front, and you're going to have to deal with reporters. You're high profile and whether you like it or not there are a lot of people who think you shouldn't be getting out of prison.'

Alan Stakeman leaned up in his chair. 'I'll deal with it.'

The intercom buzzed. 'Excuse me, sir,' said a flat, woman's voice. 'Garth Stakeman is here.'

The General hesitated before answering his secretary. Alan watched as he put on his face of authority. 'Show him in, please.' He looked at Stakeman. 'Well, I guess this is goodbye. I have no doubt that you're in good hands.'

Alan beamed as Garth came in the door.

The General walked around the desk and shook Garth's hand. 'Glad to be making your last trip out here, I'm sure.'

Garth smiled and looked at his father. 'You're right about that.'

The General shook Alan's hand and gave him a pat on the shoulder. 'Good luck to you, Alan. And let me know how you're doing.'

Alan Stakeman grabbed his bag. 'Well, General, I'm going to miss you, the bed checks, the license plates . . .'

The General escorted them to the door. 'There's nothing left to say except, be careful . . . and be good.'

Alan gave the warden a strong handshake. 'My plan, exactly.'

Garth and Alan tried to ignore the video cameras as they headed across the parking lot. Alan said nothing to the questions yelled by the reporters.

Garth gunned the Lexus and wheeled out of the parking lot for the last time. He was taking his father home. At the turnoff to the prison, he punched the engine again and accelerated past other photographers, spraying gravel behind as the car lunged toward Houston. Home.

For the first twenty minutes of the drive, his dad said little, content to fiddle with the CD player, call time and temperature on the cellular phone, and generally act like a kid at Christmas.

Alan pointed to a farmhouse sitting far back from the

road. 'There's another one. Does everybody in Texas own a satellite dish?'

Garth nodded. 'Out in the country they do. It's a status symbol.'

'What highway did you say this was?'

'Two-eighty-eight. It's fairly new. They built it about eight or ten years ago.'

'Funny, I've been living in Texas for the past fifteen years, just a couple of hours away from you, but I might as well have been in the middle of the Brazilian jungle. Nothing looks the same anymore.'

Garth laughed. 'Want to hear about tonight's agenda?'

'Belly dancers? A back rub? A gallon of scotch?'

'How about a nice quiet dinner at Vargo's? Didn't that used to be one of your hang-outs?'

'Vargo's! I could lose myself in one of their huge lobster tails!'

'Tail, claw, whatever you want.'

'Tail,' the elder Stakeman said, exaggerating the word. He nodded to himself, glancing at the passing landscape. 'Yes, after fifteen years, I could stand a bit of tail.'

Vargo's was an elegant restaurant built around a private lake. Moss-draped cedars cast evening shadows over a stunning collection of swans, peacocks, and other exotic birds, all visible through the glassed dining rooms. Vargo's was frequented by many of Houston's movers and shakers, and it was exactly the kind of place Alan M. Stakeman had ruled fifteen years ago.

Garth wondered why his normally chatty father had

become reserved at dinner. 'Is your lobster all right? You haven't said three words in the last half hour.'

'It's not the food – it's the people. Haven't you noticed the way they keep looking over here?'

All during dinner, Garth thought he had noticed the other diners staring at the two of them. There was little doubt about why they had been noticed. WIFE KILLER RELEASED was the headline that the *Houston Chronicle* used. CONVICTED MURDERER GETS FREEDOM was the header at the *Houston Post*. Both newspapers featured prominent front-page pictures of Alan Stakeman in their stories, and the *Post* had a color photo of Alan leaving the prison and getting into Garth's car.

Watching his dad pick at the lobster tail, Garth remembered the awful moment when the nightmare had begun.

'Madam foreman, has the jury reached a verdict?'

'We have, your honor. In the matter of the State of Texas versus Alan Matthew Stakeman, we find the defendant, Alan Matthew Stakeman, guilty...'

'...Garth, Garth, where are you? Did you hear what I said?'

Garth was embarrassed to be caught inattentive. 'Sorry. I was thinking about the surprise I have for you.'

'Surprise?'

Garth waved it off. 'Later,' he said. 'So, what were you saying?'

'I said, when is your talented wife coming back?'

'This is Wednesday, her show opens tomorrow. A couple of days would be my guess, though she's going to decide after the opening tomorrow.'

'Her work has really taken off.'

Garth gave a proud smile. 'Melissa is a very serious artist – and she deserves every bit of the success she's having. The International Cowboy Museum in Wyoming just commissioned her to do a new piece for their expansion.'

'What does one of her larger sculptures go for, say, this one they're placing in the Guggenheim?'

'That particular piece is larger than normal, almost forty feet tall. After transportation costs, agent's fees and the like, she'll probably come out of it with around $100,000.'

'That's one helluva cowboy statue. Look, you think we could stop off for a nightcap somewhere? Someplace loud and crazy.'

'Now?'

'Now.'

'But . . . why?'

'Are you kidding? I want to go where there are some women. Wiggly women. Lots of them.'

'Well, uh, sure. If you want to.'

Stakeman gave his son a look. 'If?'

Garth was sorry he'd chosen Bar Belle, a brass and wood yuppie hang-out with a reputation for singles action. Garth didn't go to bars much – he didn't drink – but he had heard that the Bar Belle was a nice place. The music was too loud and the smoke too thick, and you couldn't carry on a conversation, but it was what his dad wanted and at least no one was staring at them.

Garth had to lean forward to make out what his father was saying.

'I said, I'm glad to see all these short skirts back in style.'

Garth nodded. 'Dad – I was thinking that we might want to leave before too long. I still have something to show you.'

'There's plenty of time for that, I'd like to just sit here a while and enjoy the view, and the scotch!'

Garth could tell that his dad was already tipsy, but there was little he could do.

A petite redhead magically appeared on his father's left, and following a brief, shouted conversation, the two of them made their way to the dance floor.

There must have been fifty people bumping to the music, and Garth had a hard time keeping an eye on his dad. The first song ended and moved immediately into the next, and the two of them kept right on dancing. Garth ordered another Evian and watched.

When his dad came back to the table he was breathless.

'Did you see her! She's fantastic . . . and divorced.'

'She's very pretty. Go slow, though. You don't want to wake up tomorrow with a hangover.'

'I'm a big boy, Garth. Maureen, that's her name, has invited me back to her place for a drink.'

'But Dad, you haven't known her thirty minutes . . .'

'She's hot. And I think she's as horny as I am!'

Garth could see there was no use arguing. 'So what do you want me to do?'

The redhead returned, and stood three feet away, directly in front of Alan, dancing just for his pleasure. 'Go on home. Maureen can give me a ride. We'll talk tomorrow.'

'But Dad—'

'Tomorrow. Whatever it is, it'll wait till tomorrow.'

The smell of a woman in lust was driving Alan wild. Thank God she lived just a few minutes from the bar, because Alan was dying to be alone with her.

Maureen Madding lived on the tenth floor of a high-rise condominium near Hunter's Creek. Her terrace overlooked the Buffalo Bayou, and the sultry night air was breezy and clear as it passed through her windows. Alan didn't waste any time with small talk, and Maureen was just as ready as he was.

'So, you really don't remember me?'

He turned from the window and focused on her face. Her red hair fell in curls around her shoulders, and Alan's gaze was drawn to the milky cleavage at the top of her blouse. 'Sorry. I could lie and tell you yes.'

'It's not important. I was a volunteer in Mayor Hubbell's campaign. I knew who you were, of course. I was married then, and I used to have fantasies about fucking your brains out.'

Alan's lazy smile evaporated. He sat up on the bed and looked into her eyes. 'You are the sexiest woman I have ever known.'

In one motion Maureen pulled her dress up over her head. She slowly unhooked her bra and removed her hose. She'd told Alan that she was forty-six, but it was very obvious she took excellent care of herself. She stood there a moment to let him admire her, then walked over and took his face in her hands.

She leaned over and kissed him. A long, wet, probing kiss that he felt all the way down to his feet. Alan put his hands on her hips and drew her close.

She pulled away and gave him a grin. 'How's your sweet tooth?'

Alan blinked. 'My what?'

'Be naked when I get back,' she said and strolled seductively out of the bedroom. Alan didn't have to be told twice and he furiously tore at his clothing. He could hear Maureen opening cabinets and rustling around in the kitchen.

He lay on the bed and crossed his legs, his hands cupped behind his head. He could hear her humming in the other room, and could barely contain himself waiting for her return.

Maureen growled when she saw his erection. She was carrying a bottle of wine and a jar of strawberry jelly. 'Don't worry, the wine's chilled and the jelly's at room temperature.'

Alan watched her move to him. She dropped playfully beside him, setting the wine on the night stand. 'That's for later,' she said. She licked her lips, holding his gaze as she dipped her dainty fingers into the maroon-colored jelly.

'This is a little bit of fun you probably didn't see in prison.' She leaned over, reaching toward him with sticky fingers. 'Welcome back, baby.'

It was 2:35 a.m. when Garth gave up. He turned off the television in the living room and bolted the front door, making sure the porch light was on, though he felt sure that by now his father must be passed out somewhere for the night.

He climbed into bed. He lay on his back staring at the ceiling, imagining his dad with the redhead from the bar. *Guess I can't blame him,* he thought. *I wonder if he's using a condom.*

3

Alan Stakeman came awake to the soft strings of a Brahms concerto from a clock radio beside the bed. For a moment he was afraid to move, at once trying to stifle the pounding in his head and take notice of his surroundings. No doubt about it – this was not the Southeast Texas Correctional Institute.

Slowly it all came back to him, Maureen, gift from the gods, and her incredible fingers and lips. They hadn't touched the wine, but half the jelly was gone. He rolled over carefully, because of his pounding head, and found a note.

> I'LL BE OUT TILL ONE. IF YOU'RE STILL HERE WHEN I GET BACK, MAYBE WE CAN GO TO THE PARK.
>
> MO

Alan lay there for several minutes, reliving glimpses of the previous night in heaven. When he remembered Garth he groaned and pushed himself up from the bed. The bathroom and shower seemed a long way away.

* * *

Garth carefully re-rolled the orange extension cord and put the edger and yard rake in their proper places in the garage. He walked slowly down the driveway, then the front walk to be sure the yard work was up to his usual high standards.

Garth hired out the regular lawn mowing but saved the landscaping and fine tuning for himself. Most every Sunday morning, he'd spend two or three hours pruning, picking and beautifying the one-acre lot that surrounded his home. Since he was off for the rest of the week, he'd decided to get the yard work out of the way.

Garth lived in a 2,600-square-foot brick home, shaded by mature pine trees at the end of a cul-de-sac. He'd bought the home four years earlier, just after being named the creative director of Holloway & Partners, a large, respected Houston advertising agency. Garth had joined Holloway & Partners ten years before, fresh from college, where he had acquired a marketing degree to go with his 3.95 grade average from Rice University. His natural eye for design and strong conceptual skills brought him fast notice as a junior copywriter. He spent five years plugging away at various creative positions, helping Holloway & Partners build a reputation as an agency unafraid to take chances. Garth and his cohorts had made a clean sweep of the year's ADDY awards, and when the offer of creative director came his way, he accepted the promotion and $150,000 a year salary that came with it.

Garth found the mindless solitude of yard work a refreshing respite from his helter-skelter work week. He supervised a creative staff of fourteen, and his weekday schedule usually began by 7:30 a.m. and ended when it ended. A perfectionist, his soft spoken management style worked well among the volatile, pressure-packed creative team. Garth oversaw a wild and woolly group of egocentric artists, broadcast producers and copywriters, and his relaxed demeanor and leadership by example were a primary reason behind Holloway & Partners' continued success.

From his living room, Garth saw a yellow cab pulling into the driveway and he went down the hall to wash up. When he came back, his father was lying face down on the living room sofa.

'Dad, are you okay?'

Stakeman heard his son's voice, filled with concern, but he couldn't immediately respond. He had been all right when he woke up at Maureen's. He'd been okay as long as he stayed indoors. But when he hit the street, and the sunlight, he felt like his head had split open. The twenty-minute taxi ride to Garth's house had been a journey through hell.

'Dad?'

Alan felt his son's hands, gently prodding. 'I've been rode hard and put up wet.'

'Where's your . . . friend?'

'Resting.'

'Everything went okay?'

Alan turned to look at his son. 'Everything worked.' He grimaced. 'Aspirin?'

Garth went to the kitchen and returned with several aspirin and a large glass of ice water. 'This reminds me of my fraternity brothers in college. They'd go out on an all night beer bust or start drinking pina coladas at nine o'clock in the morning, then wake up the next day sick and whining about their hangovers. I guess that's why I never had much interest in booze,' Garth said.

Alan sat up, slowly. 'Thank you for sharing that.'

Garth handed over the aspirins. 'So, you got lucky last night.'

Alan sucked down the pills and gulped the water. 'Let's just say that I'll never again spread jelly on toast without fond memories.'

Garth gave him a curious look, but Alan let it pass. It wasn't an experience he thought Garth would appreciate.

The telephone rang and Garth took the portable phone out on the patio.

'Hi, honey. How bad are you missing me?'

Garth laughed, hearing his wife's voice. 'Lots. Have you sold anything?'

'Nothing yet, but Sara swears she has several hot prospects, including some big time banker from Los Angeles. Did your dad get home okay?'

'Yes. He's resting right now. He tied one on last night.'

'I think he deserves it.'

'Any idea when you'll be coming home?'

Garth listened to her chatting away, and looked out at the tall pine trees surrounding his back yard. He loved the sound of Melissa's voice. She had a deep, throaty intonation that was both husky and incredibly sexy. On the telephone, she was frequently mistaken for a man.

'...I'm arriving at 6:20 p.m. on Continental from LaGuardia. Can you pick me up?' she said.

'Don't snack on the plane and we'll all go out to eat. Any preferences on the restaurant?'

'Mexican. Some place the nutritionists warn us about.'

Garth frowned. 'Why do you like eating that stuff? You know it can't be good for you.'

'I'll have you know my arteries are just fine. Besides, you're the one with the ulcers.'

'That's true. Far be it from me to try and keep you healthy. Just make sure you sell lots of sculpture and I'll see you tomorrow. I love you.'

He hung up, padded to the kitchen for a glass of ice water, then wandered back to a deck chair. He and Melissa were an unlikely pair – he the non-drinking, clean-living health nut, she the tequila-swilling, junk food celebrant.

They had met at a rock concert on the Fourth of July in the summer between their junior and senior year at Rice University. Garth's attention had been drawn to a buxom brunette wearing faded blue jeans, a halter top, and a ten-gallon hat with a huge red feather. Melissa stood almost six feet tall and she owned a generous figure that could accurately be described as Rubenesque. She had a confident, earthy sexiness about her – not the least bit trashy but friendly, open, and overtly flirtatious.

That day at the concert, something about her had

grabbed his attention and wouldn't let go. Garth didn't try to hide his interest, and spent most of the day focusing his gaze on her ample rear end as she bounced to the music. On her hand was a leash leading to the largest dog Garth had ever seen. Several other guys in the crowd also admired her hearty, voluptuous beauty, but no one dared approach a woman with her looks and size who was also escorted by a 150-pound dog.

Garth didn't pay any attention to the rock bands, and as the concert wound to a close, he was surprised when she walked over to him and introduced herself. They left together and took a long drive around north Houston. Somehow they ended up at the golf course, where she spread an Indian blanket under the stars. She wanted him to make love to her, but he put her off – telling her he didn't believe in casual sex.

She looked at him like he was crazy, but they stayed up all night talking. She told him about her dream to be an artist. He told her about his goal to go to work with his father, the famous political consultant, Alan M. Stakeman.

Garth sipped his drink, staring blankly at the trees. Things were going to change now. He and his father, together.

Everything that had happened before was buried in the past. Ahead was a new beginning, and he and Dad and Melissa were going to grab hold of all the happiness they could.

Nobody was going to screw it up. Garth took another sip. Nobody.

* * *

Garth signed both of their names on the visitors' log in the lobby of One Shell Plaza. At night the fifty-story office building was tame and dim as Garth led his father to the bank of elevators.

Alan watched Garth press '28' on the elevator's sleek panel of buttons. His son had insisted on coming here, but was stubbornly mute about the reason.

'C'mon son, what the hell are we doing in this building at ten o'clock at night?'

'We're almost there. Just wait.'

The elevator doors opened and Garth led the way down wide, carpeted halls. Alan followed impatiently. He didn't like surprises. He didn't like the sense of not being in control. Finally, at Suite 2810, Garth stopped. With an enormous grin he handed Alan a key.

'Here,' Garth said.

Alan felt a surge of adrenaline when he saw the brass nameplate: STAKEMAN & SON.

'Go on,' Garth said. 'Open it.'

Alan unlocked the door, pushed it open. Garth reached inside and flipped the light switch. He motioned anxiously for his father to enter. 'Go on...'

Inside was a reception area with contemporary furniture, all new. Prodded by Garth, he walked through the marvelous suite. There were four offices, each furnished and decorated. At the end of the hall Garth stopped dramatically before the last door.

'The senior partner lives here,' he said triumphantly.

Alan entered a plush, wood-paneled space, at least

twenty feet square. It looked like a photo shoot for *Architectural Digest.* A bookcase covered an entire wall, filled with hardcovers that Garth had, over the years, brought to his father in prison. In front of the bookcase was a love seat and coffee table opposite two high back leather chairs. A four-foot-tall globe stood in the corner before a wall of glass. The office was commanded by a huge wooden desk centered on the window. An engraved desk plaque with Alan's name was the single ornament.

Alan's reaction was stupefied silence. Behind the desk, on the wall beside his old college diploma, was a framed photograph taken in 1972. A young and handsome Alan Stakeman grinned beside the newly elected Governor of Texas. Standing proudly between them was ten-year-old Garth. It hadn't struck him until this moment how devoted Garth was to him.

'Jesus,' Alan said, almost under his breath.

'Do you like it?'

'Do I like it?' Alan forced himself to smile. 'I know we've talked about going into business together, but I never imagined that you would have gone out and done all this.' He couldn't help himself, he had to walk around the office and touch everything. 'Garth, what does your boss at Holloway & Partners think about this? Do they know?'

'I told Doris I had leased the space, and that after your release we'd be going into business together. She asked me to stay on until the end of the year to get some things set up, and I've agreed. So for the next little while, it's going to be just you and a secretary. But in a few months,

Stakeman & Son will be more than just a name. It'll be you and me – together at last.'

Alan nodded. He should have seen this coming, he thought. Of course, they'd talked about it. That's all he thought it was, talk. But Garth was a doer. He should have remembered that.

'What about the money? This office space, this furniture, you have made one helluva investment here. Are you making this much money?'

'Dad, would you quit worrying about the money. I paid for much of this with the inheritance. Plus, I do pretty well at the agency. I've paid six months' rent in advance, all the furniture, office equipment and the computer are paid for, and there's $35,000 start-up cash in the bank. So tell me, do you like it?'

No, Alan wanted to say. He didn't like it. He didn't like his son mapping plans and making decisions for him.

'Dad?'

'I think it's wonderful, Garth.' He touched his son's shoulder. 'Truly.'

Garth's eyes lit up as if he'd heard God. He embraced Alan. 'It's going to be great, Dad. I promise you. Great.' The last words he choked out. 'Welcome home.'

At promptly 5:45 a.m., just as he had every morning for the last fifteen years, Alan Stakeman rolled out of bed. His body had grown used to the regimentation of prison life, and he resented the fact that his schedule was still tied to those long years in jail.

If he had still been imprisoned, he would have known exactly what the day would bring. First there would be a six o'clock head count, where each inmate was required to have his bed made and personal belongings stowed neatly away. Breakfast began at six-fifteen, and Alan's building was the first to be fed. Prison food was like most institutional fare – heavy on starches, healthy but bland – and Alan usually ate light at breakfast, fruit and cereal.

At seven it was time for a shower and shave followed by roll call at seven-forty-five. Each inmate was assigned specific work details and during the last twelve months, Alan had been assigned to general handyman work, one of a group of four prisoners who did painting, light carpentry, plumbing, whatever fix-up needed to be done around the facility. After a lifetime in white collar jobs, he had enjoyed the opportunity to get his hands dirty.

Alan shook off the memories of prison and looked around the bedroom for his overnight bag. His room at Garth's house was almost three times the size of his old cell, and here he even had his own bathroom with shower. Garth wouldn't understand the simple pleasure of washing or going to the bathroom in privacy.

They shared a quick breakfast before Garth rushed off to run some errands. Alan took care of the breakfast dishes, and sat down for a quiet morning with a book. He hadn't yet sorted out his feelings about the Stakeman & Son office, but decided he'd give it some time and see how matters progressed.

The ringing telephone interrupted his reading.

'Good morning, may I speak to Mr Alan Stakeman, please?'

'This is Alan Stakeman.'

'Hello, sir, my name is Joseph Farmer, and I am a reporter with KHOU, Channel Eleven television here in Houston. I wonder if I could speak to you for just a second?'

Alan was surprised by the call. The General had told him that he might hear from the news media, but he didn't think his case would draw much interest.

'Mr Farmer, I really don't have anything to say—'

'I understand sir, and I wouldn't be bothering you at all, except my boss is really on my ass for me to get in touch with you. At least let me tell you the reason I'm calling.'

'I'm listening.'

'I wasn't living in Houston at the time of your trial but I have gone back and looked through all the old stories. What we'd like to propose is a feature – kind of a "where is he now?" sort of thing. I promise we won't take too much of your time, just something so the folks can see what you've been up to all these years—'

'I've been in prison,' Alan said. 'It's not an experience that I think you can capture in a feature.'

There was a pause from the other end. 'Actually, Mr Stakeman, what we'd like to do is hear your side.'

Here it comes, Alan thought. 'My side of what?'

'Haven't you been saying, all these years, that you were innocent?'

'Farmer, what exactly do you want from me?'

'You're a cards-on-the-table guy, Mr Stakeman, I can see that. That's good. I'm—'

'Just get to it.'

'Sure, sure. An exclusive interview, Mr Stakeman. That's what I'm after. No holds barred. I'll ask you whatever I want and you say whatever you want. Live on the air, no editing.'

'A talk with a killer. That it?'

'Is that what you are, Mr Stakeman?'

'I'm not interested.'

'Why is that, Mr Stakeman? This would be an incredible opportunity for you. Get your message out. Let people see—'

'No, it's a waste of time,' Alan said. 'Please don't call me again.'

Alan hung up. For several moments he simply sat there, staring at the phone. He realized was trembling, his heart racing. He got up, walked around, and went outside.

Why does that bother you? he asked himself. *The guy's just doing his job. And it's not like it's the first time you've ever dealt with a reporter. No doubt it won't be the last. Relax, take a deep breath, control yourself.*

Alan felt better. He retrieved the book and sat back down. Patience was going to get him through this. Patience.

La Casa Verde Restaurant was on the edge of downtown Houston in the middle of a poor neighborhood.

It was little known by casual Mexican food lovers and featured the world's worst mariachi band. It was Melissa Stakeman's favorite place.

Alan had liked Melissa from the first time he'd met her. Prison was where they'd been introduced, when Garth brought her in to announce their engagement. She was everything Garth wasn't, an animated free spirit, wild and loud, a party girl with a soft heart. Garth was the Rock of Gibraltar. Melissa was a class-four typhoon.

'... so my agent takes me to this huge cocktail party the gallery organized. It was in a large banquet hall in the Trump Tower. And you know me, I'm moving around, sipping a beer, shaking hands and making friends...'

A chubby, mustachioed waiter brought a pitcher of frozen margaritas and a bowl brimming with nachos.

Melissa took Alan's glass, poured his drink and continued, crunching nachos along the way.

'Anyway, Sara, my agent, comes over wearing this big smile. She's escorting this little bitty Japanese man – I don't know how old he was, but he had to be at least ninety. He has this interpreter with him, not your everyday interpreter mind you, but this was a sweet blue-haired older lady from the Bronx. God, she was wearing this horrible perfume that smelled exactly like grape Kool-Aid. Anyway, the little guy shakes my hand and introduces himself – he had the softest, tiniest hands I'd ever seen, almost like a baby's. He's speaking Japanese and bowing, while this old lady with the Bronx accent is standing behind him telling me what he's saying. He said his name was Mr Tum-ah-tah, and that he was the chairman of the board and founder of a Japanese bank. He was in New York to acquire a number of art pieces for a bank building under construction in Los Angeles. He reaches in his pocket and comes out with a business card, and on the card, written in English, it said his name was I. M. Tomato of the Tomato Bank of North America. Well, I had to bite my lip, 'cause the first thing I thought of was, "Oh yeah, right, the Tomato Bank? That must be just across the street from the Celery Savings and Loan."'

Garth and Alan laughed.

'We're talking and the whole time he is still holding on to my hand, and because he's so short, I'm having to kind of lean down toward him. We talked a long time about art and stuff and he was very knowledgeable and genuinely interested in my work. He said that he was a big fan of cowboy movies and owned every John Wayne movie ever made, with subtitles, of course. He said his house in Los Angeles was crammed full of cowboy memorabilia.'

'He lives in Los Angeles but doesn't speak English?' Alan said.

'Half the year he's in California, the other half in Tokyo. Anyway, the Tomato Bank building is going to be a twenty-story office complex near Beverly Hills and he wanted to commission me to do a sculpture for the main lobby. He described exactly what he wanted, said that money was no object, but would require that we have a clause in our agreement that would allow him to come to my studio and watch me work.'

Melissa looked at Garth and they both chuckled.

'What?' Alan said. 'I missed something? What's so funny? What's wrong with him watching you work?'

Melissa took a huge gulp of margarita. 'Well, the thing is, Dad, when I sculpt, I always work alone. In the nude.'

Alan's eyes widened. 'Nude? Really?'

'Really,' Melissa said.

'Why?'

She shrugged. 'Because I feel like it. Do you want to hear the rest of this?'

'Oh, sorry.'

'Anyway, this guy's five feet tall, tops – puts him just about eyeball-to-eyeball with my tits.' Melissa snorted in her margarita and put her hands over her ample breasts. 'Can't you just see it? "Hey, Mr Japanese man, what do you think of *these* tomatoes?"'

Alan roared with laughter, leaning back in his chair. A tall man and his wife, passing the table on their way out, paused.

'Say, you're him,' the man said, pointing to Alan. 'Right? The guy in the paper? Stakeman?'

Alan stopped laughing. Melissa and Garth were suddenly quiet.

'This is him, Sheila,' the man said to his wife. 'Stakeman. The guy who murdered his wife. Tough guy. Blew her head off.'

The man is drunk, Alan thought. People were looking in their direction. *Let it go*.

'That's what happens when you kill your wife in Texas. Serve a few years, then get out for good behavior.'

The man leaned down till his face was inches from

Alan's. Alcohol stained his breath. 'You want to know what I think? I think they should've fried you, Stakeman.'

Alan glanced at the man and said nothing.

'You too good to talk to me?' the drunk continued. 'My name is Beets. John T. Beets, Jr. I ain't scared of you. I live on Woodway Street, near the corner of Woodway and the Loop. You don't like what I'm saying, just bring it on.'

The drunk wouldn't let it go. 'You got anything to say about that, Stakeman?'

Alan didn't look at him. He shook his head.

'I do,' Melissa said, walking up to the man. She stood several inches taller. 'You are a fucking asshole.'

The man looked at her, nodded. 'Yeah, I know. But I don't shoot women in the head.' His wife had his arm, pulling him. 'All right, all right, woman! Good behavior, he got. Christ, he must've been pretty goddamn good.'

Beets moved off with his wife. The mariachi band started up soon after, but nothing could drown out the tension left behind.

'Forget it,' Alan said. 'I'm getting used to jerks and drunks.' He looked at Garth. His face was red. A blood vessel throbbed in his neck.

'It's not a problem, Garth. Forget it.'

Garth was staring at the table. 'People like that...' He looked up at his father. 'People like him need to learn a little respect.'

'Nothing you can do in that situation, unless you want to fight every redneck drunk in Texas.'

'He's right,' Melissa said. 'You okay, Garth?'

'Yeah.' Garth nodded without looking at either of them. 'Okay.'

But it wasn't okay and Alan knew it. He could see Garth was boiling inside. He'd have to get used to it, Alan thought. This sort of thing wasn't going to end. Not for a long time.

4

He stood motionless while the deafening boom echoed in the designer bathroom. She had landed head first, a good six feet from the vanity, the body bouncing once before collapsing in a gruesome heap on the floor. Staring at her massive head wound, he could just make out a small area of gray at the center of the hole. The brain.

She lay motionless on her back, her brown hair spreading out from her face. Her face was contorted into a silly grin, her tongue peeking out from the edge of her mouth. For a moment he could swear he saw her closed eyes flutter.

His ears were ringing from the bang of the gunshot. He watched the crimson pool ooze slowly forward, spreading across one whole side of her face, inching downward across her upper body with the deliberate movement of a river overflowing its banks. He thought the deep color of the blood was an interesting contrast against the creamy sheen of her freshly cleaned skin.

Glancing toward her vanity, he noticed several small sprays of blood, making tiny upward trails on her makeup mirror. He reached down and straightened a small giraffe figurine. Satisfied, he went on with the plan.

He put the pistol in his coat pocket and walked out of the door into the master bedroom. He looked at his reflection in a full-length mirror, taking a moment to brush back some loose hairs. He admired his image in the mirror, looking deeply into his own eyes, as his mind went carefully through each of the remaining steps. Once he was certain that he had left nothing to chance, he began.

He walked down the second floor hallway, down the extra wide spiral staircase, through the large open den and past the built-in wet bar. He looked around the oversize L-shaped sectional couch in its custom-made conversation pit, and made his way to the French doors leading out to the pool. He unlocked the deadbolt, opened the door and hesitated.

Had he seen a sign of life in her body? Was it possible that she was still breathing?

He hurried back up the stairs and entered the bathroom. In his absence, the bloodstain had grown significantly, and the pool now covered an area almost five foot square around the body. He looked down at her chest and YES! She was still alive!

He retrieved his coat from the bedroom and withdrew the pistol. He cursed himself for almost making an inexcusable mistake. He ignored the bloodstain, walked over and stood directly above her. She gave no other sign of life, no sign of consciousness save for the almost invisible movement of her labored breathing. Better not take a chance.

He cocked the magnum and aimed at her left temple, at the soft spot between the cranium and the jawbone. He thought better and chose instead to shoot into her chest. This time he barely noticed the sound. Her limp body jerked as the bullet entered. He never took his eyes off her rib cage, watching for a full minute before accepting the result.

Now her chest was still.

5

For the first few weeks at least, Alan planned on getting around Houston without driving a car. Garth had offered to let him use his car for practice, even said he would buy Alan his own car. But Alan had never enjoyed battling traffic, and considering how much Houston had changed in his absence, taxis would do.

He found it invigorating to be outside, moving around the city, experiencing the sights and sounds of freedom. No one to tell him what to do, where or what he could eat.

The freedom alone should have made him happy, but he couldn't escape the paranoid feeling that people were watching him, judging him, like the drunk in the restaurant, or the snooty society-types on his first night out.

There was only one way to stop the judging, prying eyes, and that was what he was here for.

The taxi dropped him off in the parking lot on Riesner Street. The headquarters building for the Houston Police Department was huge, taking up an entire city block, where a constant stream of uniformed officers and patrol cars competed with the public for precious space. Alan headed up the steps, the building's massive shadow filling him with anxiety.

The last time he'd been here, he'd been wearing handcuffs.

Inside, Alan stood in line at the information desk, admiring a shapely pair of hips on the well-dressed woman in front of him. The girl at the desk directed him to the detective offices on the fourth floor, and told him that one of the secretaries up there would get him to the Chief of Detectives.

The elevator doors opened into a modern, surprisingly quiet entry area in front of smoked-glass double doors. A young woman in her early twenties with slicked back red hair was the first line of defense. Her office uniform was a white blouse, too much makeup and a what-do-you-want-can't-you-see-I'm-busy attitude. Her name tag identified her as F. M. Hughes. Her attention was focused on staying inside the lines as she typed on a form.

'Good morning,' Alan said. 'My name is Alan Stakeman. I'd like to see the Chief of Detectives, please.'

She didn't look up. 'Appointment?'

'No, but—'

'The Chief sees people by appointment only.'

Her attitude irritated him. 'I don't have an appointment, but I do need to see the Chief.'

'Concerning?'

He might well have been invisible. She hadn't even raised her eyes off the page.

Alan reached over and switched the machine off. 'Young lady, if you're going to speak to me, look at me.'

F. M. Hughes looked up at him, startled.

'Thank you,' Alan said. 'Now I need to talk to the Chief of Detectives. It's about a murder case.'

'A murder case?' She appeared alert now. 'Which—'

'The Chief of Detectives is the person I want to speak to about this. If you'll pick up the phone and tell whomever that Alan Stakeman is here ... please.'

He could see it dawn on her. 'Stakeman? Did you say Alan Stakeman?'

Alan nodded at her desk. 'The phone?'

She picked up the telephone and called somewhere within the offices. Alan felt better now, if a little nervous.

He had thought about this meeting for years. All the time he'd been in prison, he had looked forward to the day when he could confront his accusers and convince them that he was innocent. He went over his speech while the girl mumbled into the telephone.

'The Chief is in a senior staff meeting that is expected to let out in about thirty minutes. The administrative secretary says that if you want to wait...' She indicated with her eyes the couch behind him.

'I'm good at waiting,' Alan said, taking a seat.

He wasn't thrilled to be in this police station. After all, this was where it had all started. The very same building.

He closed his eyes and remembered.

First he had spent nine long hours in the interview room. Three detectives took turns, at first making him believe they were sympathetic. Later, they were clearly after blood.

A week after that first interview, he had found himself arrested, photographed, fingerprinted, followed, vilified, analyzed, and hounded.

Alan opened his eyes. The secretary was staring at him. She looked away, nervous.

He didn't care what anyone thought. He didn't care how stupid or pointless this might seem. He was here on a mission, and he was prepared to wait however long it took to get an audience. He had practiced his speech and was confident of its merit. Nothing was more important than clearing his name.

Alan couldn't get comfortable on the couch. As the minutes ticked by, anxiety built. What if they wouldn't see him? He'd wait until they did. What if they wouldn't listen?

He'd make them listen.

He flipped through several magazines and stared at his feet. He pulled up his socks and tied and re-tied his shoes. The secretary had said it would be thirty minutes, but anxious as he was, time seemed to stand still.

Finally the secretary called his name and pointed the way to the Chief's office. Alan knew first impressions were important, and he adjusted his tie and ran his fingers through his white hair on the way down the hall.

The Chief of Detectives' secretary nodded toward an open door, and Alan walked in. He was not happy when he saw the Chief's face.

'Well, well, if it isn't the famous Alan Stakeman,' Frieda Fishbein said. 'Saw the story about you getting out. Can't say I'm happy to see you.'

Frieda Fishbein was a true anomaly in the Houston Police Department. Not because she was a woman – Houston had its first female Chief of Police in the mid-eighties. No, Frieda was unique because she was a Yankee, a New York Jew, no less, who had managed to work without a net in the good-ole-boy world of south Texas.

Frieda had won her job the way any female outsider does – by working harder and longer, and being smarter than the rest of them. As Chief of Detectives, she now stood watch over seven hundred police investigators, and had received numerous accolades for both management skill and professional accomplishments.

Frieda Fishbein was anything but an attractive woman. She was built low to the ground, wide without being overweight, sporting a man's-length haircut and tough, inquisitive eyes. She was in her late forties, with a dark, wrinkled complexion and thick glasses. She had a Roman nose and a thin mouth, and wore the expression of someone who had heard it all.

'I, uh, didn't know you were here,' Alan said. 'I mean, I hadn't heard about your promotion. I guess congratulations are in order.'

She was staring, sizing him up. 'Yeah, I guess.'

'I appreciate you seeing me. I know how busy you must be,' Alan said.

She lit a new menthol and blew the first smoke straight up. 'Awfully polite, aren't you, Stakeman? You sure you wouldn't rather crawl across the desk and choke me?'

The idea appealed to him. 'I feel no animosity towards you.'

'I couldn't believe it when they told me you were here,' she said. 'I've been trying to imagine what you could possibly want to see me about.'

Well, she wasn't going to make this easy, that was obvious enough.

Alan sat down across the desk. Her piercing gaze unnerved him. 'I'm here because I want to clear my name,' he said, trying to keep an edge off his words. 'That's all.'

Frieda Fishbein had been a detective for two years at the time of the murder. Alan could still remember the focused, measured way she had interrogated him, and later, her unshakable testimony from the witness stand. To his way of thinking, she was single-handedly responsible for his conviction.

Her wide, ugly face suddenly lit up with a smile, and she snickered at his tone. 'This some kind of a joke, isn't it? 'Cause I know you didn't come down here to tell me that you are an innocent man?'

'It's not a joke. The justice system failed. You were wrong. I went to jail because I couldn't *prove* I was innocent!'

She laughed, and the grinning expression made her even uglier than before. Then her expression changed. 'You're out of your fucking mind. I was there – remember? I saw the crime scene, the body, the evidence. I saw the pathetic way you tried to build an alibi, and your feeble attempt to pull the wool over our eyes. You went to jail because you fucking did it! If I had had my way, you would have gotten the death penalty.'

Her intensity made the hairs stand up on his neck. 'So it

isn't possible that Frieda Fishbein might have made a mistake?'

'I've made mistakes,' Fishbein said. 'But sending your sorry ass to jail wasn't one of them.'

Alan looked down and saw that his hands were trembling. He felt like she was taunting him, trying to push him into doing something stupid.

He was determined to stay calm. 'If you would just give me a chance—'

She slammed her hand down on her desk. 'Chance? Don't talk to me about your fucking "chance"! What about your wife? What was her name – Justine? Did you give Justine a chance? Fuck you. Fuck you and every other lying, pitiful convict who starts this shit. I have no interest in anything you have to say. You did it. I nailed you. You went to jail. If the Texas Parole Board, in all its infinite wisdom, thinks it's time you got out, fine. Go out and get a job bussing tables. But stay the fuck away from me.'

Alan rose wearily to his feet. 'I'm going to clear my name, Detective.'

Fishbein grinned. 'Yeah – well, go blow your socks off.'

Garth parked his car in the underground parking lot and walked up concrete steps to a metal security door. Melissa's sculpting studio was in a rundown-looking building in the warehouse district just northeast of downtown Houston. He pushed the button on the intercom and waited for her response. He could hear country music in the background when she answered, and he knew she probably had one of her CDs blaring on the stereo.

'Who is it?'

Garth looked up at the video camera. Because her studio was in a seedy part of downtown, she'd installed a sophisticated security system with cameras, monitors, and door locks that used number codes instead of keys.

'Dwight Yoakum,' Garth said. He could hear her laughing.

'I'm in the modeling room,' she said, and he heard the buzz and click of the door electronically opening.

Melissa's studio was in a huge building fifty feet wide and over two hundred feet long. During the heyday of the Texas oil field, this building had been used to store large parts for drilling rigs.

Garth's footsteps echoed across the cavernous interior. He had telephoned Melissa just before he left the office, and he hoped she would be ready by now. The modeling room was at the other end of the building, adjacent to a small living area that had a bed, a shower and a kitchenette. The modeling room was where she did her early sketches and small scale clay versions of the larger sculptures.

Garth came into the room still immaculately dressed from the office. He wasn't surprised to find her nude and, as usual, not ready. 'Melissa, you knew I was on my way over here. We can't go shopping with you dressed like that.'

She wiped some clay off her hands and pushed the hair out of her face. 'Why not? The guys at the mall won't mind.'

She walked over, took his head in her hands and gave him a wet kiss. Her tongue slipped inside his mouth as she pressed against him. She was perspiring and had a sexy, musky smell. She put her arms around him and rubbed up against his suit jacket.

He felt his body begin to stir and he pushed her back. 'C'mon, Melissa. Are we going or not?'

Garth had always been reserved and tentative about sex, and was intimidated by Melissa's aggressive ways. She had a habit of complaining about his low sex drive and prudish manner.

Melissa giggled and came right back to him, pulling his mouth to hers. He could feel her quick breath as she kissed his cheek and neck.

'Okay Melissa, you're horny. But can't we wait until we get home?'

'For once, Garth Stakeman, would you just be spontaneous? We can go shopping anytime.'

She smiled and rubbed her face on his neck, her hot breath coming in spurts. She kissed his neck and flicked her tongue in his ear, and an uncontrollable spasm ran down his back. She felt his resolve begin to weaken, then suddenly he pushed her away.

'I don't want to do this right now,' he said, walking to the other side of the room.

'You never want to do it,' she said.

Melissa looked at the cloth that she'd spread on the floor, and fantasized about attacking him. She'd tear his suit, pull down his pants take him in her mouth. She thought about his hands and fingers and tongue on her smooth skin.

Garth sat down across the room and began flipping through a magazine. Melissa stared at him for several seconds, expecting that at any second now he would smile and tell her that he was kidding. That he wanted her as badly as she wanted him.

But the moment had passed. He was distracted and distant.

She whirled and stomped out of the room. She jumped in the shower and washed the sweat and desire off her body.

What's wrong with him? she thought. *We never have sex anymore!*

She let the cool water beat down on her tanned skin, and remembered what it was like to be loved and caressed.

It had definitely been too long. She didn't like feeling frustrated.

6

Garth wiped the director's chair with a towel, making sure he didn't get any water stains on his dress slacks. Though he knew he would be outside on location all day, he was still dressed for the office. He wore a beige wool suit, and he wouldn't loosen his tie no matter how high the temperature.

On location Garth was in his element, supervising filming of the television commercial with the production company's 22-man crew. They were filming a group of commercials for Texas Bob's Bar-B-Q, a regional chain of restaurants and one of Holloway & Partners' largest clients.

It was somewhat unusual for Garth to spend so much time personally overseeing a shoot – that's what agency producers were for – but everyone knew Texas Bob Quintell was cantankerous and Garth was the only one who could keep Quintell in line.

Texas Bob Quintell was as big as an NFL lineman, with a Marine haircut and hands the size of catcher's mitts. Though physically intimidating, he was known to be ruled by astrology and superstition, even so far as to keep a psychic on the corporate payroll.

Texas Bob spoke with a slow drawl that only came in two volumes – loud and louder. He was always around when his commercials were being shot, even though he had a great deal of professional respect for Garth. For his part, Garth knew how to make the boisterous Bob feel involved, consulting him frequently during pre-production meetings and during the actual shoot.

Bob's chair was next to Garth's under a tent in the parking lot outside of one of the Bar-B-Q restaurants. Garth had the storyboards laid out on a table and was going over the script with his client.

'This next shot is where the cowboy and his lady are entering the restaurant. To let you know where this shot is in the commercial, this is where our cowboy has won the prize at the rodeo and he and his girl are going out to eat. This is a quick little scene, probably no more than about two seconds.'

Texas Bob ran his hand across his stubby hairdo. 'Aren't we going to show them pulling up out front?'

'We don't need to. We'll cut to the two of them opening the door. We don't have to show them getting out of the truck.'

Shooting began, and Garth watched quietly while the commercial director took the actors through a dozen or more takes, changing lighting and camera angles, making sure they'd have what they needed in post-production.

Garth noticed that Texas Bob wasn't as talkative as usual and wondered if something was wrong. 'Are you alright, Bob?'

Quintell nodded over his shoulder and he and Garth walked away from the production crew. This particular shot was wrapped and the crew had started tearing down for the next location.

Bob stared off into the distance. 'Garth, did you ever feel like you're a hamster in a cage?'

Garth was startled. 'Excuse me?'

'You know, like that little rodent running on his wheel. He's running and running and running, but never getting anywhere.'

Garth didn't know what to say.

'I've gone just about as far as I can go in the restaurant business, and frankly, I'm bored to tears. Oh sure, I could keep opening up new locations from now till doomsday, but that'd just mean more employees, more travel, more headaches. I've been thinking about trying out something new.'

Garth understood. 'Any idea what you want to do?'

Texas Bob smiled and leaned closer. 'Politics.'

Garth's eyebrows arched. Texas Bob a politician?

'I've been active in politics for a long time, but always behind the scenes. I've talked to some friends in Washington with the Republican National Committee – you know I was the Texas finance chairman for President Bush – and they're all saying that I'd be great as a candidate.'

Garth agreed. 'You sure have the personality for it.'

'I don't know how much you keep up on politics,' Bob began, 'but one of the US senators, Philip Smart, is up for re-election in the fall. Now this fellow's been in the Senate for three terms – almost eighteen years – and he's so used to being on the government tit that he's out of step with the times. I've snooped around a little, and I'm starting to believe that a guy like me, a self-made man with conservative values, could beat that liberal bastard. What do you think?'

Garth knew that Quintell's family had been active in Texas politics for years. Quintell's mother was in the Texas House during the sixties, when women in public office were a rarity. And Waylon Quintell, his cousin, was the current Secretary of State.

'You certainly have the right genes,' Garth said.

Texas Bob smiled. 'I've been thinking about this for a while. I'm forming a steering committee and have started making the rounds of all the big-wigs. Since Philip Smart has been in there so long, a lot of folks are afraid to run against him. About the only other significant Republican I've heard about is Joanne Wheeler – that little fireball mayor of Fort Worth.'

Garth remembered hearing that name in the news. 'Wasn't she mentioned recently in connection with some under-the-table deal?'

'That's right, plus she's in her late forties, hasn't ever been married, and looks like a bull dyke. I don't think that conservative Republicans are gonna want to vote for a crooked queer.'

Garth nodded.

'So what I'm getting to, Garth, is that I'm gonna do this, and I was wondering if I could get you on my team. You're the best advertising man I've ever seen, and I was thinking, maybe your father might be available.'

Garth got excited. 'That's a great idea! And I'm sure Dad would love to talk to you.'

'I realize that, you know, he's just getting out and all, and I'd be less than honest if I didn't tell you that a lot of my people don't want me to even talk to him. But before the, you know, trouble, everybody knew that Alan Stakeman was about the best political consultant there was.'

Garth couldn't contain his excitement. 'He's the best. Would you like for me to set up a meeting?'

Texas Bob nodded. 'That's exactly what I'd like. And you come too. Why, I'll bet you that if the three of us put our heads together, we can elect the first United States senator who knows how to slow-cook ribs!'

Alan Stakeman had his nose in a book, a treatise, really, on the latest trends in southern politics. The author was a political science professor from the University of Texas, a weasel whose knowledge of politics was restricted to the classroom, who wouldn't know an original idea if it bit him in the ass.

In the week that had passed since Garth told him about Texas Bob's plans, Alan's interest in Stakeman & Son had blossomed.

If he could get involved in a major Senate campaign, Alan thought, that could put him back on top. The opportunity to get involved in a big race was like a gift from heaven, but he couldn't let his personal ambition blind him to the political realities. In order for it to be a good deal for

Alan and Stakeman & Son, Texas Bob Quintell had to be a viable candidate.

Alan got butterflies in his stomach just thinking about the possibilities. Politics had always been in his blood. He could vividly remember his first campaign. The brother of a good friend provided Alan's introduction into politics, and he could still feel the enormous satisfaction that came when the votes were tallied and Alan had elected a new Harris County tax assessor.

During the next decade Alan had become a star, managing no fewer than sixty campaigns in Texas, Louisiana, Arizona, Oklahoma, Missouri, and Arkansas. His impressive list of clients included two Texas governors, three Louisiana congressmen, a US senator from Arkansas, nine big city mayors, and four lieutenant governors, along with an assorted group of district attorneys, judges, and state legislators. He had handled the southern campaign for three democratic candidates in the presidential primaries.

Alan had a sixth sense about politics, realizing long ago that it was a different animal, requiring special marketing and advertising techniques. 'You can't sell a candidate the same way you sell a car, or a refrigerator,' he used to say. And the clients came in droves, anxious to take direction from the master.

Standing at the 28th-floor window in the Stakeman & Son office, he longed for the old days of glory, when his mere presence in a politician's camp gave instant credibility. But before he could return to that place of honor, he'd have to find a way to clear his name.

'Yoo-hoo. Anybody home?'

Alan wasn't sure but he thought he recognized the voice. 'Back here.'

Melissa strolled into his inner office, taking time to admire the decor. 'My stomach's growling. Want to grab some lunch?' she asked.

Alan was glad to see her, realizing that he'd been spending too much time in quiet reverie.

He glanced out the window. 'It's raining pretty hard, though.'

Melissa smiled. 'That's okay. We can take the Underground.'

'The what?'

'The Underground. It's a walkway underneath most of the downtown buildings. You can practically go anywhere and never have to stick your head outside.

'How about Italian?' Alan said. 'I'd love some pasta.'

The waiter led them to a nice table in the center of the room. The lunchtime crowd was well-dressed and animated, and Alan could tell from the aroma that the food was great.

'Garth told me that Stakeman & Son might get their first client,' she said.

Alan smiled. 'Keep your fingers crossed. He's coming in tomorrow. I hope I can talk politics intelligently.'

Melissa patted his arm. 'He'll be putty in your hands. Besides, Garth said he was really rich.'

Alan knew how important money was in the political arena, especially for a neophyte trying to build name recognition. 'Money is important, but it's not everything.

Nowadays, it's all about how good you are on television. Candidates have to be able to think on their feet, and deliver quips in fifteen- and twenty-second sound bites.'

'One thing I was curious about,' Melissa said. 'Does Texas Bob know where you've been for the last few years?'

Alan had wondered about that too. Garth said that Quintell had mentioned Alan's criminal record, and that made him start to worry. How hard a sell would Alan be? Even if the chemistry between himself and Quintell was terrific, the candidate would surely have doubters on his steering committee who would be nervous about the publicity of having Alan on the team.

'Garth says he knows everything and doesn't care. That's hard to believe, but we'll see.'

'You'll impress the hell out of him. He won't be able to say no,' Melissa said.

Alan was grateful to have her positive vibes working on his behalf. The food arrived and they chatted casually through lunch. Alan noticed that Melissa kept glancing over his shoulder, her gaze focused on two women sitting behind him. 'You look distracted,' he said. 'Is something wrong?'

'Those women at that table. They've been staring a hole through us ever since we came in.'

Alan knew which ones she was talking about. He'd noticed their reaction when he came in. 'Probably looking at me. It's all this publicity – they recognize me from TV and the newspapers.'

Melissa waited until the women were looking their way and then gave them the finger.

'What's it been like around your house? Has Garth been getting lots of calls from reporters?'

'I know a lot of them called him at the office. He hasn't said much about it, just that he'd said no to all interviews.'

'Do you think he's handling things okay?' Alan asked. 'I mean, the other night, I thought he was really mad at that guy in the restaurant.'

'He didn't say anything. But you know Garth. Trying to get him to talk about his feelings is like pulling teeth.'

Alan and Melissa finished their meal in silence, and passed up the high-fat offerings from the dessert tray.

Alan could tell that Melissa was still distracted by the way people stared at them. 'Doesn't that drive you crazy? The way people try to look right through you?'

Yes, it does, he thought, *more than you realize*. 'Nothing I can do about it.'

Melissa watched a waiter fawn over a table of businessmen. 'What was it like?'

Alan knew what she meant. 'Prison?'

She nodded.

He'd been trying to forget. 'In some ways it was better than I expected. And in others . . .'

Her face was sympathetic, concerned. 'What was the worst part?'

Alan felt a cold tingle go down his back. 'The isolation. The monotony. And the feeling that there was no one in the world who gave a damn if I lived or died. Except for Garth, and you.'

Melissa looked at him and nodded. 'How awful.'

'I remember when my lawyers were putting together our

case. I had given them a list of names, friends who I thought would make good character witnesses at the trial. I went to a meeting at the attorney's office, maybe three weeks before the trial was to start. I came into the room and the lawyers couldn't look me in the eye. They told me that they had interviewed everyone on my list – more than twenty people. Only one person was willing to testify on my behalf. That really hurt, that so many people were so quick to believe that I was a murderer.'

Alan remembered the day the police came to his office and arrested him. He'd stood in the lobby, surrounded by secretaries and office staff. The week before, he'd been on top of the world, having just elected the new mayor of Houston. His telephone hadn't stopped ringing with calls of congratulations. Then came Justine's murder and, in a matter of days, all the calls had stopped.

'Dark days,' he said, pushing his plate away. 'The worst part, I was never allowed to grieve for my dead wife. There was never time to experience the loss, the way a normal spouse would. From the moment the police arrived that first morning, I was their only suspect. Even before the funeral, I was out interviewing lawyers.'

Melissa waited until the waiter had refilled her glass of iced tea. 'What about the prison? Did you ever, you know, have any trouble with the other prisoners?'

Alan snickered. 'I was careful not to drop the soap in the shower. But no, not at all. For the first week after the trial, I was in the jail in the basement of the courthouse. Then when I was transferred out to the prison, I was isolated in this cell block that only had maybe thirty other guys.

Everyone had their own cell, and no one came on to me at all. I don't know if it was because of my age – most of the other guys were in their twenties – but no one even asked me to dance.'

'What about now? When you see people giving you the evil eye?'

Alan knew she wanted to ask him the question. 'It bothers me, but there's nothing I can do about it. Besides, I know the truth. I didn't kill anyone.'

Melissa blushed. 'Dad, I hope you know, I never thought you did.'

'It's natural to have doubts, Melissa. I mean, I was tried, convicted, and served my time. Who wouldn't have a tiny twinge of doubt?'

'I don't. And you know Garth doesn't.' She took a small bite. 'You know, my father died of cancer when I was twelve. And after he was gone, my mother started drinking and never was the same. Getting to know you, first through Garth, at the prison, and now here, well, it's like I have a father again.'

She reached across the table and put her hand over his. 'Garth has waited so long for the two of you to be together. This business thing means everything to him.'

Alan was touched by her affection. 'It means a lot to me too. It's my chance for a new start. I hope it works.'

'It will. Just wait. You'll both be rich and famous.'

Alan spent the rest of the afternoon alone in the office. The telephone company got the phones installed a little before five, and he was about leave when the telephone at the front desk sounded off. He assumed it was either the telephone company or Garth calling to make sure the installation had been done.

'Hello,' he said. 'Uh, I mean, Stakeman & Son.'

He was surprised to hear a smooth female voice. 'Alan Stakeman, please.'

'This is Alan,' he answered.

'You probably don't remember me,' the voice said. 'My name is Carolyn Seville.'

He racked his brain and came up empty. 'No, I'm sorry, I don't remember. But what can I do for you?'

'I just wanted to call and see how you were doing. I saw in the paper that you and Garth had gone into business together. I called information and got your number.'

Alan tried to place the voice but couldn't.

'I was a friend of Justine's. You remember Justine, don't you? Your wife? The woman you shot in the head? The woman you murdered?'

Alan felt his pulse start to race and he slammed down the telephone. He leaned back in the chair and closed his eyes, trying to calm himself.

He had to put a stop to all this, he thought. He had to find a way to convince Fishbein he was innocent.

Just stick to the plan, he told himself. *Stick to the plan and everything will be okay.*

7

Texas Bob Quintell stretched his long legs out and sipped hot coffee from a Styrofoam cup. He gave Alan a long look that seemed to say, 'Impress me.'

Alan had ushered his prospective client to the couch in the conversation area of his personal office. He thought that not having a desk between them might make Bob feel more at home. Something about Quintell's body language made Alan nervous, but he forced himself to make small talk.

'Glad you could come, Mr Quintell. You know, I would have been perfectly willing to drop by your place,' Alan said.

'Call me Bob. No, too many interruptions at my office. Besides, I wanted to see your home base. Y'all have a nice set-up. Garth told me that he was coming to work here, too. You should be proud – your son's very talented,' Bob said.

Alan could see that Texas Bob's respect for Garth was genuine. 'Yes, he's much more together than I was at his age. Even in my early thirties, I still had a lot of growing up to do.'

Texas Bob put his coffee cup on the small table between them. 'I've got a daughter who's just about Garth's age. Never had a son. We raised five girls – my youngest is a senior at Notre Dame.'

Alan smiled. The first meeting with a prospective political client was always a little awkward. Most of the time, they felt a need to tell you their life history. 'Well, er, Bob, let's start with the most important question. Why do you want to be a United States senator?'

Texas Bob put his elbows on his knees and let his hands lock together between his legs. 'You know, my wife has been asking me that same question. I've been active in politics since college, but it's only been in the last few years that I've started thinking seriously about running myself. I always enjoyed being a part of electing other people – you know, the kingmaker but not the king?'

Alan smiled. 'That's what I do.'

'I've been with winners and losers, in big races and small time stuff. It's a lot of fun when you're on the winning team.'

Alan knew exactly what he meant. 'Then tell me, what makes you think you can take on a guy like Philip Smart? I mean, if there ever was someone who typed the smooth, urban politician, it has to be him. He's got that look – touch of gray, tailored suits. Do you really believe you can beat him?'

'"A Kennedy Democrat" – that's what he calls himself. I'll tell you what my mother said. You know, she was in the State House for several years?'

'Right,' Alan said.

'She always used to say that any incumbent can be beaten, because he has a record. If you hold public office, there is always going to be a sizable group of people who think you're a fool.'

'Absolutely. And Senator Smart has seemed to be out of step lately.'

'The national Republican party sure thinks so. That bill he authored to outlaw some handguns is a joke. Maybe that kind of liberal crap will fly up north, but in Texas, a man's pistol is a valued possession, ranked up there with his dick.'

Alan laughed. His personal political views weren't nearly as conservative as Texas Bob Quintell's, but he couldn't help but like the folksy way this fellow expressed himself. 'You know, Bob, you shouldn't say "dick" on the campaign trail.'

Bob smiled. 'No? Well, okay. How about "cock"? Seriously though, about Senator Smart. I have pretty good connections in Washington, and the word is that the National Rifle Association and the National Conservative Movement are getting ready to let go with some big bucks for whoever wins the Republican primary. I expect that to be me.'

Alan liked his positive attitude, but wanted to see just how much of a straight shooter Bob Quintell could be. 'I'm curious, Bob, what made you come to me?'

Texas Bob stood up and walked over to the window, and looked out over the downtown skyline. 'You're the best. I have the nucleus of a campaign organization, some great people who are well-connected and enthusiastic, but I need a real pro to run the show. Everyone tells me that you're the man for the job.'

Alan knew there was more to it than that. 'Plus I'm available, and willing to take you on. All the other consultants you interviewed said no.'

Texas Bob spun around. He was obviously surprised that Alan knew he had been elsewhere looking for a campaign manager. 'Other consultants?'

A couple of old contacts of Alan's had told him about Quintell's efforts to hire two Washington consultants and one firm from Austin. All three had turned him away, saying that Philip Smart was too formidable. 'Sure. You met with the Snyder Group and David Burch in DC, and my old friend Wilson Langely in Austin.'

Bob smiled. 'Okay, so I talked to them. But I decided that I wanted to work with you. I think you're a lot hungrier than they are, with more to prove. I'll get more for my money.'

That made sense. 'Fair enough. But from now on, let's you and me have a little agreement. You don't try to bullshit me, and I won't try to bullshit you.'

Texas Bob sat back on the couch and chuckled. 'How much money do you think it will take to win this election?'

Alan had anticipated the question, and was glad he had done a bit of research. In 1994, Texas had almost nine million registered voters, scattered over a geographic area that made statewide campaigns very expensive.

'From what I can gather, there will be at least four candidates in the Republican primary. Joanne Wheeler, the mayor of Fort Worth, seems to be the front-runner, but you can't forget L. C. Wyatt, the congressman from El Paso...'

'I know L. C. He's an old drunk who is way past his prime. Joanne Wheeler is the only one we need to worry about.'

Alan agreed, but knew that it was important for Texas Bob to realize that he was a political virgin. 'You have to worry about everyone. You're an unknown, and you'll have to prove yourself to the voters.'

'I can do that.'

'In the primary, we'll concentrate all our media efforts on the major metropolitan areas. That's where the Republican base is. We'll need to buy a six-week flight of television commercials in Dallas, Fort Worth, Houston, San Antonio, Austin, Beaumont, El Paso, and Amarillo. We'll support the TV with radio spots and billboards in all those markets, and I want to do two mailings to every Republican household in the state. That means in the primary, for media advertising alone, we'll need to raise about $20 million. Figure another $5 million for travel and other expenses.'

'No problem,' Bob said.

Alan liked Texas Bob's attitude about money. He knew that this fledgling politician was wealthy, and he was curious to know just how much he had. 'Bob, what is your current net worth?'

Texas Bob walked over to the couch and sat down. 'I knew I was gonna have to put up my own money, at least to get started, so I had my accountant run the numbers for me.

Most of my worth is on paper, though I do have a little socked away.'

Texas Bob took a piece of paper out of his coat pocket. 'Let's see, the franchise company has about a hundred restaurants, with around two million shares of stock. My family and I own 1.6 million of those shares. As of last Friday the stock was trading for $18 a share, so you figure it out. I have an account at E. F. Hutton with around $3.5 million in stocks and bonds. I own my house in Houston, a condo in Florida, a ranch in Colorado, and a few pieces of investment property here and there. All together the real estate is worth about $15 million.'

Alan laughed, and didn't even try to hide his envy. At one time, he too had been a millionaire, though certainly not in Texas Bob Quintell's league. To Alan, money had never been a priority, but a tool, a way of attracting power and influence. Of course he enjoyed the material trappings of success, but he was never one to spend much time thinking about acquiring wealth.

But now things were different. Alan had nothing in the way of material possessions. All of his cash had been used up in his murder trial – $300,000 to his defense lawyer alone – and the real estate and stocks were sold off to pay his debts when he went to prison. Garth had put up the money for this office, and had bought Alan's clothes, food, even provided the roof over his head.

'I wish I had one-tenth your money,' Alan said.

Texas Bob played with his Rolex. 'If I was you, I probably would too.'

Alan and Bob shared a laugh and got down to serious

business. Alan told his new client he would need to learn how to talk to the news media. He advised him to always be available and honest, in order to build a relationship with the Texas reporters. They discussed a variety of issues – abortion, tax reform, health care, the Middle East, Cuba, Bosnia, Haiti, and Alan suggested several books and magazines that would help Texas Bob sharpen his knowledge of current events.

'You know, Bob, there's one issue that we haven't talked about. Crime.'

Texas Bob nodded. 'Crime? Oh, I'm against it.'

Alan grinned. He was impressed by this businessman. He seemed intelligent, quick on his feet. 'How do you feel about capital punishment?'

'I'm all for it.'

Alan knew he was moving into a delicate area. After all, he was a convicted murderer, and in some states, the crime for which he went to jail could have earned him the death penalty. Alan knew it was important to address the issue of his criminal record, to clear the air and make sure that it wouldn't be a source of conflict later. 'I guess this is as good a time as any to bring up my situation.'

Alan waited, hoping that introducing the subject would give Texas Bob the entree he needed to make his feelings known.

'Well, Alan, I'd be less than honest if I didn't tell you that there are a number of people in my campaign, good people, who are nervous as hell about bringing you on board.'

'I agree that it's an unusual situation, but it is something we can manage. Tell you what – let's do a little role playing.'

Alan walked over to the couch and did his best impression of a reporter. 'Mr Quintell, tell us how you can say you're tough on crime, when you have a convicted murderer running your campaign?'

Texas Bob looked uncomfortable.

Alan crossed his arms. 'C'mon, Bob, how would you answer a question like that?'

Texas Bob shifted in his seat 'I'd have to say, "Alan Stakeman has paid his debt to society, and the law says he is a free man. There is no question that he has a lot of political savvy and since I intend to win a seat in the US Senate, I wanted him on my team." How's that?'

Alan liked the response. 'That works. Now try this one. "Mr Quintell, do you believe in capital punishment? And if so, do you think your campaign consultant should have been given the electric chair?" What would you say to that?'

Texas Bob was noticeably uncomfortable. 'Listen, Alan, I'm not ready to deal with that right now.'

'You're going to have to address it sooner or later. You'll be much better off if you have thought through your response to every possible question.'

'I know you're right, but let's deal with this later. I want to solidify our deal. I assume there will be a retainer fee? What will it take to formalize our arrangement?'

That was another subject Alan had given a lot of thought to. He knew that handling this campaign would be a full-time job, and he had to have a retainer that was sufficient to cover his time and effort.

'The retainer is $150,000, with an additional fee of $50,000 a month during the balance of the campaign. For that I will perform the duties of your campaign manager, though if you want a friend to have the official title, that's probably a good idea. In addition to managing the campaign strategy and logistics, we'll produce and place all the media advertising for the standard fifteen per cent agency commission.'

Texas Bob shook his head and walked over to the couch. He opened his briefcase and pulled out a checkbook. Alan felt the familiar stirrings in his gut, as he watched the beefy hands write out the check. Three weeks out of prison and someone was giving him $150,000!

Texas Bob signed the check and tore it off the pad. He leaned forward and looked Alan straight in the eye. 'There's just one thing, Alan. I'm willing to do my part in this campaign. I'll work hard, raise money, make speeches, kiss babies, and talk to the goddamn press. I'll listen to your advice, and probably take it ninety-nine per cent of the time. I can handle the media questions, and I can take care of any pressure from my own circle.'

Alan knew what was coming.

'But I can't handle any new revelations about your past. We'll deal with your record and all, but we couldn't take the heat if something else happened that attracted the attention of the police.'

'I understand. But don't worry about that. All I'm interested in is getting you elected to the Senate. I intend to eat, drink, and sleep for Senator Bob Quintell.'

Texas Bob handed over the check. 'My wife Ellen and I would like to take you and Garth out to dinner Friday night. Check with Garth and give me a call.'

Alan walked his client to the door, thrilled at his victory. Memories flooded his consciousness. He remembered dozens of meetings and dozens of retainer fees he had collected in years past. He had received more money, but never had a check meant as much as this one.

He really was back in business again. And all he had to do was make sure he elected this overgrown cowpoke to the United States Senate. God, if they could just pull this off – the clients would be lining up!

He had turned the corner, and the first sale was under his belt. Everything was looking up. Now it was time to work on his own image. He had to find a way to get Chief of Detectives Frieda Fishbein on his side, because until he had cleared his name, he could never completely regain his stature in the business world.

He kissed Texas Bob's check and propped his feet up on his expensive desk. Yes, he had to make Fishbein listen to him. He had to find a way.

8

Garth closed his office door and sat down at his desk. His office at Holloway & Partners was nicely decorated using the simple, Shaker-style furnishings seen in the other executive suites, but Garth didn't like the rectangular desks and opted for an antique roll top desk he found at a designer studio in Galveston.

Garth knew he hadn't been focusing on work. The long list of projects waiting for his approval had grown to an unmanageable level. He was going to have to buckle down or he'd find himself so utterly behind he'd never catch up.

There was a solid knock on his door and Doris Holloway stuck her head in. 'Got a minute?'

Garth put on his best work face and nodded. 'Sure, Doris, come in.'

Garth had a great deal of professional respect for Doris Holloway. She had worked her way up the hard way, beginning as a Girl Friday, and working her way through every position in the advertising agency. Client relations became her strong point, and her grandfather, the agency's founder, had proudly turned the firm over to her in 1983. Garth hoped she wasn't here to give him a hard time.

Doris was in her early forties, with short blonde hair that, thanks to Mr Charles, showed no signs of graying. For most of her adult life she had been a competitive body builder. In work clothes she looked fit and trim, but underneath, Garth knew there was a sculpted, developed figure bursting with muscle definition. Doris had wide, light blue eyes and was used to fending off advances from many of the men she did business with.

'Garth, I've never been one to mince words, so I'm going to just lay it on the line. The creative staff is way behind, and I get the impression that you're the reason. We both know that this isn't like you – normally your department is the most organized in the office. There's got to be a reason – something's been bothering you lately. What is it?' she asked, 'and tell me what I can do to help.'

Garth was used to receiving praise for his work, and he didn't think his performance had been that poor. 'Nothing's bothering me. I just have a lot going on right now, and it's taking longer than usual to work through the assignments. Everything will be alright in a couple of weeks.'

Doris held his gaze for several seconds and Garth thought she was trying to read his mind. 'That's not good enough. I have a list here. Our television campaign for Houston Power & Light is three weeks behind schedule. We were supposed to be on the air with the new commercials by this Friday, and I've been told that you haven't released the storyboards to the production crew. We have that package design project for Grandma Taylor's Bean Mix – their marketing vice-president just chewed me out, saying the pencil roughs were due a week ago. The artists haven't received your layout instructions. I've promised the Chamber of Commerce a first draft script of their tourism video by Monday, and the copywriters say they haven't seen any notes from you. I've been dodging calls from the Texas Ford Dealers' Group, and someone just told me that Texas Bob is going to run for the Senate. C'mon, Garth, give me a clue – what's the problem?'

Garth could see she was irritated, but he didn't believe she was totally justified. It wasn't as if he had fallen behind on purpose. 'The storyboards were sent over this morning, and I've got some notes ready for the bean product. The Chamber film is at the top of my list of things to do, and as soon as I make some headway on that, the car dealers will get some attention.'

Doris stared at him for several seconds. He felt like a schoolboy who'd been called down in class. Though they were only about ten years apart, Doris had always mothered him. Her look softened. 'This is the first time I can remember bitching at you. You've always held up your end better than anyone I've ever seen. That's why I'm so concerned. I know there has to be something bothering you, and I want to help. Everything okay at home?'

The last thing in the world he wanted to do was share his feelings. 'Everything's fine.'

'Melissa's doing alright?'

He didn't want to talk about Melissa. 'She's great.'

'What about your dad? He's at home now, isn't he? How's that going?' Doris asked.

'Dad's busy setting up the office, and he's living with Melissa and me. He seems to be adjusting very well.'

'It must be hard on him, you know, after being gone for so long.'

Garth wasn't in the mood to talk about prison. 'Yes, I guess it is.'

'You visited him a lot when he was in jail, didn't you?'

Garth remembered those long drives to and from the prison. 'Every Saturday from ten till noon.'

Doris crossed her muscular legs. 'You know, I've never asked you anything about all that. What was your mother like?'

Oh God!, he thought. There were two questions that Garth hated the most. One was 'Wasn't it hard to see your father in jail?', and the other was 'What was your mother like?'. The truth was, Garth didn't like to think about Justine Stakeman – his relationship with her had been strained and difficult. He had always been tight with his dad, and after the murder, they had become even closer.

'To tell you the truth, she wasn't much of a mother.'

Doris's mouth dropped open, and Garth could see that she was stunned by his attitude. 'Oh, uh, okay.'

He pushed, hoping to shock her and put an end to the questions. 'To tell you the truth, she was a bitch. She messed around on my dad, didn't take care of me and the house. I don't think she ever loved him, and I know she didn't give a damn about me.'

Doris pulled herself up in the chair and straightened her skirt. 'Oh.'

Garth was enjoying her discomfort. He could see her little mind working, trying to decide the quickest method for getting out of this conversation.

Doris Holloway couldn't look him in the eye. 'Well, I've got a meeting across town, so I'll get out of your hair. If you need any help, let me know.'

She practically ran out of his office and he heard her quick footsteps in the hall. Garth stared at the closed door for several seconds. He could still smell Doris's perfume, and took a few moments to savor the shocked expression she had had on her face.

Garth leaned back in his chair and burst out laughing. That'd show her. Now, maybe he wouldn't have to hear any more stupid questions!

Alan still wasn't used to hearing the office telephone ring. He was standing in the outer office and sat down at the unoccupied secretary's desk.

'Stakeman & Son.'

'Hi, Mr Stakeman, this is Joseph Farmer from KHOU-TV. We talked a couple of weeks ago? Remember?'

'I remember telling you that I wasn't interested in giving an interview.'

'I know you did, sir, and normally I would take that and not call you back. But my boss is a real dyed-in-the-wool asshole, and he just won't leave me alone. All I need is just thirty minutes of your time. We can shoot it at your place, our place, anywhere you like. I'd even be willing to prepare a list of questions ahead of time – give you a chance to see what we're going to ask. Now, does that sound so bad?'

'Why do you guys give a shit about what I have to say? Where's the story in an ex-con trying to get his life in order?' Alan asked.

'C'mon, Mr Stakeman, you're certainly not the typical ex-con. Everybody in this part of the country has heard of you. You had one of the most sensational trials in Texan history.'

'That was fifteen years ago.'

'So what? People are fascinated by rich, important guys who have a fall from grace. And most defendants can't afford the legal firepower you had. You hired Morgan Villard, considered to be the best trial lawyer in the country. You brought in criminologists, psychiatrists, even that blood-pattern expert from New York. So don't try to tell me you're just a regular guy – hey man, you're news!'

Alan knew that more publicity could hurt him. 'Be that as it may, I still don't see the point in opening up old wounds.'

'This could help you. Really. I know you've said all along that you didn't kill your wife. Well, here is your chance to tell your side of the story.'

Alan knew the reporter no more cared about him than the man in the moon. And while he wouldn't mind trying to win a few hearts and minds, he knew it would cause too big a stir for the Texas Bob campaign. 'Look, I understand what you're saying, but I can't help you. Tell your boss that I have no intention of giving you an interview now or in the future.'

'Wait, Stakeman, wait. They never found the murder weapon. Where did you hide the gun?'

'Go fuck yourself!' Alan slammed the phone into its cradle and jumped to his feet, sending the secretary chair crashing into the credenza.

Alan loosened his tie and walked back into his office. He poured three fingers of scotch and knocked it back. He was angry at himself for letting the reporter get to him. He had to control himself better.

Garth, Alan and Melissa were led to the best table in Tony's Restaurant. Garth didn't think it was such a good idea to have Melissa tagging along, but there wasn't anything he could do once his father had invited her. It was obvious that Texas Bob had a lot of clout at Tony's Restaurant – the mâitre d' almost climaxed all over himself when they said they were there to dine with Mr Quintell.

The Stakemans were escorted past plush formal furnishings to a small raised area with the best view in the restaurant. The wine steward and the waiter each acted as if they were ready to lay down their lives in order to be of service to Bob and Ellen Quintell.

Alan seemed to be reveling in the attention. Garth could tell his father was thrilled to be in the company of a business giant, the man who had believed in the old Stakeman magic enough to cough up big bucks. Even though Garth wasn't much for socializing, he recognized the need to break bread with the client. Besides, Texas Bob was paying.

On the ride over, Alan had suggested that they not talk business unless Quintell brought it up first. That was fine with Garth. He watched as his father skillfully charmed the pants off of Ellen Quintell, and discreetly flirted with an attractive blonde seated a few feet from their table.

Garth was happy to see his dad so animated. It was almost as if Alan had been cured of a terrible illness. His cheeks looked rosier, his eyes were shining, and he was his old self again. In this setting, Alan looked at least ten years younger than his real age.

'Tell me, Bob – what's the story on this psychic you've got on the payroll? Is that for real?' Alan asked.

Garth had heard about Texas Bob's psychic/astrologer for years. He couldn't imagine anyone letting a weirdo like that dictate important life decisions.

'I met her when I was a senior in college – when a fraternity brother of mine talked me into going to some of the strip clubs in Dallas. It was around midnight when we got to this club, and we grabbed a table right up front. No sooner had we sat down than this loud drum roll starts and a pink spotlight hits the center of the stage. Then, this little-bitty stripper comes out. She looked like she was only about four feet tall! At first I thought it was some young grammar school girl, seven or eight years old, until she took her top off. And then I was staring at the most perfect boobs I had ever seen. They had shiny tassels hanging down from each nipple!'

Texas Bob and Alan giggled like teenagers. Ellen Quintell quietly sipped her martini and smiled politely at Garth. From the look on her face you would think they were talking about Sunday School.

'She danced for two or three songs; at one point she had one tassel spinning clockwise, and the other swinging counter-clockwise. By then we were all three sheets to the wind, and by the time she was through, I knew that I was in love. So me and my buddy sneaked around backstage, peaking in doors until we found her dressing room. By that time I was so drunk that I was ready to offer her my soul for a little time in the sack. We walk in this dressing area, and she's just coming out of the bathroom, stark fucking naked. I'm standing there drunk as hell, grinning like a fox eating shit out of a hairbrush. She strolls over, reaches down and takes my hand and just holds it. She closed her eyes and puts both of her tiny lithe hands over my big ones, the whole time never saying a word. Finally her eyes pop open, she looks me up and down and tells me that before I'm thirty, I'm going to be a millionaire. Then she turns around, puts on a bathrobe and walks out of the room. Turned out she was right too, about that, and damn near everything else she ever told me.'

A fortune-telling stripper? Garth thought that was the most ridiculous thing he had ever heard. Obviously Texas Bob believed it, and at the very least Alan was intrigued.

'Damn, Bob, you think she might be able to tell me anything?' Alan asked.

Texas Bob sucked down most of a double bourbon and water and slapped Alan on the back. 'Why, we'll just see what we can do. I'll call her tomorrow.'

Garth hoped his father was just being charming, and didn't really want to meet the psychic. He decided to change the subject. 'Tell me, Bob, what's the latest on your campaign? Have y'all decided you're going to make a formal announcement?'

'Alan and I have talked about that. The Republican primary election is September 15th. Qualifying is the first week in July. I'm thinking sometime around the middle of June. How's that sound?'

Garth couldn't remember seeing Texas Bob so easy going. He wasn't selling and there weren't any loud demands of the waiters. This wasn't the obstinate Texas Bob Quintell he was used to.

'Whatever Dad thinks. He's the expert,' Garth said.

Alan's face lit up with the compliment. Bob ordered another round of drinks, and was again disappointed when Garth asked for another Evian water. 'My father told me not to trust a man who wouldn't take a drink.'

Garth ignored the comment and tried to force himself to have a good time. Melissa was much more subdued than normal, though she was still drinking wine like there was no tomorrow. He probably should pay more attention to her, but right now, he just didn't feel like it.

Dinner arrived and Texas Bob and Alan continued to regale one another with tales of the good ole days. Bob told stories about building restaurants and making millions. Alan told stories about campaign victories and the ad business in the sixties and seventies. Garth noticed that Ellen Quintell had said little during the evening and wondered if she always deferred to her extroverted husband.

She was a lovely woman, and carried herself with the bearing of royalty. But Garth thought she had all the signs of being a hopeless drunk. She must have downed at least a half dozen martinis, though she hadn't shown the slightest sign of drunkenness. Ellen Quintell sat quietly next to her husband, occasionally smiling at his stories, more often staring blankly in front of her, obviously a thousand miles away.

Texas Bob was dominating the table talk, and Alan was letting him be the boisterous host. 'I first met George Bush about twenty years ago, when he was the head of the CIA. His cousin Richard is an investment banker and we worked together when I took my company public. George is a nice enough fellow, a bit uptight for me, but nice.'

Garth liked George Bush, but he'd loved Ronald Reagan. His political views were distinctly conservative, and he'd been a registered Republican since he turned eighteen.

Alan, on the other hand, was a lifelong Democrat, and Garth knew his father was biting his tongue in front of Bob and his Republican bravado.

Texas Bob was making a point about the Bush administration when he looked over Alan's shoulder at a bald-headed man walking toward his table. 'Well, well, Mr Mayor. So nice to see you again.'

A handsome, balding man Garth didn't recognize strolled over and shook Bob's hand. Texas Bob made small talk with the guy before introducing him to the Stakemans.

'Garth, you may not know this gentleman. This is William Hubbell. He was the mayor of Houston during the late seventies.'

Garth stood up and introduced himself. He recognized the name, and noticed that the tanned William Hubbell had seemed taken aback when Garth said his last name. 'Nice to meet you sir. Mr Hubbell, this is my father, Alan Stakeman.'

Garth glanced down at his father and saw a look of total

disgust move across his face. Alan didn't raise his eyes to the man when he spoke. 'Bill and I know each other.'

Mayor Hubbell was noticeably uncomfortable. 'I heard you were out, Alan. Don't tell me you're planning to stay in Houston?'

Garth could feel the chill all the way to his side of the table.

'Yes, I am,' Alan said.

'I hear Mexico is nice. So is Europe.'

Garth watched his father struggling to maintain his composure.

'Now wait a minute,' Garth said. 'Who the hell do you think you are? You can't talk to him that way.'

Mayor Hubbell never took his eyes off Alan. 'Young man, I'll speak to this convict any way I choose.'

Alan's jaw was clenched but he remained seated. 'Okay, Bill. You've made your point.'

Garth pushed back from the table and threw his napkin down in disgust. 'You're way out of line. You better leave right now.'

The former mayor gave Texas Bob a judgmental look. 'You should choose your friends more carefully, Quintell.'

Garth took a step closer. 'Go fuck yourself.'

Hubbell glanced at Alan, then turned and left.

All eyes in the restaurant were on Garth. He glanced toward the Quintells and saw Texas Bob sipping on his bourbon. Ellen forked idly at her dinner salad. Melissa picked imaginary lint off the tablecloth.

Alan reached up and put his hand on Garth's arm. 'Sit down, son.'

Garth was trembling, the adrenaline surging through his veins. His eyes were locked on the departing William Hubbell and he didn't blink until the former mayor had left the restaurant.

Garth realized that the entire restaurant was staring at him and he blushed.

Texas Bob spoke up. 'I never liked that man. He's a prissy, stuck-up son-of-a-bitch.'

Melissa took a sip of her margarita. 'He's a prick.'

Ellen Quintell, who hadn't said three words all evening but had knocked down ten martinis, smiled demurely and said, 'He doesn't have a hair on his ass.'

Garth felt the anger build in him like a geyser. *Fuck you, Hubbell,* he thought. *Fuck you and all the stuck-up, arrogant people who think like you!*

When are they going to leave him alone?

9

One month later

Melissa Stakeman took the last bite of the ice cream bar and licked the remaining chocolate from the stick. She was sitting cross-legged, her feet tucked under her legs, on a wooden bench under a tree at Hermann Park near the Rice University campus. Melissa had spent the last half hour at the zoo, watching a proud, male lion snooze underneath a tall tree.

She sat quietly on the end of the bench, admiring the detail on the large statue of a famous Confederate general and the city's namesake, General Sam Houston.

It was a hot, sunny day in late June. Above the brilliant green of the rolling grass and tall oak trees was a clear blue sky. The temperature was in the low nineties, with a light breeze that couldn't compete with the insufferable humidity. Melissa watched a collection of moms with toddlers tend to their small children. The mothers were huddled in the shade, trying to stay cool and keep an eye on their active children.

Melissa was crying.

She couldn't stop.

For several weeks now, she had been plagued by a growing sense of anxiety. Her marriage was in trouble – she just knew it.

Ordinarily Melissa managed to be bright and cheerful, on the surface at least, unaffected by the minor irritations of life. But there was nothing minor about this. She could feel Garth slowly, surely, consistently growing distant, pulling away from her. She was certain her marriage was crumbling, and didn't know what she could do to stop it.

It was almost noon, and Melissa headed for the spot where she had arranged to meet her agent. She walked slowly, her eyes looking down at the sidewalk, her hands stuffed deep inside her pockets. She was wearing a pair of old coveralls, a baggy, comfortable outfit that she preferred in hot weather. The faded blue jean material was soft, and the coveralls had a large, red patch in the shape of a half-moon sewn on the seat. She had chosen a bright red T-shirt and crumpled straw hat to complete her attire.

By the time she reached the 'Gorillas' Habitat' the tears had stopped.

Sara O'Donnell saw her before Melissa looked up. 'Hey, fashion plate, you better watch where you're going.'

Sara was Melissa's agent, confidante, and oldest friend. They had grown up on the same street, shared secret kisses with their first boyfriends (behind the gym in the fifth grade), and were closer than most sisters.

Melissa raised her eyes and forced a smile. 'Hi. You been here long?'

'Not long. I didn't mind.' She nodded in the direction of a tanned hunk walking nearby.

Sara O'Donnell had shoulder length wavy, red hair, gray eyes and a pale, freckled complexion. She had graduated from Stanford with a business degree, and had managed Melissa's business affairs since she first started to sell her sculpture. In addition to Melissa, Sara also represented three neurotic painters, one psychotic photographer, and she owned a gallery in the ritzy River Oaks section of Houston.

'I'm glad you could get away. I really need to talk to someone,' Melissa said.

Sara took her eyes off the hunk and gave Melissa her full attention.

Melissa was almost sorry she had called her old friend. She felt as if her relationship with Garth was falling apart, but she couldn't put her finger on exactly what was wrong. Though she dearly loved Sara, she knew that her friend wasn't the best person to give advice to the lovelorn. At thirty-two, Sara had already been married and divorced three times; she fell in and out of love with the cycles of the moon.

'It's about Garth and me,' Melissa said. 'I don't know why, but I think I'm losing him.' Her eyes teared up again and she looked away.

They entered the gorillas' area, where a wide moat separated visitors from the perfect reproduction of an African jungle. 'What's happening? I thought everything was just fine?' Sara asked.

Melissa had never expected that she could have something

as frighteningly common as marital trouble. Sure, she knew couples had fights and arguments all the time and, of course, divorce was a fact of life. But she and Garth had seemed so immune to all of that.

'How long have you been feeling this way?' Sara asked.

'I think it all began when his dad got out of prison.'

'Why don't you start at the beginning.'

Melissa hesitated, catching sight of a young couple, obviously in the first flush of love. She quickly looked away. 'Garth and I have known each other a long time, and we've always had an honest relationship. You know Garth. He's not a real talkative guy anyway, but lately he's really become, I don't know, completely withdrawn. We get into these little fights, over nothing, and afterwards, it's like he's punishing me by giving me the silent treatment.'

'What are the fights about?' Sara asked.

Melissa ran her fingers through her long brown hair. 'Sex. I want it. He doesn't.'

Sara leaned back in her chair. 'That could be serious. Do you think he's fooling around?'

Melissa shook her head. 'No. I may be naive, but I really don't. Actually, the little arguments about sex started after we'd had a big fight about something else. A few weeks ago, right after his father got out of prison, I dropped by their office and took Alan to lunch. It was a perfectly innocent thing. We went out and while we were eating, I asked Alan about prison. I swear, it didn't seem to bother Alan at all. But when I told Garth about it later, he exploded at me. He started cussing, and he called me stupid. He told me to keep my fucking curiosity to myself!'

'Why did he get so mad?' Sara asked.

'I have no idea. I've known Garth for over ten years, and you could count on one hand the number of times he's raised his voice. He's acting like a different person, a totally different person.'

Sara scrunched her eyes together. Melissa knew she always did that when she was concentrating. 'Well, maybe he just had a bad day.'

'But it hasn't stopped! We all went out to dinner last night, and I'm not exaggerating when I say that Garth didn't even look at me during the entire meal. When we got home, I waited until we were alone, in bed. I was very calm and sweet when I tried to talk to him. He wouldn't respond. He just sat there, staring at me, with this weird look in his eyes.'

'Sounds just like my second husband. The only meaningful conversation we ever had was about community property.'

Melissa was terrified that she might ultimately lose her husband. 'Don't say that. You don't think Garth and I could end up, you know, divorced?'

Sara looked away. 'Maybe.'

'I don't want that. My career's going great guns. I want to have a baby. Maybe two. But you can't get pregnant if you can't get laid.'

'Let me ask you something. You and Garth are so different – you're totally opposite. How did you two ever end up together in the first place?'

Melissa had vivid memories of every moment she and Garth had been together. She still got tingly whenever he kissed her. 'I don't know – who knows why they're drawn to someone? He was smart. Funny. Very creative. Sara, I've got to do something, otherwise I have this awful feeling that things are just going to get worse.'

Sara grabbed a handful of her red hair, and held it off her neck, letting the breeze get in. 'Maybe you should talk to someone. A professional.'

'I don't know, Sara. I don't know if it's really that big of a deal. I mean, maybe this is just something that I have to wait until it blows over'

'How long has he been acting this way?' Sara asked.

'A couple of months. What did I do that was so wrong?'

'You didn't do anything. Garth's the one who's acting like a jerk. Why don't you go to see my therapist? He's very easy to talk to, and he has a lot of good ideas.'

'I've always been suspicious of those psychiatrists or psychologists or whatever they are. I mean, aren't these the people who tell you that your life is fucked up because your mother didn't let you draw on the walls?'

'I'm talking about getting in touch with your own feelings. Right now, you're confused, angry, hurt, and you don't know which way to turn. Mitchell, he's my therapist, will help you get a clear idea of where you are, and where you need to be.'

'Is he really good?' Melissa asked.

'I think so. I've been seeing him every Thursday for the last eight years, and look how together I am!'

Melissa and Sara laughed at the absurdity of that statement. All of a sudden, the tears began again, and Melissa grabbed her friend around the shoulders and sobbed loud enough to startle the gorillas.

Sara patted her on the back, and Melissa let the flood of frustration flow from her body.

Alan checked his cummerbund and adjusted his bowtie. He had rented a simple black tuxedo, complete with shoes, for $150. The taxi pulled into Garth's driveway and he hustled out the door, giving the driver the address of Wortham Center.

Alan reached in his coat pocket and took out a pink ticket.

35TH ANNUAL BENEFIT FOR THE HOUSTON
POLICE DEPARTMENT'S
WIDOWS' AND ORPHANS' FUND
DANCING BLACK TIE
MAY 26, 1995 WORTHAM CENTER 8 p.m.

The ticket had cost him $100, a small price to pay if he could recruit Detective Frieda Fishbein to his cause.

Alan knew he had to be on his best behavior to have any chance of swaying the detective. *It'd be nice if she'd let me finish a complete sentence*, he thought.

Fishbein was one tough cookie who couldn't be underestimated. Alan had a vivid memory of the methodical, all-encompassing way she went about her investigation. How she lingered over every detail, made him repeat his story over and over, twisting his words, pointing out tiny little inconsistencies. No doubt about it, she was good at her job.

That's why it was so important that he convince her that he was innocent. If she ever did begin to believe him, his troubles would be over, because he knew that she would never let up until the case was solved.

Alan paid the driver, and joined dozens of other partygoers entering the ballroom. They were here to have fun and dance the night away – he was a man on a mission.

It did feel good to dress up again, and now that he was working with Texas Bob, it wouldn't be long before there would be other nights like this. Hopefully nights filled with celebration, congratulations and victory.

It was well after eleven when Alan entered the ballroom, and the dance floor was full and the party was in full swing. There were at least a thousand people in the hall, well-heeled society types mixing with the middle class group from the Houston Police Department. Alan stood near the back for a few moments, letting his eyes adjust to the lighting, looking out over the tables at this end of the room.

Alan assumed a big honcho like the Chief of Detectives would be at a table of honor, probably sitting with the Chief of Police or other big shots. It would be better if he waited until he could catch Fishbein alone. No sense in causing a scene or making her uncomfortable by approaching her in front of her superiors. Shouldn't be too hard to find, all he had to do was look for the ugliest woman in the room.

He walked over to one of the corner bars and ordered a glass of champagne and a double scotch. The band was pretty good, playing up-tempo hits from the sixties and seventies, and Alan's feet were tapping to the beat as he continued to scan the room.

He knocked back the scotch and sipped on the cheap champagne. God – the widows and orphans were clearing some bucks tonight, because they sure as hell didn't spend the proceeds on decent booze.

Alan spotted her. Just as he expected. Fishbein was seated at a large round table, surrounded on both sides by men. She was wearing an expensive-looking black evening gown, and no doubt was at this moment as attractive as it was possible for her to be.

Now all he had to do was bide his time and wait for her to get up to dance, or go to the ladies' room, whatever – just move away from that table full of cops. Alan finished his champagne and started to go back for another, then decided it would be better to keep a clear head.

Her table was now empty except for one man sitting across from Fishbein. Alan watched as the man leaned across the table and conversed with the detective. His excitement jumped as the man stood up and walked away, leaving Frieda Fishbein all alone.

He wasted no time. 'Good evening, Detective Fishbein. That's a lovely dress. Nice turn-out. The widows' and orphans' fund should be flush after tonight,' Alan said.

He sat down in an empty chair two seats away from her. *Don't crowd her, don't rush. Take it a step at a time.*

'Stakeman. Why are you here? And when are you leaving?' she asked.

Alan ignored the put-down. 'I'm leaving as soon as we

have a little talk. I didn't get very far the other day at your office.'

'Well, you have about two minutes before this song's over and several big, burly detectives come back. What is it?'

'I came to see you before because I want to clear my name. Whether you believe me or not, I didn't kill my wife.'

'You said that the last time,' Fishbein said.

'I know. You see, I have had a lot of time to think about everything. The night Justine was killed. Your investigation. The trial. And I can understand how someone who doesn't know me might come away believing that I murdered—'

'I certainly believe it.'

'—my wife.' *Shit, she's cocky,* he thought. *Don't let her get to you, just keep going.* 'But there are a few things that you don't know. You see, my wife's death wasn't—'

Two men in their mid thirties took seats at the table across from Alan. They looked at Alan with a glint of recognition.

'Alan Stakeman,' Fishbein said, 'meet my two top detectives. Lieutenant Mike Hollier is on the homicide squad and Sergeant Frank Lazario is in vice.'

Alan forced a smile and nodded to the tuxedos. He was momentarily torn between continuing with his plea or waiting for a time when he was alone with Fishbein. He finally decided that he might not get too many chances to talk to her, and went on. 'I realize that this isn't the best setting for a conversation like this, but it's important.'

Fishbein stood up. 'Look, let me make this easy for you. I really don't give a shit about anything you have to say. You shot your wife, I busted you for it, and that's that. Why don't you do us both a favor and stay out of my life?'

She walked around the table and put her hand on the sergeant's shoulder. 'C'mon, Frank, it's time for the dance you promised me.'

Fishbein turned and walked away, leaving Alan standing next to the homicide detective.

'Is she always like that?' Stakeman asked the detective.

Detective Hollier squared his shoulders in front of Alan. 'We don't want to have anything to do with you, fuckhead. If you don't quit coming around, you might find yourself back in jail. Or worse.'

No sense hanging around here, Alan thought. *Now what? How could he get her interested in listening to him? What would it take to get into that narrow mind of hers?*

Alan called a cab from a pay telephone and walked outside to wait. He remembered what his defense attorney had told him during the trial. The lawyer had said that all cops have a prosecution complex.

Cops believed that everybody was guilty of something, everyone dirty under the surface.

Fishbein was definitely going to be a tough nut to crack. Alan could see that he was approaching her all wrong. Maybe he shouldn't try to talk to her in person. Maybe he could put everything down on paper and just mail it to her. Maybe he could hire a lawyer to present the facts for him!

His cab arrived and Alan gave the ballroom one final backward glance.

I'm not giving up, Frieda, he thought. *You haven't heard the last of Alan Stakeman.*

10

Garth was in the kitchen when the doorbell rang. He had just finished his Saturday chores, and was about to relax. He wiped his hands, picked up his water and opened the front door.

'Hi, I'm Joseph Farmer from KHOU. I'm here for the interview.'

Garth knew nothing about an interview, but he had seen the reporter on television. 'Uh, what interview?'

'This is the Stakemans' house, isn't it? I'm here to talk to Alan Stakeman?'

'I don't know anything about it,' Garth said.

A long-haired cameraman came up the sidewalk behind Farmer, dragging a dolly loaded down with camera equipment and portable lights. 'Saturday at two o'clock,' Farmer said. 'My watch says it's ten till two.'

Garth wondered why his father hadn't mentioned the reporter to him. And he wondered why he would have agreed to an interview in the first place. Maybe it had something to do with the campaign. 'My father's not home. Truth is, I don't know where he is, or when he'll be back.'

'I'm sure he'll be here any minute. Would you mind if we stepped inside? The humidity is hell on this equipment.'

Against his better judgment, Garth stepped back from the front door and motioned for them to come in. He watched the reporter give the room a once over, in the same way a burglar might case a home for a future robbery. Already Garth was starting to regret their presence, but now that they were inside the living room, he needed a good reason to kick them out.

'So – you must be Garth. I guess that means you're the son in Stakeman & Son.'

Garth relaxed a little. 'Yes, though I haven't actually started at the firm yet. I work for an advertising agency.'

That seemed to perk the reporter's interest in Garth. 'Advertising – I took some course in that in college. Always thought I'd make a good ad man. It's so creative, and you get a chance to see your work on television. Guess it's not that different from journalism. I bet you're in the creative area, aren't you?'

'I'm the creative director at Holloway & Partners.'

'I knew it! I've heard of that agency. Good outfit. What exactly does a creative director do?'

Garth moved to sit down on the couch and offered the couch to the reporter and his cameraman. Farmer sat down near Garth's recliner, while his associate continued to wrestle with the equipment. 'We're the ones that produce the ads, whether it's newspaper, radio, television, bill-boards. The account people meet with the clients and decide on a direction, then they bring us their ideas and we write and produce the advertisements. I guess we're the artistic side of the business, though some people would say that car commercials have little in common with art.'

'Oh, I don't know – there have been some pretty fancy productions lately. Have you seen those commercials for Texas Bob's Bar-B-Q?'

Garth was glad to hear that someone appreciated his handiwork. 'I did those.'

The reporter pointed to his assistant and mumbled something, then turned back to Garth. 'Really? Well isn't that something. I think they're great – real folksy. I like the ending especially.' Farmer stood up and posed in his best impersonation of Bob Quintell. '"Try Texas Bob's Bar-B-Q. It's so good..."'

Garth finished it for him. '"...You'll think you've died and gone to heaven."'

They both laughed.

'Yeah. Great spots,' Farmer said.

'Thanks. They've done a good job for the client. You know Texas Bob is getting into politics? He's going to run for Senator Smart's Senate seat.'

Farmer's expression brightened. 'No kidding – the US Senate? Boy, that'll cost some money, taking on an incumbent.'

Garth couldn't think of any reason why he shouldn't tell the reporter about Bob's candidacy. After all, the campaign would be calling its first news conference in another week, and rumors about Texas Bob were already on the street. Garth noticed that the cameraman seemed to be setting up lights and equipment to tape. 'What's he doing?'

Farmer gave him a warm smile. 'Don't worry. We're just

going to get everything ready, so once your dad gets here we can start the interview.' Farmer nodded at the cameraman, who continued his work.

Garth was a little wary of the cameraman's activity, but the reporter seemed so friendly, he chalked his suspicions up to paranoia. 'I wonder where he is?'

Farmer dug through his briefcase and pulled out a legal pad. He scanned down the handwriting then put the pad away. The cameraman walked over and attached a clip-on microphone to Farmer's lapel. He handed him a banana-shaped hand-held mike. 'We're just going to get a level check on the video and audio feed.'

Garth watched as the reporter and his comrade ran through a series of checks. Garth was used to this routine – he had been through these tests hundreds of times while working on television commercials. They turned on the lights, and suddenly Garth's living room was as bright as an August afternoon.

'We need to leave these lights on a few minutes to warm up. Listen, Garth, while he's doing all that, let me ask you. Is your dad going to be working for Texas Bob's campaign?'

Garth was so proud that Stakeman & Son was already a success, he didn't hesitate to answer. 'Yes, and he's going to be in the driver's seat, just like the old days. Later on, I'll be leaving the agency to come in and handle the advertising. It's a dream we've had for a long time, Stakeman & Son. We're both very excited.'

'Well, that's really great. I wish you both all the success in the world,' Farmer said.

Garth didn't notice that the cameraman had moved behind the camera and framed Garth and Farmer up in the shot. Garth didn't see him turn on the recorder or quickly nod to Farmer that everything was ready. Farmer took the hand-held mike out of his lap and placed it discreetly on the coffee table near Garth. It all looked completely innocent, like two old friends sitting down for a chat, but they could capture Garth's every word on videotape.

'Tell me, Garth, what was it like, you know, with your dad in jail all those years?'

Garth remembered the banging of the cell doors, and the sweet, antiseptic smell of the Southwest Texas Correctional Institute. 'I don't really want to talk about it. That's all in the past now – we're looking toward the future.'

The reporter still had a friendly grin on his face. 'Of course, painful memories. I understand completely.' Joseph Farmer played with his tie, and crossed his legs. 'Did you go to any of your dad's trial?'

Garth had sat directly behind his father during every horrible moment of the three-week ordeal. Every juror and witness and lawyer was indelibly etched on his mind. His voice grew tough and cold. 'Oh yes, I was there. It was a circus, a farce. There was no justice in that courthouse, none at all.'

Farmer inched a little closer. 'How did you feel when the jury said "guilty"?'

Garth closed his eyes, fighting against the anger and hurt that he'd felt at eighteen and still felt as if it had happened yesterday. How could they *think* that his dad could have killed anyone? How could those twelve fools have been so blind? His voice trembled when he answered. 'I was angry, and confused. I didn't see how they came up with that verdict. The entire case was circumstantial – there was no real evidence. All they had were these theories about tiny little drops of blood on his pants – he could have gotten those when he found her! It was absurd, a complete travesty, and ever since then, I have had nothing but contempt for the American judicial system. It doesn't work, or at least it didn't work for my father.'

Farmer glanced at his cameraman, who mouthed 'rolling'. 'So you believe he's innocent?'

Garth was emphatic. 'Of course, anyone with any sense can see that!'

'And it doesn't bother you that the police said that the break-in had been staged to help conceal the murder?'

Garth vividly recalled how Detective Fishbein had mocked his dad from the witness stand, testifying that Alan had done a lousy job of faking a break-in. 'My father didn't conceal anything, because he didn't do anything! I know! There's no doubt in my mind. That stuff about a phoney robbery, that's all cops trying to cover their ass. And I'll tell you something else about that trial that really pissed me off – you're recording this aren't you?'

Farmer's expression never changed. He still looked like a buddy from next door. 'Of course. It'll be on the six o'clock news.'

It took several seconds for that to sink in. Then Garth felt a surge of fury electrifying his body. 'There never was any interview with my father, was there?'

The reporter's smile reminded Garth of a TV evangelist. 'Your old man wouldn't talk to me, but my boss is crawling all over me. Listen, let me ask you the question on everyone's mind – how does it feel to know your father murdered your mother?'

Garth grabbed the microphone off the coffee table and jerked the long cord from the recorder across the room. He leaped to his feet and jumped on top of Farmer, punching and wrestling the reporter off the couch and on to the floor. Farmer was so surprised by the physical attack that Garth was able to flail away at will. The cameraman stayed with his equipment, capturing everything. Suddenly Garth realized that he was being filmed, and he pulled off the battered newsman.

Joseph Farmer was almost unrecognizable. Blood was streaming out of one nostril, and his lower lip was already beginning to swell. The cameraman rushed to his aid, and Garth walked calmly across to the video equipment. While the newsman and his assistant were trying to stop the bleeding, Garth took the news camera off its tripod, opened the front door, and threw it out on to the sidewalk.

'Get the hell out of my house before I kill you,' Garth said.

Joseph Farmer stood up unsteadily, and staggered toward the door. 'You'll be hearing from our lawyers, Stakeman – you can bet your ass on that. You're just like your dad, one crazy son-of-a-bitch.' In a matter of seconds the cameraman had loaded up his dolly and pulled the equipment out behind him.

Garth went to the bathroom and looked at himself in the mirror. His wire-framed glasses were cocked at a slant on his head and his hair was standing almost straight up. He splashed cold water on his face and stood over the bathroom sink for a few seconds.

With trembling hands he fixed his glasses, combed his hair, and adjusted his appearance. *That'll show him*, he thought. *That'll teach that bastard not to fuck with Stakeman & Son.*

It was a thirty-minute cab ride from downtown to Lamar Suskie's office in south Houston. An afternoon shower was cooling the city, and the streets gave off steam as the raindrops fell in a steady rhythm. Alan rolled down the back window and watched the droplets fall, remembering dozens of campaigns he had worked with Lamar Suskie's professional input.

Lamar Suskie was, in Alan Stakeman's opinion, the best political pollster in the south. Give him the target and a decent research budget and he could give you the nucleus of a successful campaign. Lamar was a classic nerd, whose physical appearance bordered on comical.

Though Alan hadn't seen him in over ten years, he'd be willing to bet that Lamar Suskie looked exactly the same. Lamar was fifty-one, but depending on the day and his mood, could pass for someone between forty and seventy. Lamar was bald on top, with curly, always-dirty gray hair that started about an inch above his ear level and ended below his shirt collar. He wore very thick glasses, so thick they could have been soft drink bottles, and his clothes usually looked as if he'd just pulled them from the bottom of a laundry basket.

Lamar Suskie had a passion for children's cartoons. After he'd become successful, he had made a hobby out of collecting original cells, single frames of cartoon animation art sold at various auctions across the country. He named his polling and research firm after a running gag from his favorite cartoon, *The Roadrunner*. Lamar's company was called Acme Opinion Research.

Alan had worked with Acme since its humblest beginnings, after discovering Lamar working for a group of nincompoops at another polling firm. Alan essentially set Lamar up in business by directing all his research projects Lamar's way, making sure Acme received its fair share of media exposure.

During his time in prison, Alan had received regular correspondence from Lamar, usually a three- or four-page handwritten letter every month or so. Lamar's handwriting was so bad, Alan could seldom make out more than about a tenth of the letters, but he appreciated them anyway.

The taxi pulled on to Red Bluff Road, in front of a renovated house a few minutes from the freeway. From the outside the house looked like an average, medium-sized residence, circa 1965, with wooden exterior painted soft pink with bright purple shutters. Probably the color scheme from some cartoon, Alan thought. The only evidence that the house was really a business was a six-inch wrought iron sign placed discreetly on the front porch. The sign said 'Acme'.

The front door burst open before Alan made it up the

steps, and Lamar Suskie stood before him with his arms outstretched.

'Alan Stakeman, my friend, returned to the living.'

Alan had forgotten Lamar's tendency to be melodramatic. 'Lamar, you haven't aged a minute. You look exactly the same as I remembered. In fact, if I'm not mistaken, you were wearing that exact outfit the last time I saw you.'

Lamar laughed, loudly, in his unique nerdish guffaw. 'Probably true, probably true. Come in, let me show you around.'

Inside, the house was as cheerful as Alan had expected. One wall in the receptionist's area was covered by a large mural of Wiley E. Coyote. Alan followed Lamar down a long hallway, whose walls were adorned with original artwork of Yosemite Sam, Foghorn Leghorn, Sylvester the Cat, Bugs Bunny, and Pepe Le'Peu. Alan realized that the house was large, as they passed at least ten private offices, each with its own occupant, before making a ninety degree turn and entering Lamar's private spot.

'Have a seat – can I get you anything? Soft drink, beer, scotch?'

Alan sat down in a lawn chair across the desk from Lamar. There was another lawn chair of a different style and color on his side of the desk. Lamar's chair was an old-timey rocker, and maintained a rocking rhythm that, Alan thought, would probably drive him crazy.

'Good to see you, my friend. How long have you been out?'

Alan glanced around the room. On the wall behind

Lamar's desk was a six-foot-tall portrait of the Roadrunner posing in a Napoleon costume. 'Let's see, about two months.'

'Two months! And you're just now getting in touch! I'm hurt, deeply. But I forgive you – I never could stay angry at you. You said on the telephone that we were gonna do business again?'

Alan looked over to his right and noticed a bookshelf filled with commemorative plates, displayed with wooden stands. There had to be at least thirty plates, each one with an illustration of a popular cartoon character. 'We are. Have you ever heard of Texas Bob Quintell?'

'The Bar-B-Q guy?'

'That's him. Big Republican. He's going to run in the Republican primary for Senator Smart's seat.'

'That's going to be a big race. I hope he's got lots of money.'

'Millions.'

'My kind of man. There's a few other names I've been hearing too. The biggest one is that lady from Fort Worth...'

'Joanne Wheeler. We are assuming that she's the one to beat. But we don't want to assume anything – that's why I'm here.'

'Okay, tell me what you need and when you want it.'

'To start, we need a statewide poll to measure name recognition and job performance on Quintell, Wheeler, Philip Smart, and one or two minor players whose names I'll give you in a day or two. I need a full demographic breakdown, cross tabulated by race, sex, income, etc., and showing trial heats and second choices. Let me ask you, what would you think about doing a survey of just the registered Republicans?'

'That's fine for later on, but right now you you need to get something for fund-raising. For your first poll, I'd do everybody. He ought to look pretty good because of his restaurant advertising. By the way, you might want to suggest to him that he double his TV budget for Texas Bob's Bar-B-Q.'

'Good idea.'

'When do you want the first one?' Lamar asked.

Alan glanced to his left at a signed and numbered print of Roger Rabbit. 'We're announcing on June 18th on a whirlwind tour in Dallas, Houston, Austin, San Antonio, and El Paso. I'd like to start the telephone survey the next day. How big a sample do we need, and how much will it cost?'

Lamar adjusted his thick glasses and looked at the ceiling. 'Statewide, I'd do a six-hundred sample. With cross tabs and a narrative analysis, $45,000.'

'Done. How soon can I get the results?'

Lamar picked up his calendar and looked over the days. 'June 18th is on a Monday – so we make the calls on Tuesday, Wednesday, and Thursday. I can get you the raw numbers by Monday the 25th. The analysis will be two or three days later.'

'Good.'

Lamar stood up and walked over to a television mounted on the wall next to the plate display. 'Mind if I turn this on a minute? Somebody told me there's going to be an auction of some Porky Pig illustrations – I want to catch the six o'clock news.'

'Sure. And I guess I'll have that scotch now,' Alan said.

Lamar called on the intercom and ordered two drinks. The early edition of the KHOU news was just beginning as the drinks arrived.

'Earlier this afternoon, KHOU reporter Joseph Farmer was attacked at the Houston home of Garth Stakeman, local advertising executive and son of convicted murderer Alan Stakeman...'

Alan choked on his drink, spewing scotch all over Lamar's desk.

'In the assault, captured on video by KHOU cameraman Todd Buckelew, Garth Stakeman is shown in a violent fit of anger directed at our news crew.'

As the announcer calmly went through the voice-over, video from Garth's interview, now edited and displayed for maximum effect, filled the screen in Lamar's office.

'Channel Eleven reporter Joseph Farmer was not hurt seriously in the incident, though he was treated and released from St Luke's Hospital. A KHOU news camera was destroyed when Stakeman hurled it on to the concrete sidewalk outside his home. As of news time, Garth Stakeman's father, recently released after serving fifteen years for murder, could not be located for comment...'

11

Dr Mitchell Whitecotton's blue-haired receptionist reminded Melissa of her great-grandmother. In fact, she wouldn't have been the least bit surprised to see her pull out needle and thread and begin stitching together a large quilt.

The waiting room was tastefully decorated in mauve and gray, no doubt the colors that had been tested to be most psychologically soothing, Melissa thought. Ordinarily she could be comfortable in any situation, but she had never been in therapy before, and the idea of someone strolling through the caverns of her personality was unsettling.

The receptionist must have noticed her anxiety, and did her best to make her feel more comfortable. 'Mrs Stakeman, please help yourself to those cookies. I baked them during my lunch hour.'

Melissa followed her eyes to the end table and sure enough, there was a china plate filled with layers of homemade chocolate chip cookies. She picked up a couple and three bites later they were gone. Melissa waited until the receptionist was looking the other way before she stuffed two more cookies in her mouth. Didn't want to appear piggish.

One side of a large gray double door opened and a short, rotund man in his late sixties came out. 'Mrs Stakeman, I'm Dr Whitecotton. Won't you please come in?'

Melissa followed him into an inner office that somehow managed to be dark and draped, and at the same time warm and cozy. The heavy curtains were probably there to shield crazies from the prying eyes of the sane public.

She sat down in a high-back, blue leather chair across the desk from the psychologist. Her eyes scanned the room before noticing a cloth covered sofa at the far corner.

Dr Mitchell Whitecotton was a half foot shorter than Melissa, no more than five foot five she guessed. He was a good fifty pounds overweight, with a neatly trimmed white goatee and thin mustache. He had dark, round cow eyes over large bags of skin, and a slow gentle manner that immediately put her at ease. 'Do you mind if I smoke a pipe while we talk?' he asked.

'I love the smell of pipe tobacco. It reminds me of my grandfather.'

Dr Whitecotton laboriously selected a long-stemmed black pipe from a pipe rack on the corner of his desk. The pipe rack must have been an antique, made from wood and polished brass, and held several different pipes. Melissa wondered what had made him choose the particular pipe he was currently filling with tobacco.

Was this the pipe he always smoked on Wednesdays? The patient-with-bad-marriage pipe?

Melissa shook off those silly thoughts, noting that Dr Whitecotton was not one for small talk. That was fine with her – she didn't want to be talking about the weather when it cost her $150 an hour. 'Sara told me she has been seeing you for a long time. Did she tell you about my problem?'

He was concentrating on his lighter, carefully distributing the small flame over the entire bowl of tobacco. 'She told me you needed to talk to someone.'

This isn't going to be easy, she told herself. *Relax, take your time, and don't start crying.*

'I guess I do. I don't know where to start. Everything's confused. My life is fucked up. Oh, sorry, Dr Whitecotton, I cuss a lot.'

He gave her a small smile, and looked across the desk. 'I've heard it all before.'

She laughed. 'Thank you. I don't really know where to start. I'm worried about my husband, and my marriage. He's changed. Every day, he seems to get a little further away, a little colder. He's shutting me out of his life.'

Dr Whitecotton leaned back in his chair, puffing. His fat left hand began to make tiny notes on a legal pad in front of him, but even while he was writing, he never took his eyes off Melissa. 'I see. Exactly when did you notice this change?'

'Over the last few months, but really noticeable for the last three. It got worse when his father came to live with us. His dad just got out of prison.'

'Uh-huh,' he said, continuing to write and smoke.

'Garth – that's my husband – Garth and I have been married for five years, but we've known each other since college. He's always been very different from me, personality wise. A lot of my friends told me I was crazy to fall in love with him in the first place.'

'Why is that?'

'Well, I'm very outgoing, and I love people. I'm the kind of person who can go to a big party full of people I don't know and leave three hours later with twenty new friends. I've always been like that. But Garth is just the opposite. He's much more introverted than I am, and he's very much a homebody. He doesn't drink, smoke, gamble, or run around. He watches what he eats, he works out and jogs, nags me about my diet – you know the type.'

Dr Whitecotton nodded. 'And that bothers you?'

'No. I mean, I knew he was like that when I married him. I thought it was kind of cute. He likes to chastise me about my eating habits, telling me to cut down on the French fries, beer, tacos and tequila. I thought it was sweet, that someone cared so much about my health.'

'He doesn't do that anymore?'

Melissa scrunched down in the chair, stretching her long legs out in front of her. She picked up her ankle length skirt and draped it loosely over her legs. 'He barely speaks to me at all! He's always been quiet, and that was the one thing I've always bitched about. Garth can literally go hours without saying a word. I'm not like that at all – I probably talk too much. Garth only speaks when he really has something to say, which these days isn't very often.'

The telephone buzzed and Dr Whitecotton gave her an apologetic look. 'I'm sorry, I've been trying to reach a colleague in France. This will only take a second.'

Dr Whitecotton answered the phone and began speaking fluid French in his soft voice. Melissa couldn't understand a word he was saying, but didn't mind having a few moments to collect her thoughts. This wasn't as bad as she had expected. He seemed genuinely interested in her, and he had to be good or else Sara wouldn't have continued seeing him all these years.

The psychologist was looking toward the curtained window as he talked, smiling and nodding while he listened. Melissa watched his fat cherub profile, and decided she liked his goatee and mustache. She wondered if a woman would be able to feel those mustache hairs during oral sex.

She shook her head, trying to banish that image out of her mind. It was weird – why was she fantasizing about this rotund little psychologist? *Good God, girl*, she thought, *are you that desperate?*

Well, she certainly had reason to be. She and Garth hadn't made love in a couple of months. She loved sex, and would gladly bang away every day, if she could motivate Garth.

Was it her fault they weren't having sex? What was she doing wrong? Did Garth find her less attractive than before? She knew she didn't look any different. Oh, maybe an extra inch here or there, but her figure looked basically the same as it had the day they got married. Was Garth seeing someone else? *No*, she told herself, *put that out of your mind. You'll drive yourself crazy thinking crap like that.* There was no other woman, just another man, and Garth's warped sense of fatherly devotion.

Dr Whitecotton hung up the telephone. 'I'm sorry, Mrs Stakeman. That was a colleague of mine from Paris who is coming to Texas next month to deliver an address at a convention. He and I have been playing telephone tag for a week.'

'No problem.'

Without having to glance at his notes, Dr Whitecotton knew exactly where she had left off. 'You were saying that your husband was quite different from you – not much of a talker.'

'That's putting it mildly. Don't get me wrong, Doctor, that's not the reason I'm here. I've always known Garth and I are different. That's fine with me – variety is the spice of life. But ever since his father came to live with us, Garth acts like I'm not even there. His daddy has been in jail for the last fifteen years, and Garth has set them up in business together. He has this fixation about being close to his father, and I'm left out in the cold!'

Dr Whitecotton was re-lighting his pipe, now filled with a fresh tobacco. 'You said that your husband's father was in prison?'

'Yes. You may have heard about him on the news, it's been everywhere. His name is Alan Stakeman.'

'I didn't make the connection before. Alan Stakeman – he is certainly a high-profile individual.'

'Yes, and Garth is much more sensitive about it than his father. That was the beginning of our problems. I had lunch with Alan one day, and we started talking about prison and stuff. It was a nothing conversation, and I was just wanted to get to know Alan a little better. He wasn't offended in the least about my curiosity, but later, when I casually mentioned it to my husband, Garth went apeshit.'

'What exactly did Garth say?'

'I told him that I had seen his dad at lunch, and that we'd talked about Alan's time in prison. Garth absolutely exploded, said that I had no business dredging all that up, and told me to leave his father the fuck alone. You'd have to know Garth to realize how out of character that is.'

'Has he done any thing else lately that you would consider unusual?'

'I'll say! This past Saturday, a newsman from Channel Eleven came to the house, claiming he'd arranged an interview with my father-in-law. He sets up his camera and tells Garth he's just checking the equipment, then he gets Garth to answer a bunch of questions about his father. Now Garth isn't dumb, he's very intelligent, but he can be quite naive, and this reporter just suckered him. Garth finally figures out that he's been had, but instead of just telling the guy to leave, he punches him out. Then he goes wild and smashes the video camera!'

'And that's not the sort of thing Garth would normally do?'

'Are you kidding? He's very laid-back, unassuming. I mean, it's very frustrating to try and get in an argument with him, 'cause he doesn't argue. He'll just sit there and stare at you – never shouts, never shows his feelings. That's why the idea of him beating up a stranger is so bizarre.'

'Has your husband ever been physically violent toward you?'

Melissa shook her head. 'Oh no, that's the least of my worries. I can't imagine that, but of course, I wouldn't have imagined him smashing a camera either.'

Dr Whitecotton seemed to be mulling that one over, and

paused for a moment before making his notes. 'Tell me about the beginnings of your relationship. How is he different today from the way he was back then?'

She had to think a minute. 'I'm not sure he really is that different. Garth has never been wild and crazy like me. He's the grown-up, the one who's always reliable, always responsible. But he did used to play along with some of my hairbrain ideas.'

'Such as?'

'Our wedding, for instance. I wanted to do something funky and different, he wanted a straight, traditional ceremony. But in the end, he went along with me. We got married on Halloween. We had a costume wedding.'

Dr Whitecotton smiled at that. 'Everyone was in costume?'

'Two hundred of our closest friends. My mother came dressed as a cat, and my father was Charlie Chaplin. Garth was Napoleon and I was Josephine. The only person there who wasn't in costume was the priest, and when he first walked through the door, several people went up to him and told him what a great costume he had. And then there was our honeymoon. We spent two weeks at the Moon Bay Resort in Jamaica. It's a real laid back place just for couples. They have a nude beach – though we were there ten days before Garth finally peeled off his bathing suit. Then, on the last day there, he got a bad sunburn on his pecker.'

'His what?'

'His cock. I offered to put some aloe vera on it for him, but Garth said that a hard-on made it hurt worse.'

Dr Whitecotton choked on a puff of pipe smoke, and laughed as he made notes. 'Are you saying that he doesn't play along with you much anymore?'

'Well lately, he doesn't do anything, including talk to me, or make love to me.'

'Your sex life is a problem?'

Melissa rolled her eyes. 'The problem is that there's no sex. We haven't done it in over three months.'

'Before, was your sex life satisfactory?'

'I guess. Sort of.'

'That doesn't sound very passionate.'

'You know, with Garth, sex was always a little difficult.'

'What do you mean?' Dr Whitecotton asked.

She hesitated. 'Well, I don't think he really likes to do it, the actual lovemaking part. I have to really get him worked up, but I can't do anything aggressive like grab his dick, or he freaks.'

'I see.'

'But he gives incredible head. I've never known a man who's better at going down on a woman. Whoever taught him the technique did a really good job.'

'You mentioned that things starting changing after Alan came to live with you. Do you think your relationship would improve if your father-in-law moved out and got a place of his own?'

Melissa had given that some consideration. 'I've thought about that, but the truth is, I don't think our problem is related to his physical presence in the house. First of all, I want you to know that I love my father-in-law a lot. I probably have a lot more in common with his personality than I do Garth's. The problem, as I see it, is not where Alan Stakeman chooses to live, but Garth's obsessive desire to hover over his father, to shield him from life. We're talking about a fifty-eight-year-old man! A man who's spent the last fifteen years in prison.

'It's a fact that a jury of twelve people listened to the evidence and found him guilty. But Garth gets all hot and bothered, because he can't understand how anyone could think his father was guilty! He is so protective, so possessive that he is blocking out everything and everyone else in his life.'

Melissa could feel the emotion building. On the way over, she had promised herself that she was going to keep a rein on her emotions, and not break down the first time she met Dr Whitecotton. But she couldn't help it. The tears welled up again, and she felt the trails of moisture begin to move down her cheeks.

She got out of the chair and moved over to the couch, fighting hard to keep from breaking down completely. 'Hey, Doc, how come you didn't ask me to lay on the couch?'

Dr Whitecotton seemed to sense her desire to take a break, and didn't force the conversation. 'The only reason I have that couch is because people expect it. You're welcome to stretch out if you like.'

She pulled back the curtains and looked out the window. 'That's okay.'

'We only have ten minutes left in the hour. What do you want to happen in your relationship with your husband?'

She turned and came back to her chair. 'I want it to work. Either that, or I want to know that it's not going to so I can move on. What do you think, Dr Whitecotton? Is my marriage over?'

He took a moment before answering her. 'I can't answer that. Not yet, anyway. Right now, it's important for you to understand the feelings that you're having, while looking for the source of the conflict with your husband. Let me ask you this – do you think you could get Garth to agree to come in for a visit?'

She had already thought about that. In fact, she had almost mentioned this appointment to Garth, in hopes that he might agree to join her today. 'I don't think so, at least not easily. He is such an introverted person, not so much shy as private. He would have a difficult time talking about intimate things with someone he didn't know.'

Dr Whitecotton stopped taking notes. 'Then all we can do right now is work on your feelings, to see if we can find a direction for your life. Can you come in once a week for a little while?'

'Sure.' Melissa stood up and put her hands on the top of the high-back chair. 'Sara was right about you. You are good. I think we relate to one another.'

Dr Whitecotton tapped the burnt tobacco out of his pipe and came around the desk. He took her hand in his and gave her a firm handshake. 'I'm glad you feel comfortable. That's very important at this stage of the game. Think about what we've talked about, and next time, we'll try to probe a little deeper.'

'Do all of your patients cry the first time?'

'A lot of them do. Crying is good for the soul. It probably wouldn't hurt Garth to have a little cry.'

That was funny. 'Hah – Garth Stakeman shed a tear? It'll never happen! Never in a million years.'

12

He stuffed the large handgun in his pants, and headed back downstairs, stopping at a jewelry box to select a few of the more valuable pieces.

Down through the den to the French doors, he used his key on the deadbolt and stepped out on to the patio. Closing the door behind him, he looked out into the blackness. He breathed in the crisp night air, feeling free and exhilarated. Or maybe it was just the rush from a fresh kill.

He took several steps off the patio, careful to avoid the huge cactus and other potted plants, and looked up at the stars. He could just make out the Big Dipper, and imagined himself climbing into a spaceship and exploring the universe.

Turning back to the task at hand, he took the revolver out of his pants and removed the bullets. Using the gun butt as a hammer, he smashed a hole in the glass of the patio door, and carefully eased his hand through to flip the deadbolt.

He came back in the house and began rifling through the den. He knocked liquor bottles on to the floor, emptied drawers and shelves, and made a pile of electronics on the couch. His booty would include a small color television, a

VCR and a portable ghetto blaster. He went into the kitchen and found the antique silverware and a serving tray, and added it to the jewelry in the pillow case.

He stood back and surveyed the downstairs. It didn't look messy enough, so he spent a couple more minutes scattering papers, books and keepsakes on the floor. Satisfied with his handiwork, he took the loot to the car and loaded everything in the trunk. He had several concrete blocks in the car, and with that added weight, the goods would easily stay put at the bottom of Buffalo Bayou. All he had to do now was hide the pistol.

He was happy. He made one last tour of the house, taking a moment to look again in the master bathroom.

She was dead. He was leaving.

Everything was perfect, just as he had planned it.

13

Melissa strolled into the kitchen and flipped on the early morning news. A goofy-looking weatherman was pointing to a line of thunderstorms moving toward the Houston area, and predictions of buckets of rain were scrolled across the TV screen.

Garth was engrossed in Quintell campaign press releases and barely acknowledged Melissa's presence. *Might as well be eating alone*, she thought.

She poured herself a glass of orange juice and flipped open the morning newspaper. Maybe now would be a good time to try to talk to him.

A man's face filled the television screen as the morning news person described another murder. It took Melissa a few seconds to recognize the man, and when she did, she shouted, 'Garth, look! It's the man from the restaurant!'

Garth looked up and followed her pointing finger. Melissa picked up the remote control and turned the volume way up.

'Former Houston Mayor William Hubbell was found shot to death last night, in a parking lot near his luxury townhouse in the exclusive Tanglewood neighborhood,' the newsman read.

'Police sources say that Hubbell, sixty-two, was found near his car in the driveway at his home. There was one bullet wound to the back of the head, and investigators believe robbery may have been the motive. Neighbors reported hearing a loud bang around 1:30 a.m., but surprisingly, no one reported the gunshot to police.

'At the present time, police have few clues, and *Crimestoppers* is offering a special $10,000 reward to anyone having information about this tragic crime . . .'

Garth turned back from the television and started reading again.

'Jesus Christ, Garth. That's him, isn't it? The guy who was such an asshole to Dad?' Melissa asked.

Garth didn't look up. 'Think so.'

'Man, can you believe it? We just met him last week, and now, someone shot him.'

Garth turned a page. 'Serves him right.'

'What? What did you say?'

Garth looked her in the eye. 'After the way he treated Dad the other night, I'd say he got what was coming to him.'

A chill ran down her back and Melissa had to get up from the table. She walked over to the sink and began rinsing out her glass. Garth's cold-blooded attitude chilled her to the bone, and she ran water over her hands to try to regain her composure.

What's going on here? she wondered. *Who is this man I am living with? What am I going to do?*

* * *

The Fairmont Hotel in downtown Dallas takes up most of an entire city block, in what was once the center of the business district. Stately, elegant and classically plush, it was the ideal place for Texas Bob Quintell to announce his candidacy to north Texas.

A small crowd of two dozen supporters had been recruited to provide a backdrop of enthusiasm for the formal news conference. A cross section of businessmen, housewives, young, middle-aged and elderly were seated near the podium, between the news media, their cameras, and the candidate.

Alan Stakeman had spent the last week drilling his client on all the major national and international issues. Texas Bob knew the current balance of payments between the United States and foreign suppliers, he could talk intelligently about unemployment in Texas, the southern region, and the entire country. He was versed on the current price for a barrel of oil, renewed fighting in Rwanda, tensions in the Middle East, new health care legislation, and a myriad of other topics. Throughout the education process, Alan had been impressed with Texas Bob's willingness to learn and his almost photographic memory for detail.

Alan had learned long ago never to try to change a candidate's true views on the issues. While many candidates would listen to the advice of their consultants and change with each new public opinion poll, Alan knew he was on much safer ground if he just refined their sincere views into the most palatable form. Texas Bob was as ready as he would ever be, and Alan hoped that he would come across as his folksy self when he met the news media.

A well-known Dallas oil man and civic leader had been selected to introduce the candidate. Texas Bob had memorized a brief announcement speech, and afterwards, Alan would get to see how good a student this oversized millionaire had been.

Alan stood in the corner in the front of the room, discreetly behind Texas Bob, but near enough to see the faces of the reporters. He crossed his fingers as the oil man finished his flowery introduction and Texas Bob sauntered to the podium.

'Good morning, ladies and gentlemen. I have a brief statement and then I'll be happy to answer your questions.'

Quintell paused for effect, just as Alan had suggested, his eyes making contact with all parts of the room. 'The great state of Texas is at a crossroads, and it's time for new leadership in our nation's capital. Caught in the grip of a stagnant economy, many of our leading businesses have suffered significant setbacks. Texas's oil and gas industry has been racked by foreign imports. Over the last few years we've seen our commercial and residential real estate freefall from dizzying heights to record lows. Our once powerful financial markets have been battered and wounded, to the point where Texas consumers are afraid to put their trust in the neighborhood bank. Criminals have taken over the streets and are flooding our prisons with violent, repeat offenders.'

He paused and smiled at his pack of supporters. 'But I'm optimistic, because I believe in Texas.'

Brief applause from the back of the room. 'And while the path to success may be filled with detour signs and potholes, I know we have the strength of character to make this state great again. We, the citizens, are willing to do our part, but where is the Washington leadership? The mindless bureaucrats and professional politicians want us to believe that they hold the answer to our troubles. They do not. They have forgotten that this state and this country were built by people with vision, a vision that understands that democracy means government *for* the average working man and woman. A democracy that listens to the needs of the small businessman, and has enough sensitivity to hear the single parent who not only brings home the bacon, but cooks it too.'

Louder applause this time. Texas Bob had the crowd in his hand, and Alan looked over the reporters. Every one of them was attentive and making furious notes, except for one guy in the back, whom Alan couldn't see clearly from this angle, but who appeared to be looking at him instead of the candidate. *That's strange*, he thought.

'Our metropolitan areas are filled with gangs and killers, night-time marauders who thrive on fear and intimidation. They brazenly rob and rape and murder, because they know there's no room in the prisons to hold them.

'The federal budget deficit continues to grow, fueled by the liberal policies of men like Philip Smart, who refuse to accept that their time is past. American government has to follow the example of the American family, and learn to live within its means.'

A couple of 'Oh yeah's' came from the back of the room. Alan moved a few steps to his right and tried to peer around the group of journalists to get a clear view of the guy looking his way. His vision was blocked, though, by a large, obese woman wearing a hat.

'For these reasons and more, today I am offering my qualifications and philosophy as a businessman to an electorate anxious to return to traditional values. I'm pledging my time, energies, blood, sweat and tears, in an effort to provide true leadership for Texas in the United States Senate.'

A couple of whoops and a whistle signaled that the home folks liked what they heard. *Now comes the hard part*, Alan thought, *where we see how Texas Bob handles hard-nosed journalists.*

Alan looked through the group of maybe fifteen reporters and photographers. The woman with the hat leaned forward, and for the first time, the man came into his line of sight. He had dark hair, and he was sitting in the very back of the media group. His face seemed vaguely familiar. Joseph Farmer!

What's he doing in Dallas? Alan wondered. *The campaign is making a stop in Houston later today – why would he take the time to make a two-hundred-mile trip up here?*

The reporters were all waving their hands, trying to get Texas Bob to call on them for the first question. Joseph Farmer seemed to be paying attention to Alan, though, sitting there placidly, staring a hole through Alan's forehead. *Forget about him – he's just here to stir up trouble. Concentrate on Texas Bob's performance.*

A young female reporter from a Dallas television station stood up. 'Mr Quintell, in your statement you mentioned the incumbent, Philip Smart, and in effect called him a liberal. Does this mean that you plan to attack the senator, and turn this into a conservative versus liberal campaign?'

Alan knew Texas Bob was ready for that one. 'Well, young lady, the truth is, he is a liberal, and I am a conservative. And if I win the Republican nomination, you can bet your bottom dollar that comparison will be made during the campaign. Voters need to know who they're voting for, and how the candidates stand on the issues. They have a right to be presented with a complete disclosure of the ethics and philosophies of each of the candidates. If Senator Smart doesn't want to talk about his liberal policies and all his liberal golfing buddies, then maybe I'll have to do it for him.'

A chuckle ran through the pack of reporters. Alan figured they smelled blood at the prospect of a bare knuckle campaign. A quick glance at Farmer to see that the son-of-a-bitch was still looking his way. Well he wouldn't give him the satisfaction of knowing he had broken Alan's concentration.

A gray-haired, pot-bellied man, far too homely to be on television, got the next question. 'Mr Quintell, you talk about being in touch with the citizens of Texas, of taking their views to Washington. Everyone here knows you're a millionaire, and obviously, most of us aren't.' More chuckles. 'So how can you claim to be one of the people, when you're sitting on all those millions?'

Texas Bob gave him a big smile. 'You're right – I am rich.

I've got more money than I know what to do with, or I could ever spend.'

Murmurs ran through the reporters, and Alan started getting nervous. *C'mon Bob*, he thought, *stick to the game plan*. Farmer still wasn't paying an attention to the candidate.

Texas Bob continued. 'But let me ask you something. Isn't the pursuit of success what makes this country great? Isn't that why millions of immigrants have come to this country, and thousands more move to the USA every year? Texas Bob's Bar-B-Q began twenty years ago as a small family restaurant in west Houston. Today there are over a hundred of them and I'm damn proud of what we've accomplished. We employ four thousand people, have nine thousand stockholders, and pay a whole helluva lot of taxes. I am living proof that in America, you can make something of yourself, if you're willing to buckle down and go to work.'

Enthusiastic applause from the supporters. Alan was pleased – Texas Bob was doing very well, so far.

Another television reporter got a turn. 'There are a number of rumors that Senator Smart's seat has been targeted by the Republican National Committee and other conservative groups. Specifically, Senator Smart's recent legislation proposing to outlaw certain handguns. What is your position on gun control, and on the issue of crime in general?'

Alan was nervously excited. He knew that Bob had a great opportunity to score points if he handled himself right. Alan had told him that this would be the question most likely to be featured on local newscasts. He noticed that Joseph Farmer was talking to his cameraman, and out of the corner of his eye, he saw the video camera turn his way. *Why is he shooting footage of me? Texas Bob is the candidate. He's probably just trying to get under my skin. Fuck him. If he wants to waste his film, that's his problem.*

Texas Bob put both hands on the podium. 'On the issue of handguns, and on the entire matter of crime, Senator Philip Smart has shown himself to be out of step with reality. Now I know that there are a number of liberal legislators, Senator Ted Kennedy among them, who say that in order to stop crime we should stop selling handguns. Well, that's a bunch of bull, and everybody in this room knows it.'

Bob stepped around the podium. 'The legal manufacture and sale of firearms has nothing to do with criminals. Do you think that the average rapist goes to the mall to buy a pistol? Don't be ridiculous! Whether or not guns are sold in stores, punks and hoodlums will always find a way to arm themselves. You can't blame a .38 special for committing a hold-up. What are we gonna do next – outlaw steak knives because someone stabs their neighbor with one?'

Bob cleared his throat and continued. 'To me, this whole crime issue gets to the heart of the problem with Senator Philip Smart. Here's a man who has never had a *real* job in his entire life. He was born a fancy pants. His daddy sent him to college in England – where he probably studied flowers or bugs or something. When he was in his mid-twenties his daddy helped him get elected to the state house and he's been on the government payroll ever since!

'Philip Smart doesn't know anything about working for a living. He has nothing in common with the average, hard-working Texas family who're trying to make ends meet!'

The same reporter asked a follow-up question. 'That's all fine, Mr Quintell. But you didn't tell us what you are planning to do about crime.'

'Crime is a problem because we spend more time worrying about the feelings of the crooks than we do their innocent victims. I'll give you an example. Last week there was a trial here in Dallas that I'm sure you all covered, where a young teenage boy was accused of the rape and murder of a seventy-five-year-old woman. A *seventy-five-year-old woman!*

'Now the crime was sickening enough, but what's worse was that this thug's court-appointed defense lawyer spent three days bringing in a parade of expert witnesses who testified that it wasn't the boy's fault. Seems he was a victim of his environment. These so-called experts said that because he had grown up in a poor neighborhood and didn't have a father, that the jury ought to just pat him on the fanny and tell him, "Now, son, promise you won't do it again!" Thank God those twelve, clear-minded Texans had the good sense to see him for what he was, a no-good punk, and now he's going to the electric chair.'

More applause from the supporters. 'Youth gangs run wild in all our cities, because our society doesn't offer any real alternative to gang life. The deterrence to committing crimes, which is the assurance that if you do the crime, you'll do some time, has been removed from the equation. Adult criminals know that if they are caught, more than likely they'll get a little slap on the wrist. And juvenile delinquents can literally get away with murder, because they're not yet of legal age. I say that if you want to dance, you've got to pay the fiddler. You commit murder in Texas, by God, and I don't care how old you are, your ass is going to jail. Or even better, send them where they belong, straight to hell!'

Alan scanned the faces of the media. Even these normally jaded reporters seemed entranced by Texas Bob's sincerity, all except for Joseph Farmer, who didn't look like he cared if Bob lived or died.

'I say we commit whatever money it takes to build the prisons to remove these professional scumbags from society. If I'm elected as US Senator I'll support, hell, I'll *introduce* legislation that will provide federal matching funds for prison construction to any county that can show it needs it. And if the correction system wants to try and rehabilitate these scoundrels, that's okay with me, as long as they keep 'em locked up while they're doing it!'

Joseph Farmer finally acted like a reporter covering a news conference, and he was able to get Quintell's attention. 'Sir, all this talk about crime and such, that's all well and good. Yet you, sir, have someone in your campaign who many people would consider one of the coldest killers in the history of this state. How can you justify your tough stand on crime, when Alan Stakeman is here, apparently running your campaign?'

Oh shit, Alan thought. He felt his neck muscles tighten as Farmer glanced his way, smiling. *C'mon Bob, don't lose them now!*

No one seemed to know who Farmer was, since he was in Dallas and not Houston where his face would be well known. 'You are correct. Alan Stakeman is acting as a paid consultant to my campaign. He's on my team because he has a proven record of success in politics. Of course I am aware of Mr Stakeman's criminal record, and he has told me that he was innocent of the crime, and since his release has been working to set the record straight.

'But that is neither here nor there. The facts are that Alan Stakeman was found guilty, sentenced to prison, and he served his time. The State of Texas has said that he has paid his debt, and is a free man. As long as he keeps his nose clean, I'm happy to have him working on my behalf.'

'But how does that jive with what you said earlier? I mean, didn't you just say that you believed in capital punishment, and that we ought to send all these killers to hell?'

If Texas Bob was rattled, he didn't show it. 'What would you have me do, son? Personally execute every person who is paroled in this state?'

Other reporters jumped up and changed the subject. Farmer leaned over and whispered to his cameraman, who began packing up to leave. The newsman looked one final time Alan's way and dabbed his swollen lip with a tissue. He turned and began weaving his way through the group of reporters, and finally went out of the door.

Alan hoped this didn't mean that Farmer was going to

become his shadow, but something told him that the newsman wasn't going to forget Garth's attack.

Bring it on, motherfucker, Alan thought. *Give us your best shot – Stakeman & Son can take it!*

14

Alan Stakeman pulled his cap on and walked toward the little league baseball diamond. The stands were full of cheering parents, and throngs of spectators yelled encouragement to the home team.

Frieda Fishbein sat directly behind the home team's dugout, clapping for her son and sending obnoxious catcalls to the opposing pitcher. She was obviously one of those passionately proud parents, who wanted the world to know that her boy was playing ball and he was something special.

She probably sits by the dugout so she can tell the coach what to do, Alan thought. The spectator area immediately nearest her seat was clear of people, giving Alan an opportunity to make his case. He stopped off at the refreshment stand and bought a soft drink and a hot dog before making his way down the wooden stands. He sat on the row just behind Fishbein, a little to her left, and waited for her to notice him. When she finally looked his way, she didn't seem happy to see him.

'Stakeman,' she said, before turning back to the ball game. 'Why am I not surprised to see you?'

Alan chewed on a bite of hotdog. 'I know you probably think I'm a glutton for punishment, showing up again like this. But I've been trying to tell you something very important.'

Fishbein lit a cigarette, and left it hanging from her mouth as she clapped and yelled, 'BALL FOUR! ALL RIGHT – C'MON NOW, TIGERS, LET'S MAKE SOMETHING HAPPEN OUT THERE!' She looked up at Alan. 'How the hell did you know where to find me?'

'I saw you downtown last week with your son. He was wearing his little league uniform with Wal-Mart Tigers on the back, so I tracked down the team, and got a copy of their schedule.'

'OKAY, TOMMY, JUST A LITTLE HIT, THAT'S ALL WE NEED, JUST A LITTLE ONE!'

She blew smoke in Alan's direction. 'You're a regular little detective, aren't you?' She gave Alan the once over, like she was sizing him up for a new suit. 'That's my son at the plate. He's the shortstop. Great on defense, but not much for swinging the wood. He doesn't have to hit it very far. That kid on first base is the fastest guy on the field. If Tommy gets anything on the ball, that little fellow can fly.

'RELAX, TAKE YOUR TIME, TOMMY. MAKE HIM PITCH TO YOU, SON, MAKE HIM PITCH TO YOU!'

The thirteen-year-old boy looked over his shoulder and rolled his eyes at his mother.

Fishbein turned sideways. 'I don't suppose you're going to leave until you've said your piece. So spit it out. Don't want you to fuck up my whole afternoon.'

Alan could see that he would have to tell his story in short spurts, between pitches, otherwise Fishbein wouldn't hear what he said. There were around fifty spectators, most of them parents, and no one seemed to be paying them any attention. Maybe his days of being recognized were coming to an end.

'GOOD EYE, GOOD EYE. WAY TO WATCH, SON! WAIT FOR YOUR PITCH!'

Three or four other mothers shouted encouragement to their youngsters, but Fishbein's loud, Yankee accent stood out from the crowd.

Alan leaned near her left ear. 'For the last fifteen years, I've been stuck in prison, with nothing to do except think about my wife's death. I've played and re-played that nightmare a thousand times in my mind, and I've finally got a handle on what must have happened.'

If Fishbein was listening to him, she wasn't letting on. Her attention still seemed riveted to the ball field. The kid on first base must have a reputation as a base stealer, because the pitcher was spending more time worrying about him than he was throwing to Tommy Fishbein.

'In the weeks before my wife was killed, there had been all kinds of weird things happening in our end of town. A guy down the street had his house ransacked, two days after his dog was poisoned. A big German shepherd watchdog. A man a couple of streets over took a shot at someone he saw sneaking around in his backyard—'

'STRIKE! YOU CALL THAT A STRIKE? JESUS

CHRIST, UMP! THE BALL PRACTICALLY BOUNCED OFF THE PLATE! THAT'S OKAY, TOMMY – DON'T WORRY ABOUT THE CLOWN BEHIND THE PLATE. SHAKE IT OFF!'

Alan continued, watching as the pitcher threw ball after ball to the first baseman, trying to hold the runner on the bag. 'So all through that first year, leading up to the trial, I was just like everyone else – everyone who believed in me. I was working on the assumption that the person who killed Justine must have been a burglar, probably on drugs or something, who had been caught in the act and had panicked. But after my conviction, I had time to go back over everything, and I realized that something wasn't right. Now I'm certain that this isn't the work of a burglar. The killer was someone who knew me and Justine . . .'

Little Tommy Fishbein hit a blooper that cleared the outstretched glove of the second baseman by inches. Mr Speedball from first base was past second and halfway to third by the time Tommy arrived safely at first. Detective Fishbein was yelling and jumping up and down like she had just won the lottery. Tommy sheepishly traded his batting helmet for his game cap, giving his mother a quick smile before motioning for her to sit down.

'THAT'S MY BOY – I KNEW YOU COULD DO IT! WAY TO SMASH THAT BALL, TOMMY. UH-OH, THE PITCHER'S SHAKEY NOW! HE DOESN'T KNOW WHICH WAY IS UP. C'MON, TIGERS, LET'S KEEP IT GOING. BRING 'EM ALL IN!'

Alan let her whooping settle down before he continued.

'Justine's murder wasn't a case of burglar-gets-startled, burglar-panics-and-kills-woman. I'm convinced that it's somehow connected to another crime, from years before. An unsolved murder in Austin.'

Fishbein had stopped clapping, but Alan still couldn't be certain that she was paying any attention to him. She watched the next batter strike out to retire the side, and cursed the coach for failing to motivate his young team to score. She slowly turned around and sat staring at Alan. Beads of sweat formed a mustache on her upper lip, and she tilted her head and looked at him over the top of her glasses. 'Did you say something about *another* murder?'

For the first time since he'd been following her, Alan felt as though Chief of Detectives Frieda Fishbein was really listening to him. 'I said that my wife's murder could be connected to an unsolved case from Austin. Whoever killed Justine has killed before, and they might still be out there.'

Fishbein looked like she was torn between focusing her attention on Alan, and doing her duty as a cheerleading mom. She stood up, dusted the dirt off her wide rump, grabbed Alan by the arm and led him away from the bleachers. They ended up behind the public restrooms where no one else could see them. 'Okay, you have my undivided attention. Now what's this crap about another murder?'

Alan was delighted. 'Sorry you wouldn't talk to me earlier?'

'Fuck you, don't push your luck. I don't like you and I don't put a lot of faith in what you have to say. To me, you're just another ex-con.'

They were quite alone behind the building, and Alan was impressed that this homely woman could be so fearless in the presence of a convicted murderer. 'At least you're consistent. Okay, here it is. In 1975, almost five years before Justine was killed, a man named Edward Bailey was shot in his home in Austin. The murder was almost identical to my wife's – he was killed with a .357 magnum, shot in the head inside his home, in the bathroom. There were signs of a robbery in other parts of the house, and for a while the cops thought it was a simple burglar shooting. Later they came to the conclusion that the break-in evidence was designed to cover up a murder, though no one was ever charged.'

Fishbein's thin lips drew together in a curious smirk. 'How is it you know so much about a twenty-year-old murder case?'

'I was a suspect.'

Fishbein's eyes widened behind her glasses. 'I'm sure there's a reason why you're telling me this, but I'll be goddamned if I can figure it out.'

Alan knew she was captivated by the story. 'Edward Bailey was a competitor of mine – a consultant who worked for a number of different political action committees in the state capital. We were friends of a sort, and from time to time we even talked about merging our two companies, but we could never agree on the details. We used to see each other at different parties and fund-raisers all over the state. Back then, my wife traveled with me quite a bit, and she got to know Ed pretty well herself. Too well. They had an affair.'

Fishbein shook her head, kicking a rock with her shoe. Slowly she started laughing, then took out another cigarette. 'Goddamn – this is starting to sound like a soap opera.'

Alan wondered if she was taking him seriously. He assumed so, since she was back here with him, instead of watching little Tommy play ball. 'A few days after the murder, I get this call from a detective in Austin. He tells me that Bailey had my name in his appointment book, and a couple of cops come to see me in Houston. We talk for a while, they want to know where I was on a certain night, then they ask me if I was aware that Bailey and Justine were lovers. I wasn't.'

'Why are you telling me all this? Do you want to confess?'

'I didn't kill Edward Bailey. I didn't kill my wife either, but I know you don't believe that.'

'I don't suppose they found the murder weapon in the Austin killing?'

Alan shook his head. 'Nope.'

'And you believe it's the same gun?'

'It wouldn't be hard to find out would it? If they have an unsolved case, they probably still have all the evidence. Can't you check bullets or something to tell if they came from the same gun?'

Fishbein looked like she was in a trance. Alan could almost see the wheels turning inside that ugly head of hers. He hoped he had her interest. 'You want me to check with the Austin police and see if the bullets match your wife's. Why? What difference does it make? That wouldn't prove you were innocent of murder; it might even serve to implicate you in a new homicide?'

'Do you think I would be telling you all this if I had killed Edward Bailey?'

Fishbein's eye wouldn't let go of his. 'You say this was 1975?'

'Edward Roy Bailey III. Check it out.'

Fishbein twirled and walked in a fast clip back toward the bleachers. Somehow, Alan didn't think she would enjoy the rest of the ball game.

15

'You can go in now, Mrs Stakeman. And be sure to pick up a brownie on your way out. It's one of my best recipes.'

I've already eaten two and stuffed three more in my purse, Melissa thought. Once this situation with Garth was under control, she'd have to go on a strict diet.

Dr Whitecotton invited her in, dressed in the same black suit she had seen him in the previous four visits. She wondered if it was really the same suit, or if he owned a collection of exact duplicates.

'Do you want to sit down, or would you prefer the couch?' Dr Whitecotton asked, a small smile curling across his face.

'The chair,' she said, plopping down.

'You seem tense. How are things?' he asked.

Melissa felt like screaming. She briefly considered picking up her mauve-colored chair and hurling it out the psychologist's window. 'Things suck.'

She stood up and began pacing. The last couple of times she had visited Dr Whitecotton, she had spent more time pacing than sitting.

Dr Whitecotton picked up his Wednesday pipe and

started packing in the tobacco. Melissa knew exactly which pipe he would choose. Dr Whitecotton was very much a creature of habit, not so unlike her husband. She wondered why she thought that his little idiosyncrasies were cute, while Garth's rubbed her the wrong way.

'What is happening with Garth?' Dr Whitecotton asked.

Melissa stopped pacing long enough to put her hands on her hips and pout. 'Garth is worse. Last Friday his father announced that he's moving out – getting his own apartment across town. Of course, Garth blames me for the whole thing, as if I had anything to do with it! The way Garth is acting, you'd think his dad was leaving the planet. Personally, I don't know what took Alan so long. I mean, he's got the business up and going, making money, and why wouldn't he want a little privacy?'

Dr Whitecotton made a note. 'You said that Garth hasn't verbalized his feelings. Are you certain that he does blame you?'

Melissa sat down across from Dr Whitecotton and kicked off her shoes. 'Garth is looking for a scapegoat. He sees that his fantasy of togetherness with his father is not working out. Alan Stakeman wants to have his own life. Garth spends all his energy trying to create a false closeness. It's sort of like when the mother of a teenage daughter tries too hard to be her daughter's best friend. She puts on teenage makeup, wears all the fad clothes, all in an attempt to try and be something she can never be. That's the way Garth is.'

'That's a pretty sophisticated assessment. You sound like you're doing my job for me.'

Melissa laughed. 'Does that mean I get a discount?'

Dr Whitecotton smiled. 'Afraid not. I take it that your relationship with your husband is not improving?'

'I'm busting my ass to try and salvage this marriage while he's working overtime to sink it. Not that he's actually *doing* anything – mentally he's just not there. It's the same sad story – he doesn't talk to me, he doesn't touch me, he doesn't acknowledge my existence. I've always heard that apathy is the hardest thing to deal with, and now I know it's true. There will come a time, in the not too distant future, when I'll just say fuck it!'

She fought against the urge to cry, feeling more angry than sad, and fantasized about putting her fist through Dr Whitecotton's wall.

Dr Whitecotton grunted. 'You said that Garth holds you responsible for his lack of success with his father. Do you feel as if you are to blame?'

'Certainly not! First of all, there's something unnatural about Garth and Alan's relationship. I've got several brothers, and I can assure you that none of them have any semblance of a real relationship with our father. Men don't know how to be close. They think a close relationship is sitting together on the couch watching football. Garth wants too much! It's almost like he's still that little boy in grade school, and daddy's going to teach him how to ride a bike. Sometimes I just want to grab him and say, "Grow up for Christsakes!"'

'Have you ever said that to him?'

Melissa shook her head. 'Are you kidding? He's so absorbed in this father fantasy, he wouldn't listen.'

Dr Whitecotton turned in his chair and looked toward the window. Melissa knew that the counselor always struck this pose when he was concentrating. 'It's difficult sometimes to understand other people's motivations – to respect that we each have come from our own past, with our own set of values. It's like the old proverb that says don't criticize me until you've walked in my shoes. There may be things about your husband's past – feelings left over from his mother's death – that you're not aware of. How much do you know about the details of her murder?'

Melissa thought about it. 'Not much, really. Just that Garth never believed his father did it. He hasn't talked about his mother more than once or twice. I always assumed it was because the memories were too painful.'

'Do you know if they were close?' Dr Whitecotton asked.

'I guess they were, but I don't know really. See, now you're making me feel sorry for him, and I don't like that. Nothing could excuse the shitty way he's been treating me. I'm sorry his mother was killed. I'm sorry his father went to jail, but goddamnit, that doesn't let him off the hook for blowing our marriage.'

Dr Whitecotton nodded. 'I'm not saying let him off the hook. But the more you know about someone, where they've been and what they've experienced, the better you can understand their point of view. Tell the truth – have you really sat him down and told him exactly how you feel?'

Melissa could feel her eyes getting wet. 'I've tried, I've really tried. He never gave me the impression that he was all that concerned.'

'Perhaps if you wrote him a letter, put everything you're feeling down on paper. Would that get through to him?' Dr Whitecotton asked.

'He probably wouldn't read it.'

'You could send it to his office. In a plain white envelope. Then he'd see it.'

Melissa liked the idea. It had been a few weeks since she'd really sat down and tried to talk about everything with Garth. Maybe if he knew how she felt, realized what he was doing to their marriage, he'd straighten up and fly right. 'At this point, I'll try anything.'

Dr Whitecotton put his pen away. 'Good. Go home and compose a letter. Don't hold anything back – let him know everything you're feeling. Send it to him, and tell me next week what he says.'

Melissa pulled a brownie out of her purse and bit half of it off. 'I will, Doctor. I certainly will.'

Alan Stakeman stood backstage at the George R. Brown Convention Center. C Hall was set up to seat five hundred, and from his spot behind the curtain at stage left, most of the chairs looked taken.

A raised stage had been constructed and the four Republican candidates for the US Senate had taken their seats. The week before, Alan had accompanied Texas Bob to his favorite men's store, and supervised the selection of a gray pinstripe suit, white shirt, and maroon tie. Bob towered over the other candidates, who Alan thought were nervous and intimidated. Texas Bob's smooth, good-ole-boy charm was working well with the event sponsors, and several well-to-do ladies. The upper echelon of the Texas Republican Women's Association fawned over Bob backstage, much to the chagrin of his opponents.

Four high back chairs were positioned in the center of the platform, and the candidates did their best to look natural and friendly under the blistering television lights. The debate would be carried live on Texas Public Broadcasting, which had affiliated stations in every major city in the state. This was the first real opportunity Texas Bob had had to go face-to-face with the other Republican candidates, and Alan was anxious to see how his man did in the live forum.

The backstage area was filled to capacity with campaign workers, families, and media all struggling to find the right spot to monitor the debate. Garth accompanied Alan, and stood quietly by his side as the moderator took the stage and the crowd hushed itself.

An attractive brunette in a silver and black business suit stepped to the microphone. 'Good evening, ladies and gentleman, and welcome to the Texas League of Women Voters Senatorial Debate. We are delighted to have all our party's candidates with us tonight, as well as our distinguished panel of journalists. I'll first introduce the candidates, and I'd ask each one to stand while I read his or her resumé – if you would please hold your applause until the end. Beginning on your left is Ms Joanne Wheeler, the current Mayor of Fort Worth. Ms Wheeler is a 1969 graduate of the University of Texas at Austin, where she...'

Alan craned his neck to look out over the crowd. He was

nervously excited, hoping for a strong showing from Texas Bob. Everyone in politics knew that these debates weren't really debates at all, but more of a forum where the questions seldom elicit an extemporaneous response. Candidates were schooled and rehearsed to the point where surprises were almost unheard of. Still, it was an excellent opportunity to show this group of well-heeled Republicans that Texas Bob Quintell was someone to watch.

'. . . and finally Mr Bob Quintell . . .'

Someone whooped in the rear of the hall, and a woman's voice said, 'Go get 'em, Texas Bob,' before a stern look from the moderator regained order.

'Mr Quintell is the president and majority owner of Texas Bob's Bar-B-Q Restaurants, and this is his first race for public office. Now, let's welcome all the candidates to Houston.'

Applause filled the hall, along with a few whistles, and Alan could detect the presence of Texas Bob's more vocal supporters in the back. Alan glanced toward the table where the reporters were seated. There were three unfamiliar faces and one very familiar, sitting quietly down front. Alan didn't know how he had done it, but Joseph Farmer was seated in the last chair on the far end of the table. Alan got Garth's attention, and nodded in the direction of Farmer. Garth's face turned brilliant red, and Alan watched his jaw muscles tighten in recognition.

The attractive brunette continued, 'Asking the questions this evening is a group of Texas's most respected journalists. From the Associated Press's Austin Bureau is Mr Nick Estes. Next is the executive editor of *Texas Monthly*

Magazine, Ms Jennifer Farquhar. Here is the political writer for the *Dallas Morning News*, Mr Roy Pinto, and we were to have had Earle Lynch, the syndicated columnist from the *Houston Chronicle*. Mr Lynch had an appendicitis attack this afternoon and had to have emergency surgery. We're very lucky to have been able to have such an esteemed substitute for him, the respected investigative reporter for KHOU-TV in Houston, Mr Joseph Farmer.'

Alan looked towards Texas Bob to see if Farmer's presence had rattled the politician. Quintell smiled and nodded at the television journalist with all the enthusiasm of a political pro. If Texas Bob was worried about Joseph Farmer, he sure wasn't showing it.

Each reporter was allowed to ask a single question, which would be answered by each of the candidates in turn. The candidates rotated the order in which they responded, and the moderator kept each candidate's response to sixty seconds or less.

The first twelve questions, including those from Joseph Farmer, were as predictable as the rising sun. Bob Quintell handled himself beautifully, making the most of the meaningless inquiries, showing himself to be the kind of natural born politician Alan thought he could be.

The moderator's smooth voice filled the hall. 'And now, for this last group of questions, we're going to relax the rules a bit and allow any of the journalists to direct a question to any of our candidates. Let's see, I believe it's your turn, Mr Farmer.'

Alan sensed that something was up by the sinister glint in Farmer's eye. 'I have a question for Mr Quintell.'

Texas Bob gave the television reporter a pleasant smile. 'I hope you aren't going to ask for my Bar-B-Q sauce recipe.'

Laughter broke out in the hall.

'My question does have to do with your business. Texas Bob's Bar-B-Q Restaurants, Incorporated, went public on August 24, 1979. Last year you had gross sales of approximately $123 million, and a pre-tax profit of $11.5 million. Is that correct, sir?'

Texas Bob's smile was glued in place. 'Sounds like you know how to read an annual report.'

Farmer didn't return the smile. 'I do. In fact, I own a few shares of stock myself. That's why I feel I have the right to ask this question...'

Alan didn't like the tone Farmer was taking, and he hoped Texas Bob didn't have any skeletons he hadn't told him about.

'The company keeps a number of special consultants on retainer – attorneys, accountants, and franchise experts. But I've done a little checking, and I wonder if you could tell us who A. Rodriguez might be?'

Oh shit, Alan thought. *Athena Rodriguez*! If it came out that Texas Bob's business life was controlled by a woman who was a palm reader, his credibility would be shot straight to hell!

Texas Bob never flinched. 'Excuse me, Mr Farmer, but this is a senatorial debate, not a stockholders' meeting, and I don't think your question is relevant to the political process. Now, if you'd like to ask me that question after the debate is over, I'd be happy to oblige.'

Joseph Farmer looked determined. 'The records indicate that an A. Rodriguez is a marketing consultant, who last year earned salary and bonuses in excess of $110,000. Now I have been told by several people that A. Rodriguez is—'

Texas Bob interrupted. 'Athena Rodriguez. The person you are talking about is indeed a marketing consultant to the company. She has been with me for the last fifteen years, during which time, she's been directly involved in corporate planning, marketing strategy, site selection, and research. There's nothing sinister or mysterious about her, nor has there been any effort to conceal anything from the stockholders.'

Farmer was relentless. Alan just knew that at any moment, the revelations about Athena Rodriguez's fortune telling, and God knows what else, could be the torpedo that sank Texas Bob's ship.

'Mr Quintell, I have been told that this woman is a psychic, and that you utilize her services on a day-to-day basis.'

Texas Bob never flinched. 'Oh, that's what you're asking about. Sure, I guess you could call her that. She reads Tarot cards, does astrological charts. On Tuesdays she reads my palm. So what? You want an appointment with her?'

Laughter broke out again in the crowd, and Alan smiled when he saw that Farmer's attack had been defused. Bob Quintell was smooth. Alan relaxed.

The moderator took over and called on the next reporter. Alan felt a tug on his coat, and looked over his shoulder into the clear black eyes of Detective Fishbein.

'Your guy handled that pretty well,' Fishbein said. 'Don't know what the reporter was driving at, but he ran out of gas.'

Alan didn't know what to make of Fishbein's presence at the debate. 'I didn't know you were a Republican.'

Fishbein lit a cigarette and chuckled. 'All the nicer people are.'

Alan tried to get his mind back on the debate, but he could almost feel Fishbein's gaze locked on his back. He knew he should keep a sharp eye on Texas Bob, and he was hoping that time would run out before Joseph Farmer got another crack at his candidate.

'Listen, Stakeman, I've been doing a lot of thinking about what you said about that Austin thing. I'd like for you to come by the office tomorrow and fill in some holes for me.'

Out of the corner of his eye, Alan saw Garth staring at the woman. 'Oh, I'm sorry. This is my son, Garth. Garth, this is Chief of Detectives Frieda Fishbein of the Houston Police.'

Alan looked back toward the stage and saw tension in Garth's face.

'I thought I recognized you. You were at the trial. What the hell do you want?' Garth asked.

'It's okay, son, relax. I want to talk to her.'

Garth looked the detective up and down, then turned his back to her. 'What about?'

Alan didn't feel like going into it, especially standing backstage at Texas Bob's first debate. 'I'll tell you later. C'mon, Detective, we can talk over there.'

Alan walked Fishbein over to a wooden bench near one of the stage doors. They were twenty feet from the nearest person, so Alan felt reasonably comfortable talking to the detective. He could hear the candidates answering questions over the loudspeaker system, but he couldn't concentrate on Texas Bob, not when he had finally succeeded in capturing the detective's interest. 'I must be dreaming. I thought you said that *you* wanted to talk to *me*.'

Fishbein took her thick glasses off and began cleaning them on her skirt. She smiled. 'I thought I'd give you another chance.'

'Have you talked to the Austin police?' he asked.

Fishbein nodded. 'Only to find out if there really was a murder case involving a Mr Edward Roy Bailey III. The Chief of Police in Austin is a buddy of mine. He remembered the case, but it will be a week before he can get the file. But I want you to tell me again why you're bringing all this up. From what you told me, you'd have to be considered a prime suspect. Anxious to go back to jail, Stakeman?'

Alan could hear Texas Bob's deep southern drawl generating chuckles throughout the hall. Loud applause and the sounds of movement told him the debate was over. Damn, he hoped he hadn't missed anything. 'Not at all. I told you – I want to clear my name. I don't want to be an ex-con the rest of my life.'

A huge throng of people began filling up the backstage area, as the candidates and their entourages left the stage. Alan looked around for Texas Bob, and not seeing him, began to make his way to the hall.

'Tell you what, Stakeman,' Fishbein said, as she tagged along behind him, 'Why don't you drop in after lunch tomorrow, and we'll go over the whole thing again. And this time, I'll give you my undivided attention.'

Alan nodded yes and stepped down to the spectator area. He had no trouble spotting Texas Bob's large head above the crowd. Alan was pleased to see he was deep in conversation with the brunette moderator. Probably using his height advantage to look down her dress, Alan thought. Across the room, Alan spotted Joseph Farmer walking slowly toward an exit. Following behind, separated by a large group of Republican women, was Garth.

Holy shit! Alan thought. *Christ, if Garth gets to Farmer and starts another fight, the publicity will be terrible.*

Alan broke into a fast trot, dodging his way through the crowd as best he could. He could hear Fishbein calling out his name behind him, but he couldn't afford to stop right now.

Alan made his was past the main crowd, into a large foyer just outside the hall. He saw Farmer and Garth standing toe-to-toe outside, next to the curb. Garth was obviously angry, and Alan prayed that neither one of them would get physical.

Alan burst out the glass exit door and hustled to a stop next to Garth.

'...that was typical of you,' Garth was saying, 'to try some trick like that. I can't understand why a major television station like Channel Eleven would keep a loser like you around.'

Farmer looked like he was ready to kill, as Alan found

himself in the unique position of peacemaker. 'Look, this is no place to start something.'

Garth didn't take his eyes off the reporter. Alan put his hand on his son's shoulder, and was surprised when he shrugged it away.

For a man who had already been physically humiliated once, Farmer gave no ground, no sign of being intimidated. After a few tense moments, Farmer took his eyes off Garth, and looked toward Alan.

'Your son has some very serious emotional problems. You and your candidate would be better off without this hothead in the campaign.'

'Fuck you,' Garth said. He looked at his father. 'I'll be inside.' Without looking at Farmer again, he turned and walked away.

'Don't push too hard,' Alan told Farmer in a level voice. 'It isn't healthy, as you of all people should know.'

Farmer's face perked. 'That a threat, Stakeman?'

'I don't make threats. But it is good advice.'

'Yeah.' Farmer gave him a smile that was not friendly. 'I'll be seeing you.' He moved away, walking toward the parking lot.

Alan sighed, staring after the reporter for a few moments, then turned to return to the convention center. Fishbein stood before him, her hands clasped behind her back. 'Ah, politics,' she said with a condescending smile. 'How you must love it.'

'A couple of young hotheads. They'll cool off.'

Fishbein nodded. 'It sounded like a threat, what you said.'

'Second guessing me again, Detective?'

Fishbein shrugged. 'See you tomorrow, Stakeman. My office.'

Dear Garth

I am writing you this letter at the suggestion of Dr Whitecotton. He said that it was important that I put my feelings down on paper, to be certain that you understood where I was coming from.

I'm just about at my wits' end. The way I see it, our marriage is on the verge of collapse. You have shut me out of your life, and no matter how hard I try, I can't get you to admit that we have a problem. I know you have a lot on your mind – the new business, your father – but you have to understand that I have needs too! I'm not like you. It's not enough for me to share the same house, eat meals together, and still have to do without the closeness we once felt. It's been three months since we made love, and even then I got the feeling you were just performing out of a sense of duty.

Dr Whitecotton said that I have to realize that we are two different people, that our personalities and needs have been shaped by two different sets of life experiences. He said that that doesn't mean that one of us is right and the other is wrong – we're both right!

All that means is that we have to accept our differences, and find areas of compatibility. That's not so hard. We've done it before. I still remember the first night we were together, after the Doobie Brothers concert at the college. Remember?

Five years ago we shared our wedding vows in the middle of a room filled with drunks in Halloween costumes. But those promises were as serious for me as if they had been expressed in the Winchester Cathedral. I meant every word then, and in spite of everything, I still want us to be together.

Garth, please, please let me back into your life. Take the time to think about our marriage, and join me in making a commitment to do whatever it takes to salvage our relationship.

I do love you, Garth, so very much. I hope you still love me. Tell me where we go from here.

All my love, Melissa.

16

Melissa heard Garth turn off the television, and knew he'd be coming to bed soon. She took the large gift box out from the closet and slipped into the bathroom, closing the door softly behind her.

She stood in front of the mirror and pulled her oversized T-shirt up over her head. She stared at her naked self in the full length mirror. *Why doesn't Garth want me?* she wondered. *My body still looks good, my lips full and inviting, my breasts shapely and firm. Why doesn't he touch me?*

Her body ached for attention.

She picked up the brush and ran it through her hair. She dabbed a tiny spot of perfume behind her ears and in the valley between her breasts.

Melissa opened the box and took out the cream-colored teddy. It was an expensive, frilly thing with a plunging neckline that showed off most of her two biggest assets. The legs were cut high, trimmed in French lace, with two small snaps in the crotch. The sales girl in Victoria's Secret had promised, 'The snaps pop open automatically in the presence of an erection.'

Melissa heard Garth come into the bedroom and she quickly slipped on the teddy. She tugged and adjusted, licked her lips, and walked out of the bathroom.

Garth was sitting up in bed reading the latest copy of *Adweek.* He didn't look up when she came into the bedroom.

He'd better sit up and take notice if he knows what's good for him, she thought.

Melissa walked slowly across the room, pretending to be straightening up, giving Garth ample opportunity to glance up and see her new lingerie.

He didn't.

'What did the weather man have to say?' Melissa asked, knowing Garth had just watched the late news. 'Is it going to rain tomorrow?'

Garth looked up from his magazine. 'Just a twenty per cent chance.'

Garth returned to his reading, never reacting or commenting about Melissa's night wear.

That motherfucker! she thought. *He barely even noticed!*

She suppressed the urge to throw something at him. *Surely he'll wake up any minute*, she thought. *Jesus, my tits are hanging out, my ass is showing – what the fuck do I have to do?*

'I meant to tell you,' she said, keeping her voice calm. 'I got a massage yesterday. It was wonderful.'

'That's good,' Garth said.

'It felt good to be touched.'

Garth didn't respond.

Melissa fiddled with the jewelry on top of the dresser.

She opened and closed several drawers, making noise, waiting for him to look up and see that his sexy goddamn wife was practically naked in front of him.

Nothing happened. She was pissed off.

Melissa left the bedroom and walked to the kitchen. She poured herself a glass of chocolate milk and thought about her options.

She could go in there and demand that he notice her. She could spread ice cream all over her crotch and invite him to lick it off. Or she could take a butcher knife and cut off his balls!

Melissa downed the milk and walked toward the bedroom. She could also take a cold shower, she thought. Or go see a divorce lawyer. Or take a lover. Or do nothing and remain unhappy.

One thing was certain. She was tired of being ignored. She was going to demand change. Soon.

Frieda Fishbein told her secretary she didn't want to be disturbed and closed the door to her office. She dug around in her purse until she found her pack of Salems, lit one, and sat back to read the poor quality photocopies from the Austin Police Department.

AUSTIN POLICE DEPARTMENT
Felony Crime Data Sheet
Homicide Division
Complainant: Edward Roy Bailey III.

Fishbein's eyes scanned past the general information and

stopped at the narrative description of the detective's report.

REPORT OF DETECTIVE SERGEANT AL FURNEY – September 3, 1975. Dets Al Furney and Lt Foster Hamilton responded to a Signal 54, where we found the victim deceased on the floor in the bathroom. The crime scene resembled a suicide, due to the fact that there was high velocity blood spatter in a pattern similar to what is seen when a large caliber gun discharges at very close range. No weapon was found at the scene.

After contacting the Coroner's office and calling for the Texas Crime Laboratory technicians, we began working the crime scene. Det. Hamilton went outside to survey the exterior perimeter for signs of a break-in. I remained in the bathroom area to wait for the Coroner. While in the room, I noted a small muddy area in the bathroom carpet near the entry door. I asked the uniformed officer back to the room, and visually compared his shoe size to that of the imprint. It was obvious that the officer's shoe was several sizes larger than the footprint and I had him locate a cardboard box and placed it upside down over the print, to preserve it for Crime Lab.

Sgt. Hamilton returned and indicated that there was a rear window which had been forced open and showed pry marks. At that time the Crime Lab personnel arrived, and Sgt. Hamilton and myself

accompanied them as they photographed the scene.
(Cont. on page two)

Fishbein stopped reading and tried to visualize the situation. From the spare photographs which accompanied the police report, she saw a crime scene that was quite similar to that of Justine Stakeman's. The victim in the Austin, Texas, case had been dead for a couple of days prior to being found. The blood evidence in the room had had time to dry.

Fishbein made a note to check and see if the two detectives were still with the Austin Police Department, and to request any fragments which might still be in evidence.

Fishbein flipped several pages into the thick file, looking for the detective's references to Alan Stakeman. Scanning ahead about two weeks, she found what she was looking for.

SUPPLEMENTAL OFFENSE REPORT
REPORT OF DETECTIVE SERGEANT
AL FURNEY
September 16, 1975

Continuing in the homicide investigation of Edward Roy Bailey, III. Det. Lt. Hamilton and myself traveled to Houston to interview a Mr Alan M. Stakeman, 12392 Wells Road, Houston, 713/785-2944. Mr Stakeman's name and home telephone number had been found in the victim's personal effects. Mr Stakeman agreed to meet us at his downtown office.

He appeared relaxed and cooperative. During the interview he indicated that he had known the victim both socially and professionally for a number of years. He described their relationship as 'close acquaintances, friendly competitors'. He said that he did not know why his personal phone number would have been on the victim's body. He said he rarely received calls from the victim, and had no recollection of ever getting one at home. Mr Stakeman said that he had last seen the victim approximately three weeks prior to the homicide at a political gathering in Austin. At that time, the victim seemed normal, didn't express any concerns for his safety, though he (victim) was at the time working in a very heated political campaign and Bailey's client had received several anonymous death threats. Mr Stakeman said that the victim told him the threats had come from some Texas members of the Ku Klux Klan. Mr Stakeman indicated that in his business, it was not that uncommon to receive telephone threats, that they 'came with the territory'. It was only after the homicide that Mr Stakeman wished that he had recommended that the victim take precautions.

Fishbein put down the file and lit another cigarette. So far, everything Stakeman had told her seemed to be on the up-and-up, though she still had reservations.

The remote concept that she could have been wrong, that her actions might have been responsible for an innocent man going to prison, had given her a severe case of indigestion. Ever since Stakeman had approached her at the little league game, Fishbein had been wrestling with anxiety, and antacids were now a part of her daily regimen.

Looking over the nuts and bolts of this twenty-year-old case, Fishbein realized how much she missed actual detective work. *Oh sure*, she thought, *the title is Chief of Detectives, but the only investigations you conduct are in the search for a bigger share of the city's budget.* The Chief of Detectives' job was managerial and largely administrative. She couldn't remember the last time she had actually been to a crime scene, or interviewed a suspect.

Digging through the old homicide files got her juices flowing. Even though there was an outside chance she had made a mistake, it was the most exciting thing she had been involved in in years.

She rubbed her eyes for a few seconds before picking the file up again.

SUPPLEMENTAL OFFENSE REPORT
REPORT OF DETECTIVE SERGEANT
AL FURNEY
September 30, 1975

Continuing the investigation of the homicide of Edward Roy Bailey III.

Det.'s Furney and Hamilton returned to Houston by commercial flight, to again interview Mr Alan M. Stakeman (address in file) regarding above homicide. This was our second interview with Mr Stakeman, and he seemed less cooperative than he was previously.

Det. Hamilton explained to Mr Stakeman that certain facts had been uncovered that warranted our return. Specifically, we informed Mr S. that we had checked the victim's long distance records and noted more than a dozen calls were placed to Mr Stakeman's home phone during the five days prior to the homicide. Mr Stakeman repeated what he had said during our first interview, that he seldom received calls from the victim, and couldn't remember the last time he (victim) had called him at home. Mr Stakeman could offer no explanation for the long distance records.

Det. Hamilton then informed Mr Stakeman that a number of personal letters had been found in the victim's home indicating that he (victim) had been having a romantic relationship with Mrs Stakeman. At that point Mr Stakeman became very belligerent, and made several profane references to Det. Hamilton. We informed Mr Stakeman that the existence of the affair and the possibility that he might be aware of the same made him a suspect in the homicide. Det. Hamilton then read Mr Stakeman his rights, after which Mr Stakeman continued to express his irritation. He indicated that he would have nothing further to say without his attorney. We gave him our card and told him we would be staying in town a couple of days and where we were staying if he changed his mind.

So, Fishbein thought, *there's a flash of anger. At least*

Alan Stakeman was human and he could react like a man with feelings.

Mr Stakeman apparently thought better of his actions, and contacted us later that day at our motel. We met him in the lobby and he asked to come up to our room. Det. Hamilton again read Mr Stakeman his rights, and he indicated that he had no problem answering our questions. Mr Stakeman said that his hostile reaction earlier had been due to the fact that he was not aware that his wife had been having an affair. He said that the shock of that revelation had caused him to respond in an abrasive manner.

Det. Hamilton conducted the interview, which was recorded, during which time Mr Stakeman answered every question fully and without hesitation. He said that on the night of the murder, he had attended a victory celebration for a political client. Mr Stakeman said that he arrived at the party shortly before 7 p.m. and stayed until after 2 a.m. Det. Hamilton asked if anyone would be able to corroborate his story and he said 'only about 800 people, including the newly elected Governor of Texas'.

Mr Stakeman gave us a long list of people he had talked to at the function. Subsequent interviews with 14 persons indicated that Mr Stakeman was in fact seen by one or more of the parties throughout the evening, and place him at the party. At most he couldn't have been missing more than an hour or so. Since it is 150 miles from Houston to Austin, it would not be possible to make that trip by car in that amount of time.

Fishbein read through the rest of the file, which went on to describe how the two Austin detectives had methodically investigated the possibility that Stakeman had flown between Houston and Austin.

The detectives had checked with all the commercial airlines which fly from Houston to Austin, as well as every air charter service in each city. Private aircraft records were also investigated, and the final conclusion was that Alan Stakeman had not flown to Austin that evening and therefore could not have committed the murder of Edward Bailey.

She thought back to the first time she'd met Alan Stakeman. It was the night of Justine's murder, early in the morning, actually. The call came around 3 a.m. at Frieda's house. The crime scene had been discovered a little after midnight and Frieda's supervisor, Captain Hudson, had called her in even though she was off duty.

She remembered that her husband was very sick at the time, pneumonia the doctors said, and she'd told her captain that she couldn't leave him home alone. The captain argued with her, told her that her priorities were screwed up, before finally offering to send a uniformed officer over to Fishbein's house to baby-sit her husband.

Frieda still remembered her first impressions walking into the Stakeman house. Something about the crime scene was bogus. It showed some signs of a break-in, but it looked like kids had been in the place. An amateur did this, she thought at the time.

The body had just been taken away, though the pungent smell of blood still hung heavily in the master bathroom. Standing over the spot where Justine had died, Frieda's mind kept wandering back to her sick husband. She wondered if he had wakened to find her gone, if his fever was still high, if his cough was any better. She fought the urge to tell the captain to fuck off and rush back home to be at his side. She thought she was making a mistake leaving him there with a stranger. It was a week before he was able to go back to work, and she always looked back on that moment with a feeling of shame. *This job sucks sometimes*, she remembered thinking.

Funny how after all these years, looking back on the biggest case she'd ever investigated, that her strongest images were of her personal life, and of the personal indecision that had haunted the beginning of the investigation.

There was a knock at the door and Fishbein looked up to see Alan Stakeman at her door. She closed the file and motioned for him to have a seat.

Fishbein tried to imagine Stakeman during his interviews with the Austin detectives. She remembered how self-assured he had been when she interrogated him, and wondered if he had been the same with the capital city cops.

'So, Stakeman,' she said, 'glad you could drop by. I've been reading the file on the Bailey homicide, and so far, everything you've told me checks out. There's just a couple of small things I need to clear up. By the way, you don't by any chance have a pilot's license, do you?'

'Pilot's license? Hell no. I hate to fly.'

'Just curious. There are a few other points I'd like to discuss with you . . .'

17

Melissa woke up early Sunday morning. The bed sheets next to her were rumpled and empty.

She got out of bed, dressed in a long T-shirt, panties, and thick socks and padded to the kitchen in search of a strong cup of coffee. She found her custom blend – vanilla nut creme mixed with chocolate-raspberry – and watched the drip coffee maker do its stuff.

Garth's out jogging, she thought. *Maybe he'll run into a little emotion.*

Alan had gone on a campaign swing through west Texas and had asked them to tape Texas Bob's interview on one of the early Sunday morning talk shows. Melissa didn't feel like going back to bed, so she decided to watch. She went into Garth's study and turned on the small color television near his bookcase, sat behind his desk and propped her feet up.

'Good morning everyone, and welcome to *Houston in Perspective*, our weekly look at the people and issues of interest to the residents of America's fourth largest city. I'm Wendy Wiggins, and our guest this morning is a man whose recent victory in politics has thrust him into the forefront of today's headlines. I'm talking, of course, about the winner in last week's Republican primary for US Senator, Texas Bob Quintell. Welcome to *Houston in Perspective*, Mr Quintell.'

'Good morning, Wendy, and please, call me Bob.'

Melissa snickered as Texas Bob put on his most charming smile for the announcer.

Wendy looks like a first-class bimbo, Melissa thought. *Where do they get these Barbie dolls, anyway?*

'...now be honest, Bob, weren't you just a little bit surprised by your big margin of victory?'

The camera went to a close-up of Texas Bob as he smiled and made strong eye contact with the announcer. 'Our polls had us at or near first place from almost the beginning, though we tried to downplay that to our volunteers, so as not to peak too early. But during the last two weeks of the primary, our campaign really took off, and the tracking polls during the final days showed a very strong upsurge in support in the key metropolitan areas. And I can tell you, the night before the election, our pollster brought me a survey that had us ahead, winning with sixty-eight per cent of the vote. Of course, as you know, the final figures were a little over seventy per cent.'

Who does your hair Wendy? Melissa thought. *And my God, could you wear any more blush?*

'Okay Bob, so now you're in the big one, against Senator Philip Smart. Now my sources tell me that we're in for a real tough campaign. I'm told that the National Rifle Association, the Republican National Committee, and two or three other big conservative groups have decided that now's the time to boot Senator Smart out of office. So, just between you and me, are we about to see some serious mud-slinging?'

'Wendy, I can't tell you what the Washington groups are going to do, but as far as my plans are concerned, I'm going to try and run an issue-oriented campaign. That means I'm going use every opportunity to discuss exactly where I stand on the most important issues facing Texas – things like education, crime, job growth, foreign trade, and a variety of other concerns. And you can bet that where my position differs from that of Senator Smart, the voters will be told exactly which candidate is on the side of the people.

'Now, if you call that mud-slinging so be it. But I am not planning to conduct any personal attack on the Senator, his family, or his staff. I'm just going to tell the people the truth, tell what I think and let the chips fall where they will.'

Melissa heard a loud growl from her stomach and realized it was time for breakfast. She went to the kitchen and scrounged through the refrigerator, considering her options before grabbing a jar of pickles and a box of leftover fried chicken.

A nutritious breakfast to start the day, she thought. She skipped back to Garth's study as the interview program was coming out of a commercial.

'And we're back on *Houston in Perspective*, and we're talking to the Republican candidate for the US Senate, Texas Bob Quintell. Bob, a lot has been made out of the fact that you're a successful businessman and a man of little or no political experience. How do you expect to be able to represent Texas in a city like Washington DC if you don't have a background in public service?'

Melissa alternated between bites of chicken and kosher dill pickles.

'If you ask me, Wendy, we have too many professional politicians in office as it is. I think it's high time we got some fresh ideas in the system. Now it is true that Senator Smart has a lot of experience as a professional politician. In fact, except for about six months when he was working for his daddy, he's been on the public payroll his entire adult life!'

Melissa knew what was coming. She'd seen an early draft of a speech Alan had written on this very subject.

'Frankly, Wendy, I don't think a man who knows nothing about business has any business representing our state. Texas is hurting. Our number one priority right now has to be new jobs. We can't sit idly by and let the Japanese, the Koreans, and the Mexicans put hard-working Texans out of work.'

Melissa didn't normally care much for politics, but Texas Bob was so smooth, polished and downright folksy, she found herself clapping between swallows. She looked down at the box and realized that she'd eaten two breasts and one-and-a-half legs. She was glad Garth wasn't home to see her pigging out.

She put the food away and brought a cloth in to wipe any crumbs off Garth's desk and chair. *There will be hell to pay if he comes home and finds food on his antique mahogany desk,* she thought.

Brushing chicken remnants into her hand, she accidentally knocked a stack of manilla file folders off the desk. She bent down to pick them up and noticed that the contents of one folder had slipped out on to the floor. It was a collection of old newspaper clippings, yellowed and dried with age.

I wonder what Garth's doing with these? she thought.

Feeling like a snoop, Melissa sat down at the desk and opened the file. There were at least thirty newspaper stories, all but a couple having to do with Justine Stakeman's murder and Alan's subsequent arrest and trial.

Before she realized it she was drawn into the stories, reading each one from beginning to end. It was a complete chronology of Alan Stakeman's arrest and trial. Every aspect of the crime and prosecution was included. Sidebar items provided juicy, gossipy stories about extramarital affairs and suspicious neighbors. Several stories detailed Alan's long, successful career, and one even went so far as to list all of his assets and liabilities.

It was easy to see why the name Alan Stakeman had such an effect on people. A mysterious crime, committed in a safe, very affluent neighborhood. A rich, colorful, powerful defendant. World famous criminal defense lawyer Morgan Villard retained to represent the defendant. A three-week, circus sideshow trial, filled with titillating witnesses talking about money, sex, drugs and the interworkings of big time politics.

By the time Melissa came to the end of the stack, she felt as if she had a clear picture of what a sensation the Stakeman case had been. The yellowed stories ended, but underneath were a couple of more recent newspaper clippings. One was a front page article just a week old, detailing the robbery and murder of former Mayor William Hubbell. She felt a chill run down her spine when she remembered her very strange conversation with Garth about the killing.

The second article she hadn't seen before. It was a small story from the *Houston Post* about the killing of a man named John Beets. *John Beets,* Melissa thought, *that name sounds so familiar.*

She looked at the photo of the man which accompanied the article. A shooting, the police thought a robbery attempt, outside a bar in the Fifth Ward.

Nothing special. No reason for Garth to be keeping it. So why is it here?

She looked back at the photograph. Back at the name.

'My name is Beets. John Beets. And I think they should have fried you, Stakeman.'

John Beets, the drunk who mouthed off at Alan in the Mexican restaurant, the first week after he'd been released. Holy shit! Melissa thought.

She checked the date on the article, then counted backwards in her head.

That guy turned up dead just a few days after seeing us in the restaurant. Why would Garth have a copy of that article?

She could understand how Garth might want to keep the stories about his father, but John Beets? It didn't make any sense.

'Find anything interesting?' Garth was standing in the

doorway, shirtless and wearing jogging shorts, drenched in sweat.

She jumped at the sound of his voice. 'Garth, oh, um, I was just watching Texas Bob's interview on Channel Two. And, uh, this file kinda fell open while I was straightening up.'

'I see.'

'No, really!' she said. 'It just slid out.'

'Looked like you were reading through my stuff.'

'I wasn't prying – if that's what you mean.'

Garth's eyes never left hers as he walked over and took the file out of her hand. He picked up the newspaper clippings and stacked them neatly inside, then put the file back on top of his desk.

'I guess you've already had breakfast,' he said, thumping a small piece of chicken crust off his desktop.

Melissa felt like a little girl caught with her hand in the cookie jar. 'I was hungry. I had a snack.'

'I was going to see if you wanted to go out and get something.'

She was stunned by the invitation. 'Uh, yeah sure. Let's go out. I only had a couple of bites. Breakfast would be great.'

Garth nodded and walked out of the room. In a minute she heard the shower running in the bathroom, and she realized that she'd been holding her breath.

Did he think I was spying on him? she wondered. *Of course he did, you idiot. What else could he think, under the circumstances?*

Melissa went into the bedroom and looked in her closet.

She pulled on a pair of black walking shorts and a white cotton blouse. She applied a little make-up and ran a brush through her hair. By the time she'd finished her primping, Garth was out of the shower.

He walked into the bedroom with a towel around his waist. She watched him pass by in the mirror.

'Where d'you want to go for breakfast?' she asked, her eyes following his movements.

Garth glanced her way. 'How about Le' Peep?'

'Great!' she answered.

Garth took a pair of khakis out of his closet. He pulled a dark blue polo shirt over his head and combed his wet hair down.

'You know, my mother was nosy like that,' Garth said. It felt like a kick in the stomach.

Your mother, Melissa thought. *Where did that come from?*

She could count on one hand the number of times Garth had ever said the word 'mother'. Melissa had learned long ago that he was not forthcoming on the subject of 'mom'.

'I used to catch her going through my stuff all the time. She'd go through my books, homework, anything she could find. I'd write notes to her in my diary, stuff like "Hello, Mother", just to piss her off. I tried to convince her that even a teenager deserved a little privacy. She laughed in my face.'

Melissa didn't want to be put in the same category as Justine Stakeman. Not that she knew much about the woman.

'Look, Garth. Don't make a big deal out of this. I was

watching Texas Bob on TV. I accidentally knocked open the file. I'd never read all those stories about the trial. I was curious.'

Garth wiped his forehead with a small towel. 'How was it?' he asked.

He was making her nervous. 'How was what?'

Garth sat down on the bed and was putting on his shoes. 'The interview. How was the interview?'

She must be imagining things, because she could swear that his eyes had somehow changed color. Instead of their normal green, now they looked dark brown, almost black. 'Oh – good. Really good. Bob seemed very relaxed. Knowledgeable. Y'all have been working with him, haven't you?'

'Dad has. I've been busy at the agency, trying to get everything in order so I can leave.'

Oh my God! Melissa thought. *Is Garth talking to me about his work?*

'How's your latest project coming along?' Garth asked.

She was shocked and delighted with his sudden interest. 'It's been moving slow up to now. I haven't felt much like working on it. But the deadline is staring me in the face and I'll be moving into high gear.'

'This is the Mayan thing?'

She went over to the walk-in closet and grabbed her sketch pad. A few months earlier she'd been given a commission by the Mexican government to do a twelve-foot-tall Mayan figure for a new museum in Mexico City.

She flipped to her latest pencil sketch and showed it to him.

The drawing was of a Mayan priest. A man standing in profile, wearing an extremely tall hat which towered three feet above his head. The hat looked like a combination of a stovepipe hat and a Mexican sombrero. The face of the Mayan priest was regal, with a very wide, exaggerated, long nose. The figure's eyes were closed in prayer. 'I've just started the clay modeling. It will be a few weeks before we're ready to pour any casts.'

Garth's eyes moved from the sketch pad to her face. He reached out and touched her cheek. 'You know I'm proud of you, don't you?'

She couldn't believe what she was hearing. His eyes were green again, warm and loving, his voice calm and affectionate.

She stepped forward, put her hands on his shoulders and kissed him lightly on the lips. She was surprised when he grabbed her and kissed her back, his tongue finding its way inside her mouth.

Garth pulled back and smiled. 'You taste like a pickle.'

She melted in his arms. *God it's been so long,* she thought.

Garth planted short, soft kisses across her face. She felt tears start to fall gently out of the corners of her eyes.

He kissed the tears away. Her body was on fire.

She pressed her body against him. His hands reached up to cup her face, and her legs grew weak with desire.

Garth pulled back from the kisses and looked at her. They stood close, her nipples visibly erect through the fabric.

She didn't know what was going to happen next. She was

afraid to let him stop kissing her. Afraid to give him a chance to withdraw back into his shell.

He had kissed her with an eagerness she hadn't felt in years. Her body ached for his touch, and she felt her growing wetness.

He reached across and cupped her breasts in his hands. His fingers gently pinched her nipples.

She sucked in a deep breath of air and closed her eyes. His hands squeezed and fondled her. She felt herself swoon.

Garth dropped his hands from her breasts and took her hand. He led her over to the edge of the bed. He reached down and began unbuttoning her blouse.

Melissa leaned back on her hands and closed her eyes again. She was determined to feel every sensation. She felt his warm, strong fingers working on the cotton fabric. Her head was full of his clean, fresh smell. She thought she might faint.

Garth pulled the tail of her blouse out and worked through all the buttons. He gently pulled her arms out of the blouse, leaving her topless. She kept her eyes closed as his hands began working on the shorts. When his hand grazed across her upper thigh, she opened her eyes.

She whimpered as he lifted her butt off the bed and pulled the panties down her long, tan legs. He was on his knees now, kneeling at the altar of her womanhood. She fell back on the bed, ready.

'I want you inside me,' she whispered.

He made no move to get up. Instead, Garth planted tiny kisses across the top of her thighs. His fingers kneaded and stroked the inside of her legs. His hand grazed the top of her pubic hair.

She spread her legs.

The kisses started again just above the knee, leaving a warm, wet trail up the inside of her thigh. Her head rocked from side to side. Her moans grew louder as his tongue flicked near the opening.

'Fuck me. Eat me. Do something!'

She writhed on the bed as his mouth and tongue found her. He spread her with his fingers as his tongue moved in a slow, soft rhythm.

She came within seconds, her hands ruffling his hair as he worked his magic.

Melissa rocked with the continuous flood of sensations as Garth performed miracles on her neglected sexuality.

18

Melissa parked her twelve-year-old Harley-Davidson in the grass next to a picnic table in a small, secluded city park. Two teenagers were lying on a blanket across the way, paying absolutely no attention to anyone but themselves.

She took her motorcycle helmet off and lay down across one of the benches. She took out her portable stereo, popped a Tom Petty cassette into the tape player and lit a big, fat joint.

She took a hit off the joint and held her breath.

Am I crazy? she thought. *I know I'm acting like a bitch. I piss and moan and complain about no sex, then the minute Garth pays it on me, I get suspicious.*

Okay, so it was a little strange. Garth came home, found me poking around in his stuff, but instead of getting mad and storming away, he throws me across the bed and licks me like a sugar cone?

The pot was doing its job. She could feel the stoned wave roll over her, and for a few moments at least, she didn't think about anything but rock 'n' roll. Melissa adjusted her headphones and turned the music up louder.

What's wrong with this picture? she thought. *Why am I so confused? I feel like such a weak sister, like some mousey little woman who cries to get her way, but is never happy when she gets it.*

Does Garth really love me? she wondered. *Do I even want this marriage to work?*

Am I ever going to be happy with this man? Should I just cut my losses and move on. And why does my gut tell me that there is something evil bubbling just beneath the surface?

Melissa rang the buzzer on the outside security gate and waited for Alan to let her through. She knew she should have called first, but what the hell, he'd either be here or not.

Her hair was standing out from her head, mussed from the motorcycle helmet and the wind. The dope had made her pensive. She wanted to talk to Alan, to see if he had any insight into his son's state of mind.

Alan was smiling when he opened the door. 'Melissa, hi. C'mon in.'

Alan was dressed in a dark blue suit, apparently just home from the office. Melissa had been to his townhouse when he was moving in, but this was the first time since he'd finished decorating.

Alan fixed her a drink and pointed to the couch while he excused himself to change.

She looked around the room. The townhouse was open and roomy, two stories, decorated in earth tones with lots of leather furniture. A tall cactus plant stood near the sliding glass patio door, and numerous other house plants made the place feel comfortable and lived in.

I can see where Garth got his good taste, she thought. *Am I making a mistake by being here? Maybe I shouldn't bring my troubles to Dad.*

Alan came back more casual in a beige sweat suit. 'Much better,' he said, pouring himself a highball.

She hoped she would be able to open up and tell Alan everything on her mind. 'I love the way you've decorated – and all the plants.'

'I know what you mean. I wanted lots of greenery in my place. That's one thing you miss in prison. Nothing much grows inside those concrete walls.'

She could feel her heart racing in her chest, and had to sit on her hands to keep them from trembling.

He propped his feet up on the coffee table. 'So, what brings you over here?'

Here I am running to Dad with wild suspicions about Garth, she thought. *Alan will probably think I'm an idiot.* 'I was at the park. I hope I'm not disturbing you.'

'No, I'm glad to see you. If you hang around long enough you can meet my date.'

Melissa smiled. 'Oh? Someone special?'

Alan patted down his thick, white hair. 'I think so. I met her at one of the news conferences about a month ago. She handles sales for the downtown Hyatt.'

'Oh really? How old is she?'

'I don't know. Late thirties, early forties. Old enough to have a daughter in junior college.'

'You look casual.'

Alan grinned. 'That's the way I like it. We're going to hang out here this evening. Grill a couple of steaks, eat a salad. You're welcome to join us.'

'Thanks anyway,' Melissa said, taking a deep breath. 'Dad, I need to talk to you. About Garth.'

'I figured as much. What's wrong?'

She turned up her glass and gulped down the cold scotch. The liquor warmed her throat but it did little to calm her nerves. 'I don't know if you know this or not, but things haven't been good between Garth and me.'

Alan nodded. 'He told me you were unhappy. I tried to get details, but you know Garth. He basically said that you were upset with him because he's so quiet.'

Melissa shook her head. 'It's much more involved than that. There is something very deep going on here.'

'Like what?'

'I don't know exactly. Garth's changed. I can't put my finger on it, but he's definitely not the man I married.'

'Everyone changes as they grow older. You two have known each other a long time.'

'I know, and for a while, I sort of wrote it off as my imagination. But the man I fell in love with is gone. He's been replaced by a very distant, almost completely withdrawn Garth. You must have seen it too. You're around him at work. How does he seem to you?'

'Now that you mention it, he does seem quieter than usual. Though for me, all this freedom is so new, I sometimes feel like I'm gonna have a sensory overload. When did you first notice a change? I really haven't noticed anything.'

'It all started about a year ago. But it's gotten much worse since you got out of prison.'

Alan looked startled. 'What are you saying? That somehow I am to blame for Garth's behavior?'

She hoped he wasn't offended. 'No, not at all. He seems edgy all the time. And he gets angry at the tiniest thing. A couple of months ago, I told Garth that you and I had gone to lunch, and he got very mad. Didn't talk to me for a week.'

Melissa could see he was confused.

'I don't understand,' Alan said. 'What upset him?'

'I told him that we had talked about your time in prison. He got pissed because I had brought up your past.'

'That's ridiculous. I'll say something to him.'

'No, please don't. He and I have to work this out between us.'

'Garth's just being overprotective, like a mother hen. But come on, Melissa. There has to be more to it than that. What happened that made you want to come to see me?'

She told him the story of watching TV in Garth's study, not going into detail about the newspaper clips. Alan smiled as she hesitantly mentioned the sexual interlude. 'Has he ever said anything, you know, about me? Or about our marriage?'

'Only that he's proud of you. I thought I had noticed some tension between you.'

Melissa took a deep breath. 'There's something else, something I can't put out of my mind. You know I told you about finding the newspaper stories. Well, I read them. And most of them were about your trial.'

Alan took their glasses to the bar for a refill. 'So, he kept the articles about the trial. That doesn't sound unusual to me.'

'It wasn't just the trial. It was more like a scrapbook. There were stories from the society pages, stuff with you and your wife. It looked like every story that ever ran, from the time Mrs Stakeman was found dead right through all your appeals.'

Alan refilled the drinks and sat back down. 'You know Garth doesn't do things halfway. I remember during the trial, the way he was ... well I don't know what I would have done without him. Here I was, an innocent man on trial for my life, and no one, I mean no one, except Garth, believed in me. Garth became almost a hired hand on the defense team, though he was only eighteen. He latched on to Morgan Villard, my lawyer, with a vengeance. Called him at all hours of the day and night with ideas for my defense. Every day, all day, he sat in the same chair right behind me in that courtroom, his eyes and ears glued to the proceedings. He took extensive notes and every evening he would hand over pages and pages – about certain testimony, witnesses, ideas. He was something.'

Melissa tried to imagine what it would be like to be an innocent man charged with murder. 'Dad, let me ask you something. Do you know who killed your wife? I mean, you must have thought about it.'

Alan shrugged. 'I think it was a burglar. Some thief, probably high on drugs, looking for something to steal. Justine was just in the wrong place at the wrong time.'

She was relieved. 'There's something else about the

stories I found in Garth's office. There were three other articles about a murder that was even older than your wife's, something about a man in Austin. There was an article about Mayor William Hubbell, then another story, only a couple of months old. It was about John Beets.'

Alan shrugged. 'Who?'

'John Beets. You probably don't remember. You know that first night we all went out – right after you got out and I got back from New York? It was me, you and Garth and we went to La Casa Verde, the Mexican restaurant?'

'Yeah?'

'Remember? We were all drinking and having a good time when this drunk comes by, and starts mouthing off, you know, pointing at you, talking about how they shouldn't have let you out of jail.'

'Vaguely. For a while there, everywhere I went, people did that to me.'

'I know. And you handled it fine. But it really got to Garth. He talked about it for days. He even said he wished the guy would die.'

'I'm sure he didn't mean it literally,' Alan said. 'So, what happened, anyway? Why was the guy from the restaurant in the paper?'

Melissa reached for her drink, and took a long pull. 'John Beets was murdered. Shot. A few days after that night.'

Melissa could see Alan's mind turning.

'I want to ask you something,' Melissa said. 'Do you think Garth is capable of murder?'

Alan's eyebrows arched. 'What! Garth?'

'Beets, the drunk from the restaurant. Mayor Hubbell.'

'Jesus, Melissa, that's one helluva leap. Just because Garth saved a few news clips doesn't mean—'

The intercom buzzed, breaking the tension of the moment. Alan sat staring at Melissa for several seconds before he got up. He pressed the button opening the front outside gate and walked to the front door.

'I don't see it, Melissa. I just don't see it.'

Alan opened the front door, and a petite blonde dressed in a white sundress planted a wet kiss on his mouth.

'Hello, stud, ready for Round Two?' the blonde said. The woman ran her hands across Alan's chest before she noticed Melissa.

'Oh, excuse me. I didn't know you had company,' the woman said.

'Charlotte Price, I want you to meet my daughter-in-law, Melissa,' Alan said.

The blonde's face was bright red as she walked over and shook Melissa's hand. 'Didn't expect anyone to be here.'

Melissa smiled and took the opportunity to exit. 'I was just about to leave. Thanks for the drink, Dad.'

Alan looked puzzled. 'Wait. You can't leave now. We haven't finished our conversation.'

The truth was, she was grateful for the opportunity to get away. 'Just give it some thought. And please, keep this conversation between us. No telling what would happen if you-know-who found out.'

Melissa walked over and gave Alan a kiss on the cheek. 'Nice to meet you, Charlotte. Dad – I'll call you tomorrow.'

She bounded down the outside stairs two at a time, happy to get out of the townhouse. The wind was kicking up in front of a thunderstorm, and the outside air had the smell of the coming rain.

Melissa pulled her motorcycle on to Memorial Drive and ignored the speed limit. She got on the loop heading for West University. She gunned the big motorcycle around a slow moving truck, hitting eighty miles per hour as she weaved through bottlenecks.

The Harley felt powerful between her legs, and she made the short drive to her exit in five minutes flat.

But she didn't slow down when she got to her exit, keeping the bike pointing south. She needed time to think, to be alone, to decide what she should do next.

Galveston and the ocean seemed like a good destination. She still had half a joint left, maybe a little toke by the ocean would make her feel better. She flipped on her headlight as she downshifted through the busy, early evening traffic.

19

Don't drive over the speed limit, he told himself. Come to a complete stop at all stop signs and use turn signals when you change lanes. It wouldn't do to get stopped right now, he thought, though unless they looked in the trunk, there would be no reason to be suspicious.

The plan was to avoid the main streets whenever possible. Traffic should be light at this time of night, and if he stayed on the neighborhood streets, cars would be few and far between.

This is almost too easy, he thought. A lot easier than the last time. Of course, Austin was tougher because he wasn't in his house, and he had to rush to do the deed and get out in a small window of time. Here, he didn't have to watch the clock. No one was at home except Justine. He used his own key, slipped in, did his business, slipped out. The house was remote enough that there was very little chance that even a loud gunshot would be overheard.

I wish it had lasted longer, he thought. I should have stuck that big fucking gun in her face, just to watch her eyes bug out. I could have waved the pistol around, made her think she had a chance. Watched her crawl, cry, beg for mercy.

Fuck, why didn't I think of that? It would have been a lot more satisfying.

Oh well, he thought, at least the cunt was out of his life. I won't have to listen to her constant bitching anymore. Most of all, I won't have to find ways to avoid having sex with her.

I should have cut her throat, he told himself. That would have been great, watching her thrash around, spewing blood all over the room.

Or maybe I could have choked her to death.

God, that would have felt good, wrapping my fingers around that scrawny little neck, cutting off air to that fucking sick brain of hers.

Oh, well. At least she's gone.

Bye-bye Justine. You fucking cunt!

20

Sara O'Donnell picked the jalapenos off her nachos, while Melissa systematically stabbed the throwaways with a toothpick, popping them in her mouth one at a time.

'Jesus, Melissa, how can you eat those things? If I did that, I'd have the runs for a week.'

Melissa could tell that Sara had recently gotten laid. Her complexion was absolutely glowing, even in the muted restaurant lighting.

Sara tossed her hair back and leaned close across the table. 'Did I tell you about my latest conquest?' Sara's fiery red mane and low cut blouse had been drawing admiring looks from across the room. 'He never knew what hit him. He's a firefighter, twenty-four years old. Wide shoulders, flat stomach, buns of steel. Bedroom eyes and a smile that would melt ice. He's so young he doesn't have much control and will come the first time in about thirty seconds. But he gets rock-hard again immediately, and I'm showing him the finer points of carpet munching. Last night, I had at least a dozen orgasms!'

Sara chugged her frozen margarita, and ordered another round.

'Oh, and one other thing about this fireman,' Sara said. 'He's huge. As a matter of fact, I have some pictures.'

Sara began digging around in her purse.

Melissa hadn't been paying very close attention. 'Sara, what are you looking for?'

'Ah, here they are.'

Sara handed Melissa some instant color photos. Melissa was caught completely off guard. Each picture was a cheesecake shot of the fireman in the buff.

'Oh my God!'

Sara laughed and pointed to the top photo, which showed the fireman leaning back on the bed, his erection in full bloom. 'Yes, my dear, this is a cock. Or as Robin Williams put it, "A heat-seeking missile of love".'

Melissa had to laugh. 'He looks very ... talented.'

'Nine inches. I measured it.'

'Impressive,' Melissa said.

Sara smiled. 'Enough about me. What's going on with you? If you'll pardon me for saying it, you look tired. Aren't you getting any sleep?'

It had been two weeks since Garth had found her looking through the newspaper clippings, then given her a few wonderful minutes of oral sex. But immediately afterwards, he'd gotten back into the pattern of long periods of silence, avoiding her and playing like nothing was wrong.

'I have been having trouble sleeping this week,' Melissa said, 'but I've called the doctor and he's getting me some pills. That should take care of it.'

Sara gave her a suspicious look. 'How are things with Garth? Anything new?'

'I'm going to ask for a divorce.'

'What?'

'Garth doesn't know if he wants to be married to me or not.'

Sara sipped her drink. 'So you're just going to end it?'

'I want to be loved. I want to be treated like a human being. And I refuse to do like so many other woman do, where they stay in a lopsided relationship with a man who's either insensitive to their needs, or incapable of fulfilling them. I'm sick and fucking tired of his bullshit. I'm gonna go home tonight and tell him we're through. If Garth wants to be married to me, then he can get off his lazy ass and do something. Otherwise, that's it.'

'I don't remember ever seeing you like this,' Sara said.

'I am fucking angry. Garth has done nothing except act like a confused little boy. He expects me to sit by and hold his fucking hand and wait for him to get his act together. Well, I'm more than willing to meet him halfway. I want this marriage to work. But I'm not going to do it alone. He has to try, too.'

Melissa couldn't stop thinking about the newspaper stories she'd found in Garth's desk, in particular, the ones about John Beets and the Mayor.

It just doesn't make sense. Why would Garth keep an article about those murders? she wondered. *Is it just some kind of morbid curiosity or is there more to it?*

Melissa didn't want to think about it right now.

'Let's get drunk,' Melissa said, motioning for the waitress to bring them two more margaritas. 'And let me have another look at that fireman's cock.'

* * *

Garth found his spot in the parking garage and backed the Lexus into its assigned slot. He'd been gone from Holloway & Partners for almost a month now, and was just returning to town after filming a series of television commercials for the Quintell campaign. It had been a busy, run-and-gun session, capturing Texas Bob on film in many urban and rural settings across the state. Dawn to dusk shooting schedules, late night flights and long drives between cities, an exciting production that Garth was confident would result in powerful, memorable TV spots.

Traveling between locations, Garth had pondered his future. What did he really want in a relationship, he wondered. Was he really happy with Melissa? Why did he act like such an idiot when it came to sex? Why was it so hard to feel intimate with his wife? Did he even love her?

Beginning a few months before his father was released from prison, Garth had found himself re-evaluating everything in his life. He had been married for several years, but he didn't feel happy. He had achieved much in the ad agency world, but now it only bored him. If he was honest he'd have to say that he felt empty and confused, anxious, unsure of what he believed or what he expected from life.

The only clear, positive feelings he had been having these days related to his father. He was thrilled that Alan seemed to be adjusting to life on the outside. The idea of creating Stakeman & Son was a sound one, for it accomplished several things in one fell swoop. First, it gave Alan a focus, an opportunity to pick up the pieces and make something of himself. For Garth, it offered a new professional challenge, a chance to build a business and test his skills and intellect in an entrepreneurial setting.

Stakeman & Son was an undeniable success. The mix of business expertise between him and his father was perfect. Garth had been very impressed with Alan's leadership skills, admiring the way he commanded a room full of political insiders and swayed them to his way of thinking. Both Alan and Texas Bob seemed very happy with Garth's advertising skills, and the campaign's position in the polls was testament to its effectiveness.

Stakeman & Son was running on all cylinders, with money in the bank, and several new employees hired to keep up with the work load.

Now, if he could just get his personal life on the same, positive keel as his professional one.

Garth opened the trunk of his car and grabbed an armload of videotapes, half-inch copies of the raw campaign footage. He locked his car and headed toward the office, anxious to run the images for Alan.

Garth rounded the corner and walked into the main lobby of the Transco Tower, balancing an armload of three-quarter-inch videotape cassettes. As he passed a large bank of elevators, he saw his father about thirty feet away, deep in conversation with a woman. For a moment Garth couldn't tell who she was, then she turned and he saw her profile. Detective Fishbein.

Why does she keep showing up? Garth thought. *Hasn't Dad been through enough? He served his time, got his parole. She's going to spoil everything!*

Garth stepped back against the wall and watched. The detective was repeatedly referring to a file folder, occasionally taking papers out to show Alan. The longer Garth watched her, the more angry he became. Weren't there laws against this kind of police harassment? Didn't his father have the right to live his life and be left alone? Besides, this detective didn't care about the truth. She'd been the one who told all those lies on the witness stand. The cops were all alike, he thought. They weren't out for justice. They just wanted the glory, the prestige of making a big bust. It didn't matter to them if an innocent man went to jail, as long as they got their picture in the paper.

Garth thought his dad looked worried, as if maybe the detective was threatening him and had him backed in a corner. Garth tried to read her lips, he couldn't make out what she was saying.

The more he watched, the angrier he became. He wanted to run over there and push her away. Knock her lights out the way he did that reporter.

Garth turned his back as the detective passed near him on her way out to the street. He fought the urge to run and grab her, to take hold of her head and slam it into the sidewalk. He watched her get into a dark blue, four-door Oldsmobile, and he didn't take his eyes off her until she drove out of sight. Maybe it was time he had a little heart-to-heart with that bitch, he thought. Maybe he should set her straight on a few things.

I'll be seeing you, detective Fishhead, he thought. *You and I are going to have to have a little talk.*

21

Texas Bob Quintell worked his way through the big group of smiling people, laughing, shaking hands and slapping backs as he headed toward the bandstand. *Awful lot of pretty women in San Antonio*, he thought, admiring the well dressed lunchtime crowd. Texas Bob was such a big man that he had no trouble negotiating his way through throngs of people, escorted along the way by several uniformed San Antonio police officers.

Bob was thrilled with the big turnout. The campaign organizers had estimated that at least a thousand people were jammed into the courtyard of the picturesque River Center Mall. The Quintell campaign had arranged for an outdoor stage and brought in free hot dogs and soft drinks, hoping to attract the white collar workers during the lunch hour. The perfect weather on this late October afternoon had helped, and the crowd had munched on food, watched magicians, and listened to twenty-minute sets from a number of musical groups. At a quarter till one, the Republican nominee came through, pressing the flesh on his way to the backstage area.

Texas Bob waited until the song was finished before he

jumped out on stage, taking the microphone off its stand. 'Did everybody get something to eat?'

The crowd answered with enthusiastic applause.

'Well, don't worry. I'm not going to ruin your meal with a long-winded campaign speech.'

Good-natured cheers broke out among the spectators. Nothing like free food and toe-tappin' music to put them in the mood, he thought. Remember what Stakeman said – when you're speaking before a large crowd, pick out four or five faces in different parts of the group and maintain strong eye contact with them.

Texas Bob pulled a piece of white paper out of his sport coat pocket, and held it up to the crowd. 'We're just two weeks away from the most important election of this decade. You know what this paper is? It's the results of the latest poll. Among Texas voters who have made a decision, fifty-one per cent say they're for Philip Smart, and forty-nine per cent, say they're for your buddy Texas Bob. Ladies and gentlemen, this race is a dead heat!'

On cue, dozens of campaign volunteers scattered throughout the crowd began enthusiastic applause. That encouraged the whole audience to join in, and a thousand pairs of hands slapped together.

'We've come a long way since June, and our momentum is going to carry us to victory in November!'

More cheers and yells. Bob wasn't sure how many undecided voters there might be in this audience, but he knew he had to be winning over the large majority.

He again remembered Alan's coaching, and lowered his voice for dramatic effect. 'We are on the threshold of a great victory for Texas. With me as your US senator, you're gonna have a friend in Washington. Someone who knows what it means to work for a living. Someone who knows we need to cut taxes and keep those liberals from spending us into the poorhouse.'

He paused and let the applause die down. 'And someone who believes that it's time to put a stop to the wave of crime and drugs that is sucking this country dry.' More loud cheers broke out. *If you want to win them over, just talk about stopping crime*, he thought. 'I am the only candidate who can give Texas a new beginning. Tell your wife, tell your husband, tell your significant other to please vote for Texas Bob Quintell for the United States Senate!'

At that point the band struck up the first familiar chords of *America the Beautiful.* From behind the stage, a huge American flag – sixty feet wide and forty feet tall – was raised as a backdrop to the bandstand. Huge fans blew wind on to the oversize flag, making it move dramatically in the artificial breeze. Then, a tumultuous roar went up from the crowd as Willie Nelson appeared from behind the amplifiers. Willie waved to the audience and walked over to Texas Bob. The two men embraced center stage and stood together, posing and smiling for the cheering audience. Then Willie Nelson took the microphone from Bob's hand and began singing the first verse of the song. Within moments, Texas Bob, the stage band, and the audience all joined.

Texas Bob had practiced with a voice coach to make sure he wouldn't make a fool of himself on stage. Even though he had rehearsed and was comfortable with the song, he wasn't prepared for the sound of a thousand Texan voices joining in. Bob had tears in his eyes as he sang at the top of his lungs.

'...For the land of the free, and the home of the brave.'

Alan and Garth Stakeman were standing just off stage during the San Antonio rally, congratulating each other for another brilliant public relations event. It had been Garth's idea to get Willie Nelson to make a surprise appearance, and with good news coverage, it would be well worth the large fee the campaign had to pay him. Alan tapped Garth on the shoulder, and pointed to several television crews in the audience. With any luck they could count on coverage in San Antonio, Houston, Austin, and Dallas.

Just before the rally had started, Texas Bob had given Alan a check for $3.6 million – money to pay for a huge television and radio advertising blitz during these final critical days. Stakeman & Son, Inc. would clear $540,000 from that check alone.

Alan felt rejuvenated. They had run a political neophyte against a powerful incumbent and the race was dead even. If they succeeded, and the momentum was definitely on their side, Alan would quickly regain his reputation as a political genius. Stakeman & Son would be the hottest new consulting firm in the south, and prestige and money would follow.

Alan also had other reasons to feel like he was on top of the world. He was in the first bloom of new, passionate lust with the vivacious Charlotte Price. He had spent so many years in prison that he had forgotten what it was like to have the love of a beautiful woman. Alan and Charlotte were almost inseparable, spending almost every night together, either on the road working in the campaign, or back home in Alan's luxury townhouse.

Alan had to smile. If all that wasn't enough, it had become clear that Detective Fishbein was now putting in overtime to clear his name. Once that happened, Alan knew, even the most conservative holdouts would welcome their old friend back into the circles of power. A return to power, new money, sweet love – Alan's smile got bigger and bigger. It was as if God himself had looked down and said, 'You've suffered enough. Here's a little good fortune.'

Yessir, Alan thought, *everything is going just according to plan.* Nothing could stop him now, and that was why he wasn't the least bit concerned to see KHOU reporter Joseph Farmer walking toward him.

There's that smug son-of-a-bitch, Farmer thought. *Look at him standing with his asshole son. You think you've got this campaign in the bag, don't you, Stakeman? Boy, are you in for a rude awakening.*

Over the past few weeks, Joseph Farmer had been putting in overtime too. Only he was looking for ways to dig up dirt on the Stakemans. Obviously, there was plenty to work with about Alan, but the story of the Stakeman murder case was old news, and Farmer wouldn't get anywhere by regurgitating it.

Farmer then spent a couple of weeks looking into Garth's background. What he discovered there didn't satisfy him either. Respected in the advertising community, never even a hint of criminal wrongdoing, Garth Stakeman seemed disgustingly clean. That meant Farmer would have to effect his revenge by taking the indirect approach, and he set out to get the goods on Texas Bob Quintell.

Bob Quintell also seemed, at first glance, to be free from the kind of dirt Farmer was looking for. But after a few weeks of questioning, bribing, and romancing current and former employees, business associates, and enemies of the king-sized candidate, Farmer had found what he was looking for. Now, with the smell of victory hanging heavy over the River Center Mall, Joseph Farmer was about to exact his revenge and blow the Quintell Campaign right out of the water.

'Well, well,' Farmer said, 'glad to see the Stakeman and the Son together in one place.'

Garth stepped in front of Alan. 'When are you going to get a life?'

Farmer laughed. He was going to enjoy this. 'Oh, I just dropped by to tell you guys about a little story I'm working on.'

'We're not interested in anything you have to say,' Garth said.

Alan stepped up and put his hand on Garth's shoulder. Farmer could hear the sarcasm in Alan's voice. 'Wait a minute, son. This is a distinguished member of the news media. Give him a chance,' Alan said.

Farmer smiled. They were both so smug, so cocky. *We'll see how cocky you are five minutes from now,* Farmer thought. 'Thank you Mr Stakeman. Quite an impressive rally, though I thought that corny patriotic crap went out with the Reagan presidency. Still works on Texas yee-hahs, I guess.'

Alan put his hands in his back pockets. '*America the Beautiful* gets 'em every time. What can we do for you, Farmer?'

You can kiss my ass, Farmer thought. 'Just a couple of pieces of business I wanted to discuss. Could we go somewhere private?'

'We have a meeting room inside. We can talk there.'

Farmer followed Garth and Alan into the mall, to a private conference area where the campaign had set up its San Antonio headquarters. Rows of black telephones were positioned every few feet on rows of rectangular tables set end-to-end. Later that evening, Quintell volunteers would come in to operate the phone bank, and during a three-hour period between 6 and 9 p.m., over 1,000 San Antonio voters would be called and encouraged to support Texas Bob.

'Okay, Farmer,' Alan said, 'no one will bother us here. What's on your mind?'

Joseph Farmer had waited for this moment since he first got the goods on Texas Bob. 'You might want to sit down, Stakeman. This isn't going to be pleasant.'

Alan shrugged and leaned against the edge of the table. Garth stood facing Farmer, his posture stiff.

'You remember that debate in Dallas? The one where I was on the panel of questioners?' Farmer asked.

Alan nodded. 'Yes.'

'I asked a question then didn't get an answer. I asked Quintell about this woman, Athena Rodriguez, who is some kind of psychic and works in his company.'

He paused to see if that got a reaction. Alan's expression gave no clue to his thoughts. Garth was still standing at attention.

'Since Quintell dodged the issue that day, I decided to do a little checking on my own. Would you like to know what I found out about her?'

Alan smiled. 'What, that she likes to read her horoscope?'

Farmer chuckled. Stakeman's bubble was about to burst. 'Athena Rodriguez got her start as a stripper, going by the name of Princess Fortune. She got a fake ID and started dancing in a topless bar in Dallas when she was sixteen. She worked at a place called Fat Jack's for three years, turning tricks on the side, and when she was nineteen she moved to Waco and opened a massage parlor. She did that for a couple of years – was arrested four times for prostitution – and in 1970 moved back to Dallas. In 1973, while working as a fortune teller and palm reader, she gave birth to identical twin boys. One baby she named Bob, and one she named Quint. Sentimental, isn't it?'

Alan's mouth was hanging open.

'It took some work, but I did manage to get my hands on a copy of the twins' birth certificate. In fact, I just happen to have a copy right here.' Farmer reached into his coat pocket and took out a folded piece of paper, handing it to Alan. 'You might want to take a look at the space for the father's name.'

Alan glanced at the certificate, and there in bold type, next to *father's name*, it read: ROBERT G. QUINTELL.

Farmer watched with delight as all the color left Alan's face. 'There's more. So much more.'

From another coat pocket Joseph Farmer took out three more pieces of paper, handing them over to Alan. 'These documents are just a part of the paper trail covering Texas Bob's support of his adoptive family. The first page is a copy of the paid mortgage on Athena Rodriguez's Dallas home, which has a current assessed value of $225,000. The second page is a copy of last year's admission report to the Dallas Christian Academy, a very exclusive private school which the twins attend. You'll see that the tuition is $10,000 per year per pupil, and you'll also note who pays the bill.'

Alan glanced down and saw a notation that a check in the amount of $20,000 was issued by Texas Bob's Restaurants, Inc., and received by the Dallas Christian Academy on August 23rd, 1994.

Farmer looked over at Garth, who was reading the papers over his dad's shoulder. 'Page three is a copy of the registration of three different automobiles. The one on the top is a 1992 Mercedes, which she drives, followed by a 1995 Camaro Z-28, and a 1994 Acura Integra. All three vehicles are owned free and clear, and were paid for with checks drawn on Texas Bob's Restaurants, Inc.'

He stared at the two Stakemans, savoring the moment, wishing he could see inside their heads. 'So, the bottom line is, your client is fucked, and the Quintell campaign is going down the tubes. I've got him playing house with a stripper, fathering and supporting two bastards, and since Texas

Bob's Restaurants is a public corporation, illegal use of stockholder funds. I'm sure the Securities and Exchange Commission and maybe even the IRS will be interested to know about Bob and his hooker lover.'

Alan and Garth looked at each other without speaking.

'So, Mr Stakeman, and son, I'll be using some of the footage of today's rally as a backdrop for my piece. Be sure to have someone tape tomorrow's early and late news. It will be the lead story.'

Joseph Farmer turned and strolled out the door. He started whistling, and grinned with satisfaction at a job well done.

Garth stuffed his hands in his pants pockets. 'Is this as bad as it sounds?'

Alan sighed. 'Do you remember Gary Hart? Something like that will blow us right out of the water.'

Garth sighed, his eyes following Farmer as the reporter got lost in a crowd of people.

22

Fishbein took off her glasses and rubbed the tender area on the bridge of her nose. It was after 7 p.m., but since her ex-husband had gone on vacation, taking her son, she was free to work late. Since early this morning she had been holed up in her office, poring over every piece of information on both the Stakeman and the Edward Bailey murder cases.

Her desk had become a mountain of paperwork, covered by yellowed and musty files, retrieved from storage in two separate cities. The files for Justine Stakeman's homicide greatly outnumbered those for the Austin murder. That came as no surprise, since the Stakeman investigation resulted in an arrest and conviction, and included the extensive trial preparation, lab reports, and other pertinent homework. The Austin homicide of Edward Bailey was still technically an open case, though there hadn't been any work done on it since three months after the original shooting, in late 1975.

In her prime, Frieda Fishbein was as good as they came, an intuitive investigator, who found the right balance between by-the-book technique and gut instinct. She played off the nuances of a case, realizing that every homicide had its own character and its own signature of detail. Fishbein also liked to spend as much time as possible actually seeing and touching the physical evidence, believing she could somehow psychically connect with the killer.

But this investigation was a real stumper. The only evidence she had from the Bailey case was a single bullet, mostly intact, which had been removed from the victim's brain during the autopsy. Luckily, it had held together during its journey and Fishbein ordered a ballistics test. The results hadn't surprised her. The bullet that killed Edward Roy Bailey III, was fired from the same gun that shot Justine Stakeman.

Fishbein picked up a small plastic bag in which the Bailey bullet was stored. She held the bag up to the light, moving her dark eyes over its surface, concentrating on the tiny, unique grooves the mysterious gun had left on the shell. It fascinated her to know that eighteen years ago, this small piece of lead had ended Ed Bailey's existence.

Why was Ed Bailey killed? Where is the gun? What about Justine Stakeman? Were there any other victims in this spider web of motive?

In her heyday, Fishbein never thought much about motive, she was too busy trying to catch the bad guys. But lately, even before she'd gotten involved in reinvestigating the Stakeman case, the issue of why had started to call to her.

Why do so many people use violence to settle their disputes? What is it about human nature that drives someone to murder?

There was nothing in the Bailey homicide file that addressed the issue of motive, except for the very obvious and previously discounted fact that Bailey had been having an affair with Justine Stakeman. *Of course*, Fishbein told herself, *we've apparently ruled Alan Stakeman out of the Bailey case, and, considering the new, irrefutable ballistics match, that surely puts him in the clear for his wife's death.* Of course, he could have hired someone else to do it, but her instincts said no.

So where does that leave us? she thought. *Who else would have the motive and opportunity to kill both Bailey and Justine Stakeman?*

Don't think, *feel*, she told herself. Use your instincts, listen to your gut. Problem was, her instincts were still sputtering, suffering from the effects of atrophy. But she did have one vague idea, a suspicion that had first occurred to her when Alan Stakeman had talked to her at the baseball game. If the Bailey homicide and the Stakeman homicide shared the same killer, then who would be in a position to know both victims, and perhaps have reason to kill? There might be others, but one person that came to mind was Garth. *But that's crazy,* she thought. *Since the Bailey murder happened in 1975, Garth would have had to kill when he was thirteen years old!*

Garth may be a little strange, Fishbein thought, *but is he a killer?*

She had had a funny feeling about Garth from the moment she met him. There was just something about that young man she couldn't put her finger on, but it was definitely there. Maybe it was the way he hovered over his father, as if Garth were afraid that, without his constant vigilance, the world might try to swallow up Alan Stakeman. To Fishbein that was misplaced devotion, an obsession the likes of which she hadn't seen before.

No, she told herself, *I don't have a single piece of information or evidence that even remotely ties Garth to either killing. And while I might be able to put together a circumstantial case involving Justine Stakeman, why would Garth have killed Ed Bailey?*

She sighed, and stretched her arms over her head, realizing for the first time how tired she was. She decided to call it a night, looking over the mountainous homicide files to consider which, if any, she would take home for the evening. Her eyes were drawn to a thin yellowed file on the Stakeman side of the desk. It was about halfway down in the stack, its tab barely legible. It said: FAMILY HISTORY.

Fishbein knew she had read through every file at least twice, but now she could look with a fresh perspective. There were only eight or ten pages inside, and she flipped through the contents, glancing at birth certificates, death certificates, and other government documents. But the last piece of paper in the file was out of place. It was page four from a nine-page police report filed by Fishbein's investigative partner at the time of the Stakeman killing. She pulled the document out of the file, intending to find its proper spot in the stack, when her eyes were caught by a brief notation at the bottom of the page.

Detective Paul Pace, her comrade during the late

seventies, had interviewed several relatives of the Stakemans' during the week following the homicide. His comments, mostly family gossip and other useless information, were summarized in the final paragraph.

> . . . and Mrs Inez Dollzey, 62, said that she was an aunt of the deceased, and was a bridesmaid at the victim's first marriage. She stated that the victim previously was married to a Mike Wainwright, of Beaumont, Texas, and that Mr Wainwright was the natural father of the victim's son, Garth . . .

Alan Stakeman wasn't Garth's father?

Fishbein didn't know what difference that made, but it did spark her interest. *I wonder how old Garth was when his mother and father were divorced?* she thought. *Hell, for all I know, Garth may have been raised by Wainwright.*

Instinct. That old familiar feeling took over as this newest piece of the puzzle showed itself. She felt the hair stand up on her arms. This was important, she knew it.

She could feel adrenaline energizing her tired body. She picked up the telephone and called long distance information. Beaumont, Texas, was only about a hundred miles from Houston, and as Fishbein gave the name to the operator, she decided that she would drive over tonight if need be.

She was elated when the operator gave her the number for a Michael J. Wainwright. Fishbein glanced at her watch, noticed it was almost 11 p.m. A deep male voice with a heavy Texas twang answered on the third ring.

'Good evening, is this Michael Wainwright?'

'Yeah. Who's this?'

'My name is Frieda Fishbein. I'm the Chief of Detectives at the Houston Police Department. I wonder if I might speak to you for just a minute.'

'It's kinda late. What's this about?'

'I'm calling about your ex-wife, Justine.'

'Justine? Hell, she's been dead for years. Her second husband just got out of jail for the killing.'

'I know. But we have reason to believe that Mr Stakeman was unjustly convicted of the crime, and the real killer may still be on the loose. Could I ask you a few questions?'

'Stakeman innocent? You're kidding!'

'No sir, I'm not. I'm trying to get a little family background. Can you tell me, sir, when were you and Justine married?'

'Oh gosh, that's a long time ago. Uh, let's see, I think it was May something, in 1960.'

Fishbein was taking notes with one hand, smoking with the other, using her shoulder to hold the telephone against her ear. 'Uh-huh. And what about Garth, do you remember when was he born?'

'Garth was born two years later. September 1, 1962. It's easy to remember, 'cause it was on Labor Day. We laughed about it, you know, Justine being in labor on Labor Day.'

Fishbein listened to the man giggle at his own joke, making notes as fast as she could. She hoped he wouldn't start asking her a lot of questions about the investigation.

'Now, how old was Garth when you and Justine were divorced?'

'Let's see, Garth was six, about to start to school. I moved back to Beaumont and went to work at the Texaco Refinery. Still do. We filed for divorce at the end of that summer, just before he started grammar school.'

Fishbein lit another cigarette off the butt of the one she was smoking. 'I see. And pardon me for asking this, Mr Wainwright, but did you and Justine have an amicable divorce? I mean, was it friendly?'

She could hear him laugh on the other end. 'It started out to be friendly, but it sure as hell didn't end that way. We went to war over Garth.'

Fishbein put down her pen. 'Garth? What do you mean?'

He sounded guarded. 'Oh, I don't know. Let's just say there were some problems.'

Fishbein was intrigued, but knew she had to go slow if she wanted to draw out the information. 'To tell you the truth, Mr Wainwright, Garth is the reason I'm calling. We're looking into his background, childhood and adolescence, trying to get a fix on the type of person he was.'

'Why?'

She didn't want to explain. 'I can't really get into that right now. If you feel uncomfortable talking on the telephone, I could come see you.'

'Look, you called me out of the clear blue sky and start asking a bunch of questions about my son. Now, I think I have the right to know what's going on.'

'This is an official investigation and I can't go into the particulars on the phone.'

'I'll tell you one thing. Just because someone dies, they aren't automatically a good person.'

What the hell does that mean? she thought.

'If you want to talk to me you'll just have to come to Beaumont,' Wainwright said. 'Now I got to get some sleep.'

She heard the telephone click. She flipped open her desk calendar and wrote a memo to her secretary. '*Cancel all my appointments. I will be in Beaumont all day.*'

Fishbein lit another cigarette. *Okay, Mr Wainwright*, she said to herself. *I guess I'll see you tomorrow.*

The Texaco Refinery outside of Beaumont, Texas, takes up four square miles. More than 125,000 gallons of gasoline are processed each day, and around 5,000 people work three shifts, around the clock, 365 days a year.

Michael Wainwright was a senior systems analyst, and spent most of his time as a trouble shooter in the vast network of pipes. He was on his back, up underneath a valve connection when he got the word that there was a Houston police detective waiting to see him in the administration building.

He cursed under his breath and headed for the visitors' lounge. He wasn't happy to see the smiling face of Frieda Fishbein.

'Mr Wainwright, I'm Captain Fishbein. We talked on the telephone last night.'

'Christ, lady. What the hell are you doing coming down to the refinery? If I had known you wanted to talk to me this bad, I could have met you at the house!'

Fishbein wasn't about to cut him any slack. She took out her notepad and a pen. 'I have some friends with the Beaumont Police. We could go to the police station if you'd prefer.'

Wainwright shook his head and sat down. 'What do you want to know?'

Fishbein smiled. 'Thanks for your cooperation. As I told you on the telephone, I have re-opened the investigation into the death of Justine Stakeman. I have very good reason to believe that Alan Stakeman was wrongly convicted. But what I need to know from you are facts about Garth. When Garth was younger, say before you and your wife got that divorce, did he ever display any action that you considered, oh, say abnormal?'

There was a long silence. Wainwright was fidgeting. Fishbein was certain she had hit a nerve.

'What do you mean by abnormal?' he asked.

'Just anything, however minor, that you thought might be unusual.'

Wainwright cleared his throat, and sounded nervous. 'There was something that happened at the day care center. This would have been just a few months, maybe a year before the divorce. It's been so long now, I can't remember the details.'

'What exactly do you remember?'

'Nothing. I mean, that's it. Must not have been that big of a deal if I can't remember.'

Fishbein thought he was holding out. 'What was the name of the day care center?'

'I don't remember. It was run by a Catholic church. St Joseph's, St Mark's, something like that.'

Fishbein wrote that down and underlined it. 'And when do you think this, uh, incident occurred?'

'Oh gee, Detective. Let's see, Garth was around five or six, so it would have been around '67 or '68.'

'Tell me what happened.'

'Excuse me, m'am, but why are you so interested in Garth as a little boy? No matter what kind of trouble he might be in today, it can't have much to do with what happened twenty-five or thirty years ago.'

'Sir, when you're trying to solve a murder case, you have to look at everything. You never know which piece of the puzzle will be the one to make the picture come together.'

It was as if she'd turned on a faucet. 'He was a very sad little boy. He didn't laugh and cut up the way most kids do. I never knew why. I had my suspicions.'

Fishbein frowned. 'I don't understand. What do you mean?'

'Okay. All right. I'll tell you.'

Wainwright took a big gulp of coffee and exhaled. 'One day, I got off work early and I went to the day care center to pick Garth up. Usually, Justine did it, but I thought, "I'm off early, I'll go get him." When the head sister found out who I was, she took me off and talked to me. We walked to the back part of the playground, sort of away from everything where the other kids wouldn't notice us.'

'Uh-huh,' Fishbein said.

'There were about thirty kids there, all about five or six years old. All the children were running and playing, swinging on the swing, climbing on the monkey bars, playing ball. That is, all the kids except Garth. He was off by himself, sitting alone on the ground, staring off into space. The sister told me he did that every day.'

Wainwright hesitated. Fishbein could see the memories rushing back in his face. His countenance changed, became more serious, as if he were in pain.

'The sister pointed to Garth and said, "Do you know why he acts that way?" I told her no. I could see from the expression on her face she didn't believe me.

'The sister told me that she had found marks on Garth. On his genitals. I could see her watching me, judging me, trying to see how I would react. I told her I didn't know anything about it, but that I would talk to Justine as soon as I got home. The sister just stood there looking at me, not saying a word.

'We stood out on that playground for a long time. Finally, I remember her saying, "This child is innocent. He is a child of God. If I ever see any other marks on him again, I will call the police." I felt like I had been hit with a baseball bat.'

Fishbein watched as tears began streaming out of Wainwright's eyes. 'I drove Garth home, not wanting to think about the accusation. I remember making small talk with Garth, asking him about school and stuff. He seemed so calm, almost serene.

'I went home that night and thought about what the sister

had told me. I went into the bathroom and looked in the dirty clothes hamper. I found several pairs of Garth's underwear and looked. In a couple of pairs, there were bloodstains in the crotch. I literally got sick to my stomach and threw up all over the bathroom floor.'

'Garth had been molested?' Fishbein asked.

'I knew I hadn't done anything to the boy, so that didn't leave many suspects. I tried to talk to Justine about it, but I didn't do it very well. She played ignorant, claiming that she didn't understand what I was talking about.

'Not long after that, I decided to move out. Get a divorce. I knew I wanted to get Garth out of there, away from her. But I wasn't fast enough.'

'What do you mean?' Fishbein asked.

'I came home from work about a week later and there were police at the house. A woman from Child's Protective Services was there, and she accused me of molesting Garth. Apparently Justine, covering her own ass, had filed charges against me.

'I told myself that I could fight back, get a divorce, then come and take Garth to live with me. The investigators made a lot of threats, but never filed any formal charges.

'During the divorce hearing, Justine's attorney repeated all the sex charges in front of the judge. I didn't get custody, of course, but I couldn't even visit Garth without a chaperone. The public accusations ruined me, and I was weak. I just went away. Garth, of course, was left to survive any way he could.'

Fishbein thought of her own thirteen-year-old son. She had a funny taste in her mouth.

Wainwright continued, 'As long as I live, I will never forget the day I moved out. It was on a Sunday. Justine and I weren't speaking. We both knew who was guilty. I packed some clothes, loaded up my car, and then Garth came in from the back yard and asked me where I was going. He was just a little boy, but he could carry on a conversation like an adult, and we'd talk to him as if he was one of us. So I just came right out and told him we were getting a divorce.

'I said, "Son, your Momma and I aren't getting along, and for her sake as well as yours, it's better if I just go live someplace else." I said, "Now I'll still come visit you, and this doesn't mean I'm not your daddy." I hugged and told him, "I will always love you."

'Well, he went nuts. Garth started screaming and carrying on like I've never seen before. He was yelling, "No Daddy, please don't leave me, Daddy," at the top of his lungs. He was totally hysterical, that's the only way you could describe it.'

Fishbein didn't move.

'Justine and I tried to get him to calm down, but he wasn't having any of it. Finally, I picked up my stuff and headed for the door and he grabbed a hold of my leg with both of his arms and wouldn't let go. I mean he had a hammer lock on my leg that practically cut off the circulation. It took all of our strength, both of us, to pry him off. Justine took him upstairs until I could get in the car and pull out of the driveway. Justine told me later that when she finally let him out, he went on a rampage, went through the house breaking stuff and crying. Then he broke free, ran outside and tried to follow my car down the street.'

'Did you have much contact with your son after the divorce?' Fishbein asked.

'Off and on, for the first three or four years. But it was a tough situation. The court order wouldn't allow me to be alone with him.'

'Do you think she continued to abuse him?'

Wainwright looked very nervous, and his face turned beet red. 'Well, I know for a fact that Justine and Garth slept in the same bed all during that time. And somebody told me that she was still giving him baths after he was twelve, thirteen years old.'

Oh my God, thought Fishbein. *How fucking sick can you get?*

'I told her the boy needed a psychiatrist,' Wainwright said. 'Justine did too, for that matter. But I'm sure neither one of them ever saw one.'

Fishbein felt drained. 'You've been a big help, Mr Wainwright. I appreciate you sharing that with me. I know it was hard.'

'Can I tell you something?'

'Of course,' she said.

'You said that y'all were thinking that Alan Stakeman didn't kill Justine. I never did believe he was guilty anyway.'

'It looks like you're right,' Fishbein said.

'I could have killed her myself. Dreamed about it a time or two.'

She thanked him again for his time and went out to the car. Even the polluted air next to the refinery seemed refreshing after that conversation.

Fishbein pulled her car out of the parking lot and headed for Interstate 10.

Justine Stakeman, Fishbein thought. *Did he do it?*

One thing's for sure. She got what was coming to her.

23

Joseph Farmer was shut up in Edit 3, a five foot square cubicle housing a television monitor, two three-quarter-inch and two half-inch video cassette recorders, a small switcher, and various other assorted goodies. When he arrived in Houston from the San Antonio Quintell rally, he'd gone straight to the station in hopes of getting at least a rough cut of his blockbuster story ready for next morning's assignment meeting. *The other reporters will be green when they see this,* he thought.

Farmer had finished writing his story on the airplane and was now looking for visuals to go along with his script. Stopwatch in hand, he read through the material for time.

'Texas Bob Quintell epitomizes the American entrepreneurial success story. Raised in a family that was middle class but hardly rich, he got his start when his grandmother died, leaving behind a modest but successful barbecue restaurant on the northern edge of downtown Houston. The flamboyant Quintell, who legally changed his name to Texas Bob after his restaurants became successful, parlayed his grandmother's simple recipes into a $100 million business.'

Farmer checked the watch – twenty-six seconds for that portion of the voice-over. That meant he would have to go through his raw footage and search for an equivalent amount of matching video, old photos and pictures of Bob in his early twenties.

Farmer cleared his throat and continued. 'Along the way, Quintell's interest in politics was influenced by his mother's experience as the first female member of the Texas House of Representatives—'

The telephone intercom interrupted him, and a voice told Farmer that line three was for him.

Irritated, he put down his script. 'Joseph Farmer.'

He could tell that someone was on the line; he could hear faint traffic noises in the background, but the caller didn't speak.

'I said this is Joseph Farmer.'

The voice was gravely and muffled, as if someone were trying to disguise their voice. 'Farmer...'

'Yes, who is this?'

'Your house is on fire.'

'What?'

There was a click and he knew he'd been disconnected.

What the fuck was that? Farmer thought. He looked at his watch. *Some asshole is calling me at 11:45 at night to tell me my house is on fire?*

He picked up his script again, and continued with his work. But he found that he couldn't concentrate and decided to check with the newsroom, just to be on the safe side.

KHOU-TV had college interns on duty around the

clock, monitoring police and fire transmissions on the electronic scanners. Farmer stuck his head around the corner and yelled toward one of the interns. 'Hey, have there been any fires called in during the last thirty minutes?'

The kid looked up. 'Uh, yeah. Some duplex a few blocks from here. I sent a cameraman.'

It can't be, Farmer thought. 'What's the address?'

'3878 Allen Parkway.'

'Sonofabitch! That's my house!'

He ran back to the editing room, gathered up his Stakeman material and loaded everything into his workout bag. Then he and the bag hustled out the back door toward the parking lot.

The stolen pickup truck was parked just outside the television station. The driver was wearing a black sweat suit, black gloves, and a dark ski mask. The driver's side window was rolled down, and he found the crisp evening air invigorating.

He could see the reporter's car parked in the last row of the station parking lot. He knew the man wouldn't be driving it to his house – all his tires were flat.

He waited patiently as the reporter ran to his car, saw the slashed tires, and began cursing. He could hear the vulgarities as the man screamed at the city. He snickered and waited.

The reporter looked around, took a few steps back toward the TV station, then draping the strap of his exercise bag over his shoulder, began a steady trot toward his burning duplex.

The man slumped down in the driver's seat as the reporter jogged directly past the front of the truck. He waited a few seconds, then raised up and started the engine.

He knew it would be easy to overtake the runner and he took his time pulling out and running through the first few gears. He looked all around for other cars. He was humming, driving without headlights, his vision sharpened by the adrenaline of the chase. An early evening shower had left puddles on the dark concrete, the reflection of occasional street lights reflecting off the wet blacktop. Shifting into fourth gear, he was up to thirty miles per hour now, quickly gaining on the jogging Joe Farmer.

He made one final check for traffic. No one in sight. Except for Farmer, about thirty yards ahead.

He accelerated slowly, careful not to rev the engine and make too much noise. He saw the reporter glance over his shoulder, and smiled as the newsman moved off the street and on to a sidewalk. The reporter was about two-thirds of the way home, keeping a steady pace as he ran down the walk. He had barely seemed to notice the truck, now bearing down at forty-five miles per hour.

When the truck's front tires bumped over the curb, the reporter turned back to look. The driver turned on his headlights, momentarily blinding Farmer. Farmer's face first registered surprise, then fear. The driver accelerated more as Farmer frantically looked around for a way out.

At the moment of impact, the reporter's body was hurled

ten feet up in the air and forward, slamming into a telephone pole before bouncing off and ricocheting down off the side of the truck.

The reporter landed face down on the sidewalk, blood pouring from his mouth and ears, the left side of his face a bloody mass of tissue and bone.

The truck stopped. The driver looked around again for traffic. The impact had made little noise – Farmer never made a sound.

Crumpled in a heap on the street, the body of Joseph Farmer looked twisted and broken, almost comical under the streetlights. The driver climbed down from the truck and pried the workout bag off the reporter's bloody shoulder. He checked the bag and smiled when he saw the videotapes inside. Then he pulled a long-barrel .357 magnum out of his belt and fired one shot into the back of Joseph Farmer's head.

[illegible]

[illegible] for almost [illegible]

[illegible] before the

[illegible] between the [illegible] command,

[illegible] knocked twice and came in the door.

[illegible] plain. Chapel [illegible] writing [illegible] interview room

[illegible] picking up [illegible] of cigarettes

and [illegible] briefcase. She told [illegible] secretary where

she would [illegible] that she was not to be interrupted.

Outside, [illegible] closed door of the interview room, she [illegible]

24

Frieda Fishbein had been on the telephone for almost an hour, mostly listening. Apparently reporters were camped out at the Mayor's office, causing a scene over the fact that Joseph Farmer, one of their own, had been murdered.

'Yes sir, Mr Mayor,' Fishbein said, 'I can certainly understand your concern. You can tell them that I have ten homicide detectives assigned to the case, and we will work around the clock to uncover every possible lead. As a matter of fact, I am personally interviewing a suspect this morning. With a little luck, we'll have something before the day is out.'

Fishbein listened for a couple of minutes before she could get off the telephone. Her second in command, Lieutenant Case, knocked twice and came in the door.

'He's here, Captain. Got him waiting in interview room C. And the visitors are in position also.'

Fishbein nodded, picking up a fresh pack of cigarettes and grabbing her briefcase. She told her secretary where she would be and that she was not to be interrupted.

Outside the closed door of the interview room, she

stopped for a moment to collect her thoughts. Fishbein entered the room and nodded to the uniformed officer.

'Thank you, Sergeant, I won't be needing you anymore,' she said.

The interview room was bare bones, a green tile floor, government issue rectangular table and four chairs, two on each side. There was a small window positioned high off the floor opposite the door. A large ashtray was in the middle of the table, next to an old cassette recorder. A four-foot-wide mirror took up the center of one wall, and Garth Stakeman sat facing the mirror. 'Good morning, Mr Stakeman, thank you for coming.'

Garth's voice was even, his hands clasped together on the table in front of him. He was fashionably dressed, wearing a gray Hugo Boss suit and a floral tie. 'Do you want to tell me why I'm here?'

Fishbein had played the interrogation game hundreds of times and she knew she had a distinct advantage over an amateur like Garth Stakeman. 'Didn't the detective tell you?'

'He said that you wanted to talk to me about a homicide investigation.'

Fishbein shook her head. 'Joseph Farmer was murdered last night.'

'Oh.'

Fishbein watched him.

Garth pointed to the large mirror. 'Is that a two-way mirror?'

'Yes.'

'Who's behind it?' Garth asked.

Fishbein pulled a chair out and opened the new pack of Salems.

'I'd appreciate it if you wouldn't smoke,' Garth said.

Fishbein took out a cigarette and lit it. 'Did Sergeant Drummond read you your rights?'

'Yes, he did.'

'Would you like to speak to an attorney?'

'I don't need a lawyer. I haven't killed anyone.'

'It's your right to have an attorney present.'

'That's okay.'

'Mr Stakeman, someone has murdered Joseph Farmer. That someone stole a truck, set fire to his house and slashed the tires on his car – all to ensure he'd be on foot. The killer ran him down, then shot him in the back of the head. It's no secret that you and Mr Farmer had your differences. We know that there was a scuffle between the two of you a few weeks ago, and I was told that you and your father were seen arguing with Farmer yesterday in San Antonio. That makes you a prime suspect.'

'We weren't arguing. We were having a conversation.'

'That's not what I was told,' Fishbein said.

'Well, you were told wrong. Have you ever met this guy, Detective? He's a real asshole. I'm sure there are plenty of people who would have liked to kill him.'

She reached over and turned on the tape recorder, staring at the microphone while she spoke. 'This is Captain Frieda Fishbein of the Houston Police Department. It is October 30th, 1995, and I am in conference room C with Mr Garth Stakeman of 1137 Bissonnett Road in West

University Place. Mr Stakeman, have you been informed of your rights?'

'Yes.'

'And are you aware, sir, that you are being recorded?'

Garth ran his hand through his hair. 'Yes.'

'Mr Stakeman, do you know a man named Joseph Farmer?'

'Yes.'

'How do you know him?'

'He is a reporter for one of the Houston television stations. I met him in conjunction with a political campaign that my father and I are working on.'

'Have you ever been to Mr Farmer's house?'

'No.'

'Has Mr Farmer ever been to your house?'

'Yes, sometime around the middle of June. It was on a Saturday, and he said he was there to interview my father.'

Fishbein knew some details of Garth's run-in with Farmer, but she wanted to get more. 'Did you have an altercation with Mr Farmer that day?'

Garth smiled. 'You could say that. He told me that he was there to see my father, but after a few minutes I realized that he was lying. I threw him out of my house.'

Fishbein probed. 'What was he asking?'

She saw Garth's eyes dart nervously to the recorder. 'He asked me how I felt when my mother died. If I believed in Dad's innocence. And what it was like to have my father go to jail for killing my mother.'

Fishbein put out her cigarette. 'Stepfather.'

'Excuse me?'

'Stepfather. Alan Stakeman is your stepfather. Your natural father is Mike Wainwright.'

Garth didn't say anything for several moments. His voice was almost a whisper. 'He is a *father* to me.'

'What about your natural father?' Fishbein asked.

'What about him? He moved out when I was very young. He didn't give a damn about me.'

Fishbein pressed. 'He was around till you were six. And he came to visit – at least until your mother remarried.'

Garth was squirming. 'Alan Stakeman is my father. I love him very much. Michael Wainwright? He's the man who ran off and left me. Excuse me, but did I misunderstand something? I thought we were here to talk about Joseph Farmer?'

'I just find it interesting that you're so close to your stepfather.'

Garth frowned. 'I don't know why.'

'Okay – back to Joe Farmer. What happened that day at your house, when he came in asking all those questions about your stepfather?'

'Why do you keep using that word?' Garth asked.

'What word?'

'Stepfather. I don't like that word,' Garth said.

'I'm sorry. What happened after Farmer started asking questions about Alan?'

Garth cleared his throat. 'Once I realized what was going on, I terminated the interview.'

'You attacked him, didn't you?'

'I physically threw him out of my house. He was there under false pretenses.'

'Is that how you handle conflicts in your life? With physical violence?'

'Hardly. I'm not a violent person, Detective.'

Fishbein lit another cigarette. Garth curled his nose.

'Did you see Joseph Farmer on October 29th – yesterday?' Fishbein asked.

'You already know that.'

'Please answer the question.'

'Yes, he came up to Dad and me at a political rally in San Antonio.'

'What did he want?'

'To annoy us. He liked doing that.'

Fishbein was quiet. Waiting.

'He wanted to schedule an interview with our client,' Garth finally volunteered.

'Did you get into an argument with Joe Farmer?'

'No.'

Fishbein looked him in the eye. 'Did he say or do anything yesterday that made you angry?'

Garth broke the eye contact. 'Everything he says pisses me off. I can't help it, I don't like the guy.'

'What time did you get back to Houston last night?'

Garth was looking at his hands. 'We took a seven o'clock flight. I got home about eight forty-five.'

'You went straight home from the airport?'

'Yes.'

'Was your wife at home?'

'No.'

'Did anyone see you come home?'

'I don't know. Maybe the neighbors.'

'Did anyone call?'

'Not that I remember,' Garth said.

Fishbein stood up and paced. 'You want to know what I think? I think that Farmer said something that pissed you off in San Antonio, and you decided to kill him. I think you came home, changed clothes, went out and stole a truck, started a fire at Farmer's house, waited for him, and ran him down.'

'Do you really think I could do all of that?'

She nodded. 'I certainly do.'

If Garth was nervous he wasn't showing it. 'I didn't like the guy, but that doesn't mean I killed him.'

'But you're happy he's dead, aren't you?' Fishbein asked.

'I'm not all broken up about it.'

'You've always believed in your stepfather's innocence, haven't you.'

'There's that word again,' Garth said.

'What?'

'You know. Stepfather.'

'But that's what he is, isn't he?'

'To me, he's just Dad,' Garth said.

'Whatever you call him, you don't believe that he killed your mother?'

'I know he didn't do it.'

'How could you know that? Were you there?'

Garth's eyes moved around the room, stopping at the mirror. 'No.'

'Then how can you say for sure that he didn't do it?'

'Because I know him. I know him better than anyone, and I know he couldn't have done it.'

'You just know – is that it?' Fishbein asked.

Garth was still looking straight into the mirror. 'Who is behind the mirror?'

'You didn't get along with your mother, did you?'

Garth's eyes returned to Fishbein. He didn't answer.

'Were you and your mother as close as you and your father?'

Garth just shook his head. 'She was a difficult woman.'

'Was she a good mother?'

'She wasn't Aunt Bee.'

'Did the two of you fight?'

'Not really.'

Fishbein pressed. 'Did she ever mistreat you?'

He didn't answer right away. She waited.

It was a full minute before he spoke. 'I don't remember,' he said.

'After your father moved out, it was just you and your mother?'

'Uh-huh.'

Fishbein noticed tiny beads of perspiration on his upper lip. 'Garth, I talked to Mike Wainwright a few days ago.'

He stared at her without speaking. She stared back.

'And Mr Wainwright had quite a few interesting things to say about you and your mother.'

'I really don't see what any of this has to do with Joseph Farmer,' Garth said.

Fishbein glanced at her watch. The interview had only

lasted twenty minutes, but she felt like she had been sitting there for hours. 'Mr Wainwright told me that your mother mistreated you. And that to cover that up, she filed charges against him for sexually molesting you. Is that true?'

'It's true that she filed charges.'

'But did Mike Wainwright molest you?'

'No.'

'Did your mother?' Fishbein asked.

Garth took a deep breath. 'You know, I don't see how any of this could have anything to do with Farmer.'

'Before your mother died, did she and Alan ever have any business meetings at the house? Maybe parties where they entertained clients?'

'Yes.'

'Did you ever meet any business associates of your dad?'

'I'm sure I did. There were lots of parties.'

'Did you ever meet a man from Austin named Edward Bailey?'

'I don't remember. Doesn't ring a bell.'

Fishbein decided to go for the jugular. 'When I saw Mike Wainwright the other day, he said your mother sexually molested you for several years. And that she made you sleep in the bed with her, that she even gave you baths after you had become a teenager.'

She could see his face flush but he said nothing.

'What else did she make you do?'

He looked at his hands. He fidgeted in his chair.

'Mike Wainwright said that once he found blood in your underwear. Did your mother ever put things inside you?'

Garth was looking down at his feet.

'Did she touch your penis?'

No response.

'Did your mother make you touch her?'

Garth's eyes burned into her. 'I don't know what you think you're doing here, but I'm not playing. My mother was a very disturbed woman. I was not sad when she died.'

'Did you ever wish for her to die?'

'Probably.'

'Did she force you to do things with her? Sexual things?'

No answer.

'Did she make you have sex with her?'

He kept his head down.

'Did she, um, did all that stop after she married Alan?'

He nodded.

'So when Alan came along, the bad stuff stopped?'

'Pretty much. She'd sneak in my room sometimes. But not as often.'

Fishbein softened her voice. 'So you were grateful to your dad for being there, for protecting you from her?'

'Yes.'

'Did you ever talk to Alan about your mother's, um, problems?'

'No,' Garth said.

'Do you think he knew what she was doing?'

'No.'

'Did you say you did meet Edward Bailey?'

'I said I don't remember the name.'

'That's the man in Austin your mother had an affair with.'

Garth's voice was sarcastic. 'Oh – one of those. Then that would be pretty hard to keep track of. Mom was a whore.'

'You love your dad, don't you?'

'Yes.'

'And you'd do just about anything to protect him, wouldn't you?'

'Of course.'

'Lie. Cheat. Even kill.'

Garth sat up straight in his chair. 'Is this the place where I'm supposed to fall down on the floor and confess to murder?'

'Do you have something you want to confess?'

'No.'

'You want to know what I think, Garth? I think Alan *is* innocent of killing your mother.'

'Oh really.'

'Yes, I do.'

'That's not what you said at the trial.'

'That was then. I've changed my mind,' Fishbein said.

'Just like that?'

'Uh-huh.'

'Well, what are you going to do about it?' Garth asked.

'I'm going to make it up to him. I'm going to tell the world that Alan Stakeman is an innocent man. Then I'm going to arrest the real killer.'

'And what are you going to do about the fifteen years you took away from my father?'

'There's nothing I can do to give them back to him,'

Fishbein said. 'So – do you want to know who I think killed Justine?'

Garth looked again at the mirror. 'Let me guess. Was it someone in this room?'

'You want to tell me about it?'

'There's nothing to tell.'

'Where did you hide the gun?' Fishbein asked.

'I don't know what you're talking about.'

'You said yourself that you hated Justine.'

'I don't want to talk to you anymore.'

'Doesn't it bother you that I know you're a murderer?'

Garth shook his head. 'I don't care what you think. You sure as hell don't have any proof.'

'I think you killed Joseph Farmer, too.'

'Think what you like.'

'How many other people have you murdered?'

'Are you going to arrest me?' Garth asked.

She hesitated.

He pointed at the mirror. 'I want to know who's back there. Who's behind the mirror?'

'A police psychiatrist.'

Garth's eyes moved slowly to the mirror. 'A shrink?'

'A doctor on retainer to the department.'

Garth stared at the mirror. 'Is he here to tell you whether I'm crazy or not?'

'He's there to observe.'

'Do you think I'm crazy?'

Fishbein shrugged. 'I don't know yet. Did you kill Joseph Farmer because he had something on your father?'

Garth didn't answer.

Fishbein pressed on. 'What time did you get home the night your mother was killed?'

'That was a long time ago.'

'You remember, though, don't you?' Fishbein asked.

Garth suddenly pushed back from the table and stood up. 'I think this conversation is over.'

Fishbein pushed. 'Garth. I know your mother was sick. I know she abused you and I know you killed her. You know, Garth, the court will take into consideration what your mother did to you.'

'Please don't try to act like you understand. Or that you care.'

'It must be hard walking around all those years with the guilt hanging over you. You would feel better if you got everything off your chest.'

'Can I go now?' Garth asked.

She didn't move or answer.

His eyes darted to the mirror, to the tape recorder, and back to her face. His voice was low and calm. 'Did you hear what I said? I want to leave.'

He waited for a few seconds. When she didn't move, he stepped around the table and walked over to the door. His hand grasped the doorknob and he stopped, glancing back over his shoulder. When she didn't move he opened the door and walked out.

Fishbein realized that she'd been holding her breath and she let out a sigh. For a moment, she just stood alone in the room, then she turned to the mirror, ran her fingers through her short hair, and waved for the visitors to come in.

* * *

'Well, what do you think?'

Dr Irving Perlman was a forensic psychiatrist on retainer to the Houston Police Department. Perlman had helped the department catch several serial criminals, primarily by preparing a psychological profile of the perpetrator. 'It's hard to tell from this one observation. Clearly, he was uncomfortable with the whole father-stepfather issue, and it's just as obvious that he doesn't care much for the mother.'

'What about the incest between him and his mother? Is that as rare as I think it is?'

'Father-daughter abuse is much more common, but the other does occur. You told me that Garth's father had said that the mother continued to give the boy baths when he was thirteen, fourteen years old. That's a common characteristic in these cases. A lot of mother-son incest happens that way. It may not necessarily be rooted in sexual intercourse. It could be rooted in things like bathing, or giving him frequent, unneeded enemas, constantly taking his temperature with a rectal thermometer, inspecting his genitals, even mutual masturbation.'

'That's disgusting,' Fishbein said. The idea of a mother doing that to a young boy made her nauseous. 'Would that be something that would make him angry, want to strike back?'

'It's hard to say. Most incest victims remain victims, and rarely have the courage to stand up to their abusers.'

'Can you tell, doctor, if Garth Stakeman is the kind of person who could kill?'

Dr Perlman shrugged. 'A lot of us have the capacity for violence, given the right stimulus. But you saw how touchy he was when you were talking about his stepfather?'

'Yeah.'

'Well, I found it interesting that he chooses to identify more with the stepfather than the father or the dead mother. I would guess that the abuse got worse after his natural father moved out, and it ended, or at least greatly tapered off, when the mother remarried. That would explain why he was distant from the real father and close to the stepfather.'

Fishbein paced the room, trying to put the rest together. 'What we're really talking about here are psychological theories. How does that translate into my building a murder case?'

'All I can say is that this young man appears to have all the classic symptoms of sexual abuse. In my mind, he certainly *could* be capable of violence. And that violence would be directed at his mother, both in retaliation for the abuse, or if he thought that she was going to cause him to lose his protector, the stepfather.'

Fishbein turned to the other visitor. 'Well, Alan, what do you think?'

Alan Stakeman had his hands stuffed in his pockets. He shook his head. 'I'm speechless. I just can't believe it.'

'What is it that you can't believe? That Justine molested Garth, or that Garth would strike back and kill her?'

'All of it. Any of it. To think that Justine would do that. It's just too bizarre for words.'

Dr Perlman spoke up. 'I'm sure your wife was abused as a child. This sort of thing always runs in families.'

Alan looked at Fishbein. 'When I approached you and told you I wanted to prove my innocence, I had no idea...'

Fishbein could see that Alan was in incredible pain. 'He needs help, Alan. He's obviously carrying around a lot of guilt, and the best thing you can do is to convince Garth to get the help he needs.'

'I don't know,' Alan said. 'It's just so hard to believe.'

The psychiatrist spoke up. 'I've seen many, many cases where a child was sexually abused by a parent. As horrifying as incest is, it is treatable. But clearly the young man needs intense therapy. If he doesn't get some help, and he himself becomes a parent, it's likely that he will fall into this pattern and end up abusing his own children – or someone else's.'

Alan sighed. 'I can't talk about this right now. I've got to have some time to think about everything. I'll see you later.'

Alan walked quickly out of the room and out of sight. The psychiatrist gathered up his notes and likewise left, leaving Fishbein alone with her thoughts.

She could feel Alan's pain, and knew that this revelation would be haunting him for a long, long time. From the point of view of the criminal investigation, the interview had gone as well as could be expected. She had told Garth that she was on to him, and he would either confess his crime or she would have to build a solid case against him.

It was going to be hard to get the District Attorney interested in reopening the Justine Stakeman case. DAs were political animals who didn't savor the idea of publicly admitting their mistakes.

Fishbein knew she'd have to build an airtight case against Garth before she even approached the prosecutors. And that was going to be hard, considering that Justine's case was over fifteen years old.

First things first, she told herself. *Concentrate on the Farmer investigation for now. Pin that on Garth and you'll be on your way toward reopening the others.*

One thing is for sure, Garth is one cool customer, and you can't expect him to crack.

25

He parked the car under a large oak tree, near a winding curve a few blocks off San Felipe Boulevard. He'd already scouted the location of a small bend in a secluded part of Buffalo Bayou. From his earlier trial run, he knew that at this time of night, he could safely unload the stolen goods from the trunk of his car and dump them ten feet below into the murky water.

It was peaceful here in the dark. Just a couple of hundred yards from major streets, the large lots and tall trees gave him the feeling of being alone deep in the woods. He rolled down his window and let the night air blow across his face. The breeze was cool against his skin, and he realized that he'd been perspiring. Nervous sweat, he told himself.

Justine liked the outdoors, he recalled. For a while there, the three of them had made regular camping treks into the Texas hill country. They did it right, staying away from the crowded campgrounds, preferring the ruggedly beautiful rolling pasture land of Justine's uncle. They'd put their sleeping bags on the ground near a small brook, stare up at a bright evening sky full of stars, and pretend that they were a close-knit family. The illusion would hold for a few short hours, maybe even as long as a day, before Justine would crank up her bullshit and the good times would evaporate like raindrops on a parched desert landscape.

Everyone who knew Justine agreed that she was fucked up. No one knew why she was the way she was, though theories abounded about her strange father and equally bizarre mother. It was assumed that she had come from an abusive, disgusting childhood. Why else would an otherwise smart, attractive woman be so goddamn impossible to live with?

Fuck you, Justine! A shitty childhood doesn't excuse your actions as an adult, he thought.

This is what you get, Justine. Be glad I did it quickly and painlessly, because after the crap you put me through, you surely deserved worse.

26

Melissa spread margarine across the top of the baked chicken, using a frayed basting brush that was her favorite kitchen utensil. She lifted the pan cover and stirred the black-eyed peas, simmering in water and ham pieces, then pulled a large stem of broccoli out of the vegetable bin.

She heard Garth's car pull into the garage and she took a deep breath. *This is it,* she thought. *If I don't do it now, I never will.*

She was standing over the kitchen sink, broccoli in her hand, when she heard his car door shut. She heard his key in the back door, and listened to his footsteps coming inside and walking across the hardwood floor. Melissa waited for him to stick his head in the kitchen and say hello, giving her a chance to gage his mood. Instead she heard him pass down the hall, past the open door to the kitchen, never even acknowledging her presence.

Maybe he doesn't know I'm here, she told herself. *Bullshit, of course he knows. He had to park next to my motorcycle in the garage, and he can smell dinner cooking!*

In the quiet house, over the gentle sound of bubbling peas, she heard water running in his bathroom. By now she had his routine down pat. First Garth would wash his face and hands, brush his teeth, then change clothes, carefully draping today's suit across a wooden valet.

She had been tense all day, clear in her mission to have it out with him, knowing tonight was the night. 'I want a divorce,' she would tell him, ready to listen if he had something to say, ready to walk if he didn't.

She heard him coming down the hall. She kept her back to the door. He said nothing, didn't make a sound. She would not turn around. She would not be the first one to speak. She'd wait him out, make him start a conversation. She heard him opening the mail, tearing into the envelopes with loud determination. He still hadn't said a fucking thing!

'How was your day?' she said, irritated at herself for being so weak.

The only response was the continuing sound of paper tearing.

'Garth?'

'Huh?'

She turned from the sink. His back was to her as he looked through the mail. 'Is something wrong?'

'Nope.'

She put down the steamer. Actually, what she wanted to do was throw it at him.

'Would you now look at me, please?' she asked.

He turned and looked at her. His face was void of expression. Nothing. His green eyes held her gaze for a moment, then he glanced away. 'Nothing's wrong. Long day. When's dinner?'

Stay calm, she told herself. *Yelling won't do any good.* 'Ten minutes.'

He turned and left the room. She heard CNN on the living room television.

That's it! she told herself. She didn't think she'd be able to hold her tongue. He was an insensitive jerk and deserved to be told off.

She cut up the broccoli and boiled water. She made a large salad with fresh spinach, tomatoes, celery and feta cheese, all the while biting her lip, trying not to cry. She set the table, and peeked around the corner to see him in front of the television.

You can't lose it now, she thought. *It won't make you feel better. It won't get any response from him. Just swallow it and wait until after dinner.*

During dinner Garth ate in silence. No what-did-you-do-today-honey. No guess-what-happened-at-the-office. Nothing. Not a fucking thing.

After dinner, he helped her bring the dishes into the kitchen, and while she put away the leftovers, he rinsed the dinner dishes and loaded the dishwasher. Once the kitchen was clean, he went back into the living room, and she heard him changing the channel to one of the movie stations.

Frustrated, she went and drew a hot bath. She poured an extra capful of her favorite French bubble bath, and undressed as the fragrant steam and tiny bubbles built around the faucet. When the tub was filled and covered with a layer of pink bubbles, she pinned her hair up and eased into the steaming water.

She laid her head back on the curve of the tub, with only

her face visible above the surface. She closed her eyes, squeezing them tightly shut as tears streamed out the corners.

After a while, she had no idea how long, the tears stopped.

How would it feel to let my head slip below the water's surface, she wondered. *Would the sweet release of death be easier than living this shitty life in this shitty marriage? What would Garth think if I killed myself?*

She shook her head, erasing that ridiculous image from her mind. She sat up in the tub, sloshing water out the sides, and grabbed the wash cloth. She soaped up the cloth and scrubbed her face. *Fuck you Garth,* she thought. *I'm not some stupid little girl who needs a man to make her happy. I'm an intelligent attractive woman and I can get along just fine without you!*

The knock on the bathroom door caught her by surprise, and she wiped the soap off her face and pushed back her hair.

Garth stepped inside and closed the door behind him. 'Melissa, can I talk to you for a minute?'

She sat up straight, exposing her grapefruit-sized breasts above the bubbles. His countenance was serious, and she wondered what he had on his mind. 'Sure.'

'I just wanted to ask you something,' he said. He put the lid down on the commode and sat down.

She picked up the bar of soap and, her eyes locked on his, began to slowly soap her exposed breasts. 'Ask away.'

She saw his eyes move across her chest, then fall to the floor. He pulled a piece of paper out of his shirt pocket and held it in front of him. 'I was looking at the electric bill. Usually it's around $140. It's never been higher than $150, and that's in the middle of summer. But this month it's $197.24.'

She couldn't believe her ears. *Was he talking about the electric bill?*

'Excuse me?' she asked.

He looked flustered. 'The electric bill. It's a lot higher than usual.'

She took the soap in her right hand and threw it as hard as she could. Garth managed to duck and the soap whizzed by his ear, splattering against the bathroom wall, leaving a sudsy smudge on the wallpaper. 'You motherfucker!'

He stood up. 'Jesus, Melissa, what's wrong with you?'

She couldn't believe her ears. 'What do you mean what's wrong with me? What the fuck is wrong with *you*?'

He looked confused. 'What's the deal? Is it that time of the month?'

In one swift motion she pulled herself up out of the water, jumped from the bathtub and lunged across the room. Slippery and covered with bubbles, she slammed into him with all the force her 142 pounds could muster.

The momentum carried them across the bathroom until they hit the closed door, sliding down to the floor. She landed on top of him, her hands slapping his face, the loud slaps sounding furious in the small bathroom.

She was out of control, crying and screaming loud, unintelligible sounds as she hit him. Garth struggled to get away from her and she grunted as her slaps turned to closed-fist blows. He freed his arms and used them to shield his face against her attack. After she had landed a dozen or more punches, her arms got tired, and Garth took advantage of the situation to give her a shove and she rolled off him. She landed on her butt in the middle of the floor, wet, naked, wailing.

'You fucking bastard!' she screamed. 'You motherfucking bastard! I've had it with you. I'm leaving you – you hear me? I'm getting a divorce!'

Blood trickled out of one side of Garth's nose as he touched a tender place over his left eye. 'You've lost your mind.'

She wanted to hit him some more, and started trying to get to her feet. Her slippery skin, coupled with too much adrenaline, kept her clumsily on the floor.

'You don't care about me!' she cried. 'You never did. All you care about is yourself. Oh, and don't forget Daddy! That's always the way it's been with you. It's Daddy this and Daddy that. Well, fuck you!'

He stared at her for a moment, and she prayed he would open up, yell at her, hit her, do something. Instead he turned and left the room, slamming the door behind him.

She couldn't remember ever being this angry. With some difficulty she managed to stand, her legs rubbery, her hands and body trembling. Bubbles still clung to her full figure, making her look like she was covered in pink cotton candy. She didn't stop to towel off, and stormed naked and dripping down the hall.

'I'm your wife, you little jerk! I don't deserve to be treated like this!'

She stomped into the bedroom, her fists clenched, ready for a fist fight. Garth wasn't there.

She stormed back down the hall and looked in the study, the guest bedroom, the kitchen, and the living room. No Garth.

She looked across the room and spied a photograph on the bookcase. It was she and Garth on their honeymoon.

'Do you remember the day we got married?' she said out loud, picking up the photograph. 'I had to practically beg you to fuck me on our honeymoon!'

She moved down the bookcase, grabbing a bookend, the figure of a dog. 'Remember this, you fucking prick? You gave me this when we were dating.'

She held the photograph and the bookend under one arm while she took a small painting off the wall with the other. 'Remember this, you cocksucker? You bought this for me in New Orleans!'

She walked to the French doors which led out to the patio. She flung one of the doors open and threw the bookend outside. The ceramic figure bounced twice on the concrete patio before shattering into pieces. Melissa used the framed photograph like a frisbee, sending it flying across the backyard, the glass breaking when it hit the ground. She took her fist and punched two holes through the painting before hurling it out the door.

She heard a car pulling out of the garage, and jogged across the patio toward the driveway and saw Garth's car back into the street and drive off.

She started to jump on her motorcycle and go after him. She giggled at the mental image, her nude on a motorcycle, paralleling his car as he drove down Kirby Drive.

She went back into the house and grabbed a bottle of tequila. She dug around in her purse and took out a bottle of Valium. She popped two tiny pills in her mouth and took a big swig.

She almost gagged on the tequila and stood over the kitchen sink until she was sure she wouldn't throw up. Then she took the pills and booze down the hall to the bedroom.

There'll be no more tears over that loser, she thought. *No more anger. No more hurt. Nothing.*

She sat down on the bed and took another gulp of tequila. She put the bottle and valium on the night stand and turned off the light.

She closed her eyes and thought about her marriage. *It's over now,* she told herself. *It's one hundred per cent over. Nothing can make me change my mind.*

Fuck him! Fuck him and the horse he rode in on.

27

First Tuesday in November. Election day.

Texas Bob Quintell had already been awake for an hour when his radio alarm clock went off. His wife Ellen lay curled up next to him, in sleep more forgiving than she had been since he told her the truth about his psychic Athena Rodriguez and his 'other' family.

He turned his head toward the large glass wall which separated the master bedroom from a two-acre, landscaped backyard. Ellen spent much of her free time keeping the yard in bloom, working a variety of bulbs, bushes and flowering plants, that added constant color to the immaculate grounds. Texas Bob gently pulled back the covers on his side of the king-sized bed, leaned over and kissed his wife on the forehead while feeling around with his foot for his house shoes.

He slipped quietly into his bathroom, took care of business then stepped up on to his digital scales. Down to 245, he noted, thirty pounds lighter than when the campaign began. The only other physical sign of the last six months was a large bruise on his right hand. An area the size of a quarter was purple and blue, on the palm between his thumb and pointer finger, caused by shaking so many hands. He considered wrapping a bandage around the hand to discourage more shakes, then decided he could endure the discomfort for one more day.

Texas Bob pulled out his matched, sterling silver shaving kit and began lathering up. The new blade made sure, smooth swipes, turning and following the contours of his rugged face with even strokes. He wasn't certain how he was supposed to feel, here on the morning when several million Texans would choose a US senator. He felt strangely calm, and he remained grateful that nothing about Athena Rodriguez or his illegitimate sons had made the television news.

The last week of the campaign had been a blur of frenzied media events, rushing to catch tour buses, grabbing limousines and racking up air miles, criss-crossing the state, often appearing in ten cities a day. He'd received a real lesson in the Lone Star state's geography, gaining a new appreciation of the true vastness of his home region. From Texas's most western city, El Paso, to one of its most eastern, Texarkana, it was more than eight hundred miles. It was even further from the top of the northern panhandle near Oklahoma, southward to the Rio Grande River at the Mexican border. Thank God they'd had that private jet, supplied by a big contributor to the Republican National Committee. With that aircraft at their beck and call, they could move at will, often changing their itinerary mid-air.

Texas Bob shuffled into his kitchen, opened the refrigerator and looked over his options. Ordinarily, he wasn't much of a breakfast person, but this morning he was famished. At his request, Ellen had given the maid and cook the day off, giving Bob a chance to putter around in his own kitchen.

He found a large bowl and went to work. First he cracked five eggs, carefully removing the yolk from three, and beat the eggs until frothy. He added a dob of milk, then dropped in a few chunks of Monterey Jack cheese. He found half an onion in the bottom of the refrigerator and diced it up, adding some chopped bell pepper, a little picante sauce, then sprinkled black pepper over the top. He put a little butter in a cast-iron skillet and was pouring the concoction in when his wife came down.

'Bob, what in the world are you making?'

He looked over at her, noticing that she was wearing his favorite nightgown, a low-cut red satin job that made her look especially delectable. 'Just cooking my baby a little Mexican breakfast.'

She smiled briefly, then caught herself. 'I'm not gonna eat that.'

Her hair was going in all directions, her face clean and scrubbed of all makeup, her small breasts outlined against the flimsy material. 'You look beautiful this morning,' he said.

She blushed, and unconsciously smoothed her hair with her hands. 'It's too late for flattery, Bob.'

He didn't want to break up. 'Now, c'mon baby, you know you don't mean that.'

'I do,' she said.

'Let's not talk about that right now.' He stepped over to

where she was sitting and gave her a peck on the cheek. 'This is going to be the best omelet you've ever put in your mouth.'

'What all did you put in there?'

'A little of this, a little of that.'

'Looks like too much that,' she said, retrieving a glass from the cabinet and pouring herself some juice. She walked over and stood next to him at the stove.

'Are you in love with that woman?' she asked.

He wasn't surprised at the question; in fact, he had expected it to come earlier. Ever since Alan had told him that the reporter had learned about Athena, Bob had been taking a hard look at his life; in particular, his feelings about the 'other woman' he'd been supporting.

'I told you the other night that you were the only woman I loved.'

Ellen Quintell was much calmer than she'd been the night he'd told her about his relationship with Athena. Her initial reaction had been predictable enough. She'd thrown an ashtray at him. Then she'd cried. Then she'd got drunk.

She was rightfully angry and hurt, and had seemed solid in her intention to end their marriage. But this morning, the early sunlight reflecting on those round eyes, he sensed a change. A weakening. Maybe, just maybe, he could save their relationship.

She watched his eyes moving over her figure, and he could see her trying to look inside his mind. *She knows I still find her very attractive,* he thought. *Maybe she just needs to be convinced.*

Bob took his hand off the skillet and pulled her close. He moved his free hand down her back, letting it rest on her soft bottom.

'Stop it,' she said, playfully slapping his hand away. Her mouth was saying no but she wasn't pulling back.

'After we eat, why don't we slip back into bed? We don't have to be at the voting booth till ten thirty.'

She looked up at him, her eyes shining with suspicion. He knew she wanted to resist, to punish him for the ultimate indiscretion.

'Is that supposed to make everything all right? A little roll in the hay and all's forgiven?' she asked.

He sighed. She wasn't going to make this easy, he thought. Who could blame her? He deserved to lose her. He deserved to lose the election. 'I love you, Ellen.'

She moved across the room and sat down at the breakfast table.

Bob stirred the eggs a couple more times and took down two plates. He put four pieces of bread in the toaster and got out plates and silverware. All the time, he could feel her eyes burning into his back. He didn't know what to say, what to do.

He divided up the omelet, putting a third in her plate and the rest in his. He buttered the toast and took salt and pepper to the table.

He turned to face her. She was still standing by the stove, staring at him. 'I really am sorry, Ellen. I love you. I don't want a divorce. I want us to be happy together.'

Ellen Quintell's expression didn't change. She glanced down at the food, then picked up her fork. She ate the omelet without talking, occasionally glancing up at him with tears in her eyes.

After they'd eaten without saying a word, she took Bob by the hand and led him out of the kitchen, upstairs toward the master bedroom.

In her dream Melissa heard ringing. The ringing of bells? A front door? A telephone.

Melissa rolled over on to her back and grabbed on to the bedspread. She felt the room spinning, as a deep, painful headache took hold and refused to let go.

She opened one eye to the bright, sunlit morning. An inconsiderate bird tweeted outside the window, and a clear blue sky was visible over the tops of the trees.

She felt like throwing up.

And the ringing wouldn't stop.

She grabbed the telephone off the night stand and mumbled, 'What?'

Alan was on the line, talking from his car phone. 'Melissa? Is that you? What's wrong? You sound terrible.'

She rolled over and put the pillow over her eyes. 'I had a run-in with a tequila bottle.'

'Oh. Uh, where's Garth?' he asked.

'I don't know and I don't care.'

There was a long pause. 'Well, did he say anything about the police?'

That's funny, she thought. It sounded like Alan said 'police'. 'The what?'

'Didn't Garth tell you? Chief of Detectives Fishbein? She called Garth in.'

She threw the pillow off her face and sat up. The sudden movement made her head feel worse, and her stomach sent a taste of bile up her throat. 'Garth? Police? What for?'

'They brought him in for questioning. That reporter who was shot.'

Oh my God, she thought. *I was right!* 'We had a big fight and he drove off. I don't know where he is now.'

'He hasn't been to the office in three days, and today is election day for Chrissakes. We have to find him. Captain Fishbein wants to talk to him. She thinks he was involved in Justine's murder.'

'Garth, accused of murder?'

'I know,' Alan said. 'I still can't believe it. Look – do me a favor. Check around the house. Maybe there's something there that will tell you where he's gone to.'

'Hold on,' Melissa said, and she forced herself out of bed. Her legs felt unsteady at first, but seemed to stabilize once she started moving. She shuffled through the house, looking for any sign of where Garth might have gone. There was none.

She picked up the extension in the kitchen. There were letters all over the floor in the front entryway. The mailman had been shoving stuff through the mail slot and it looked like no one had picked it up for a week. She flipped through the bills and junk mail looking for a clue. Nothing. 'There's nothing here. I don't know where he is.'

Alan sounded worried. 'We've got to find him. I'm on my way to meet Quintell for the photo op at the polling place. You take a shower and get dressed. I'll come by in an hour or so and we'll put our heads together.'

'Dad, wait,' she said, but she heard the cellular phone click off.

Why did I drink so much? she thought. *I need a clear head for this kind of shit.*

She staggered toward the bathroom. Suddenly the churning in her stomach grew worse, and she barely made it to the toilet.

She threw up. A bowl full of disgusting liquid that was probably fifty per cent booze.

She sat back on the cool tile floor and wiped spittle from her face. She wondered where Garth could be, and vowed never again to drink tequila on an empty stomach.

Garth ran past a slow-moving, chatty couple on the Memorial Park jogging path, irritated that he had to swerve off the gravel to get around them. The air was crisp in the early morning, with unusually low humidity for south Texas. The fall weather had given the trees a beautiful brown and orange glow. A perfect morning for running, and Garth hadn't noticed.

His breathing was easy as he passed the three-mile mark, running past the congregation of young singles flirting near the exercise bars. A busty blonde and her overweight girlfriend were stretching their legs near a tall pine tree, their curves straining at the form-fitting fabric.

This is not the way it was supposed to go, Garth thought. *A failing marriage, accusations of murder, this is definitely not what I had in mind.*

He knew things hadn't been right between him and Melissa. And he acknowledged that it was primarily his fault. *But how can she expect me to get everything right?* he thought. He was trying, really he was. There were a lot of things going on in his life.

Garth had imagined that once he and his father were business partners, their personal relationship would take off. It had been hard to try to remain emotionally connected to a man locked away in a prison. Once Dad got his freedom, Garth had assumed, he and his father would be closer than ever.

But it hadn't happened. Somehow, for some reason he didn't understand, he and Alan still weren't thinking, feeling as one.

I've risked so much to be there for him, Garth thought. *I've put everything on the line, just to give him the chance to once again take his place in the world. Why doesn't he acknowledge me? After all this, why does he make me feel like the bastard stepchild?*

Garth never envisioned becoming the target of a police investigation, never thought that he'd have to beat off an attack from his own wife. *Why did Melissa act like that?* he wondered. *Doesn't she understand the pressure I'm under? Why has she turned into such a bitch?*

He had tried to be patient, to put up with her constant nagging, but over the last couple of months, that incessant complaining had really taken its toll. He knew he was in a vicious circle with Melissa, but he didn't know how to get out. Their patterns were as predictable as the seasons. He'd be quiet, thinking about work, she'd get on to him about being so introverted, which would only serve to make him that much quieter. Then he'd be quieter, she'd start to get irritated, and she'd become even more demanding.

Christ, didn't she realize that she was pushing him away? Didn't she know that?

A young redhead was running toward him going the opposite way. Garth caught himself admiring the way she dug into the running path. A group of society ladies walked by, their hair and faces perfectly made up, their designer jogging suits repelling any sign of perspiration or dirt.

What made Melissa go nuts? he wondered. *It's not like I've been messing around behind her back. And that stuff about Dad and me. If I don't watch out for Dad, who will?*

She's probably spilling her guts right now, tattling to her friends on the phone. Yeah, she's telling everybody how her life is ruined because she's married to an asshole.

He didn't want his marriage to end, he knew that. But he felt like events were spiraling out of control, that he actually had nothing to say about whether or not he got a divorce.

Melissa's bitching had reminded Garth of the ugly side of his mother, the way Justine would get herself all worked up over nothing, then break loose with a long-winded harangue that might last a few minutes or could go on for days. Garth was convinced that it was Justine's nagging that had made Mike Wainwright move out. Just as he was certain that Alan and Justine had been headed down the path to divorce in the weeks preceding her death.

Yeah, he thought, *Melissa wants the marriage to be over. Is there anything I can do to save it? Is it actually worth saving?*

Maybe we would both be happier just to call it quits, he told himself. That would certainly be the easiest thing to do. Besides, he had a more pressing problem right now.

Captain Frieda Fishbein.

Garth jogged around a fat woman running her German Shepherd and wiped the sweat off his forehead. He tried to remember everything he'd said during his short, tense conversation with Fishbein. He replayed the conversation in his head, trying to get a vivid mental picture of the two of them in the interrogation room together.

He never should have agreed to talk to her in the first place. Certainly not with a tape recorder running.

He wondered how his voice sounded on the recording, if he seemed nervous or anxious when the tough questions came. Garth knew how incriminating someone could sound on tape. He vividly remembered how confused and guilty his father had sounded when Fishbein played Alan's interrogation during the murder trial.

Garth was in the last half mile of the run, and he accelerated around a slow-moving cluster of seniors. He passed an open, treeless area and felt a cool breeze hit him in the face. He noticed a young boy playing with a puppy, tossing a stick on the edge of the woods near the jogging path.

Why did Fishbein bring up all that stuff about Mother?

he wondered. *And what made her go all the way to Beaumont to talk to Mike Wainwright? Who was watching behind the mirror? Was there really a police psychiatrist back there, or was Fishbein playing mind games?* he wondered.

Garth was afraid of Fishbein. He knew how tenacious she could be. He remembered how she had bulldogged her way through his father's investigation, how relentless she'd been once she got on the trail. *I need to talk to a lawyer*, he told himself. *A damn good one.*

Garth jogged through a stand of tall pines, into another clearing about fifty yards from the end. He gradually slowed to a walk.

He walked past the front of the Memorial Park tennis courts. He noticed a dark-haired woman and a young boy dressed in tennis clothes getting out of a black BMW. The woman was attractive, thirty-fiveish, and the boy looked to be around twelve. The woman was fussing over the boy, handing him tennis rackets and paraphernalia, all the while brushing back his hair and straightening his clothes. The boy seemed embarrassed by the attention, humiliated to be mothered in public.

It reminded Garth of the way Justine had treated him.

He kept walking, glancing back to see the boy trying to distance himself from his mother. Garth stopped at a drinking fountain near a large, open exercise area where runners stretched and socialized. He took several long sips of the iron-rich water, spit and swallowed, then put his body through a series of post-run stretches. The image of Justine was stuck in his head and wouldn't leave.

He put his right foot up, heel down, on the back of a sit-ups bench in the exercise area. He leaned forward, running his hand down his leg towards his toe, feeling the stretch in his hamstring.

He closed his eyes and felt the stretch. As soon as his eyes were closed, Justine's face was right there in front of him. She was smiling and laughing, seemingly normal, in a scene he had replayed a thousand times.

In his mind's eye, Garth was now a skinny young boy, ten years old, standing naked in ankle-deep water in the bathtub. Justine was nude also, sitting on the edge of the tub. She was talking a mile a minute as she held his small, uncircumcised penis between two of her fingers. He'd not yet grown any pubic hair, and his little penis looked like a flesh-colored worm in her womanly hands.

This inspection was a daily routine. It was preceded by her reciting a litany of strange instructions, how he had to be careful with his 'dirty parts', that one day 'whores and sluts' would try to give him diseases that would make it turn black and fall off.

As Justine talked on about 'being sanitary', she would pull back the foreskin and, using soap and the soft fingers from her other hand, gently cleaned around the exposed head. She always did a good job, taking her time, he could recall, 'To make sure we get all the germs...'

Garth's eyes were squeezed shut as he remembered how she soaped his tiny testicles, then sloshed cold water to rinse it off his genitals. After that came the worst part. She ran warm water from the faucet, holding a bar of soap under the gentle stream. She would lather up her hand and put an extra dab of soap on her index finger. Then, ignoring his pleadings, she would make him lean across her naked lap and work her lubricated finger up inside his 'nasty little behind.'

Garth opened his eyes and looked at his surroundings. Other runners were stretching and exercising all around him. He could tell he was blushing, embarrassed at the memories. He walked quickly toward his car, paranoid that someone would discover his dirty family secret.

He got in the car, turned on the engine and pulled away. He shook his head, trying to get rid of the images.

Even today, more than twenty years later, Garth vividly remembered every detail, each physical sensation, particularly the way his young body was involuntarily excited into spasms.

In his mind, he could still see the brown curl of her hair, falling in waves around her shoulders, the full red lips, whispering, encouraging, seducing him. He breathed in and remembered the musky odor of her womanhood, mixed with a hint of perfume, a fragrance at once enticing and nauseating.

During the bathroom interludes, she manipulated me like a toy, he thought, *an animal to be stroked and excited for her own amusement. How many times did she play out that exact scene? Two or three times a week, starting when I was ten, lasting for years, even after she and Alan got married.*

Did Alan know how she was abusing me? Surely he would have stepped in and done something if he had!

Garth remembered how, as she grew even bolder, she would guide his hand to her, showing him the proper stroke for her clitoris. Later she taught him how to use his mouth on her, often appearing at his bedroom at night for a session of mutual masturbation.

Where was Alan during all of that. Didn't he know?

But Justine never actually had intercourse with Garth – that wouldn't be right, she said.

She never had to tell him to keep these encounters a secret. Even in the beginning, before he grew to realize the true horror of her act, he understood that she was forcing him to commit unspeakable acts.

Garth drove through Memorial Park and remembered it all. Joggers and walkers were everywhere. Happy couples playing with dogs and small children, lovers stretching together after a leisurely run.

No one knew. Not one person in the park knew about his shameful past. No one judged him or blamed him or felt sorry for him.

He hated his mother for what she had done. He was glad she was dead!

Melissa stepped into the shower and turned the water on full force. She alternated between excessively hot and chillingly cold settings, trying to shock her system toward lucidity.

It was partially her fault that things had gotten out of hand with Garth, she thought. During these last long months, the last couple of years really, all he had heard from her was a litany of complaints. 'You never talk to me anymore ... we never make love ... you're always pushing me away.'

Yeah, she told herself, *no wonder he's pulling away. All you ever do is bitch. What man wouldn't get tired of that kind of constant harassment?*

Not the time to be blaming yourself, she thought. *Not if Garth is in trouble with the police.*

Did Garth kill the reporter? she wondered. *Is he going to be arrested?*

She tried to fight off the belief that Garth could have been responsible for the reporter's death.

She lifted her face to the shower, and flipped on the cold water. She turned the shower massage to pulse and let the icy liquid flow across her head and neck. She switched from cold to warm and turned around, her back under the water's flow.

Maybe it was just too late, she thought. Maybe the best thing would just be to pack up, move out, and hire a good divorce lawyer.

No, running out on him now would be the chicken thing to do. First she had to find him, sit him down and make him tell her everything. Then, if he refused her help, if he continued to push her away, then she could leave, knowing she had done her best to try to stand by him.

But was leaving what she really wanted? Was she ready to give up? If she knew Garth, that was probably what he was thinking. Garth hated confrontation, and wasn't good at facing up to problems. No, he'd be looking for the quick, easy way out, she thought.

She got out of the shower and toweled off. She combed

her wet hair straight back and walked over to the bed. She put lotion all over her body and rubbed it in. She dug a pair of blue jeans out of the closet. She grabbed one of Garth's dress shirts and stuffed it in her pants, rolling the sleeves to her elbows.

Oh shit, I can't forget to go vote for Texas Bob, she thought. With all the turmoil in her life, she had almost forgotten that today was election day.

Melissa scrounged around the kitchen and fixed a bowl of cereal. She looked at the front page of the paper but couldn't concentrate. She went into the living room to the front entryway and gathered up all the mail that had been shoved through the mail slot. She absentmindedly flipped through all the letters. Nothing but bills and credit card statements and junk mail, she saw. Then something caught her eye. It was one of those envelopes with the clear window. The return address said First National Bank of Diboll, Texas.

She looked at the front of the statement and saw that it was addressed to Garth.

Diboll, Texas? she thought. *Why would Garth have an account up there?*

Melissa had a vague idea that Diboll was a small town a couple of hours north of Houston. Outside a car honked and Melissa put the statement on the counter.

Alan was just getting out of his car and waved as he came up the sidewalk. After months of being taxied around town, he had finally broken down and started driving again. His brand new Lincoln Continental looked like it had come straight from the car wash. It sat gleaming in the driveway, its dark, tinted windows and shiny, black finish giving it a mysterious aura.

'Did you talk to Garth?' Melissa asked.

'No. I went by the office. No sign of him there. I really don't know where to look.'

They walked into the house. 'Dad, do you really think he killed the reporter?'

She could read the worry on Alan's face. 'I honestly don't know.'

'You should see the way his eyes look whenever anyone mentions Farmer's name.'

Alan sighed. 'Detective Fishbein believes he's guilty. I talked to her last night and again this morning. She's building a case. She wants to arrest him.'

Even though Melissa had toyed with the idea that Garth was guilty, it was still shocking to hear it from someone else. She felt a little better, knowing that she could talk it over with Garth's father.

Alan had huge bags under his eyes, and she could tell that he hadn't gotten much sleep. She realized that she had been so focused on her own problems, on the marriage, that she hadn't considered what a strain this was on Alan.

'He might really be arrested?' she asked.

Alan nodded. 'If Fishbein thinks she can prove it, she will. If he is involved, I don't think it's his fault. There's a lot of stuff about Garth's childhood that you probably don't know. He needs psychiatric help. You should be careful.'

Melissa took a deep breath. 'Garth wouldn't hurt me.'

Alan didn't seem so sure. 'I'm sure you're right.'

Melissa walked over and gave him a wet kiss on the cheek. 'I'm not staying here anyway. My studio has a nice little apartment. I'm going to take some clothes and stay over there for a while.'

'I can't say as I blame you,' Alan said.

'I've got to spend a few days sorting things out. God knows when, or if, Garth will come back. My friend Sara is on her way over to help me get organized. I'll hole up at the studio and get my head on straight.'

'Do you need any help moving?' he asked.

She could feel the anxiety building. A twinge of nausea stabbed her gut. 'No, I'm not taking furniture or anything. Just clothes. Besides, this is election day and I'm sure you have a full plate. I'll be okay. Sara is my best friend, and she knows Garth. If he shows up, she'll help me deal with him.'

Melissa picked up a pencil and a piece of scratch paper. She wrote for a moment then handed the paper to Alan. 'This is the phone number at the studio. The other number is just in case. It's the security code that opens the front door of the studio. The door has one of those number things – you punch in the number instead of using a key.'

Alan glanced at the paper then put it in his coat pocket. 'I'll call you later, just to make sure you're making it all right. And if you do hear from Garth, will you call me immediately? You've got my cell phone number?'

She touched her right temple with her finger. 'I remember it. Thanks for everything, Dad.'

He walked over and kissed her on the cheek. Immediately she started tearing up. She leaned forward and gave him a big bear hug. She realized that she was taller than Alan and probably weighed as much as he did. She put her long arms around his back and squeezed him tight.

Alan mussed her hair and walked to the front door. 'Talk to you later,' he said.

She stood in the doorway and watched him pull out of the driveway. She strolled to the kitchen and poured herself a glass of juice. She sat down at the breakfast table and stared blankly in front of her.

Melissa sipped the juice in silence. Her left hand brushed against the stack of mail she'd left on the table. The bank statement was sitting on top. She picked it up again.

The First National Bank of Diboll. *That's over a hundred miles from here,* she thought.

She stood up and walked over to the window. She held the envelope up to the light and tried to read through the thin paper. She couldn't make out what it said so she tore open the envelope.

It was a statement for a savings account. There was a balance of $1,493.32. A passbook savings account, earning a puny rate of interest.

It doesn't make sense for Garth to have an account like this, she thought.

She looked down the rest of the page. No deposits or withdrawals, though there was a credit for a small amount of interest earnings. At the bottom of the page there was a debit notation. $19.95 had been deducted from the account, it said, for the annual rental fee on a safety deposit box.

Safety deposit box? she thought. *That's weird. Strange that he would have an account at some po-dunk bank. Stranger still that he would have a safety deposit box there.*

What is he keeping in the box?

Melissa gulped down her juice, folded up the bank statement and put it in her purse.

What the fuck is going on? she wondered.

28

Melissa turned off the radio and flipped open the tinted face shield on her motorcycle helmet. She used one hand to wipe the tears while the other hand popped the clutch to let her downshift the Harley. *Why does every song on the radio make me cry?* she asked herself.

Melissa had called her friend Sara back and told her that she was going for a drive in the country. Sara offered to drop by and pack up Melissa's clothes and drop them off at the studio. Melissa promised to be back by five in the evening.

She drove her motorcycle hard out of the city, blasting by Houston traffic like it was standing still. She'd gone about thirty miles, driving on automatic pilot, before she realized where she was heading.

North on Highway 59. Straight toward Diboll, Texas.

What do you think you're going to find in that little town? she asked herself. *Garth? Answers? What?*

She made sure to slow down to the forty-five-miles-per-hour speed limit at the edge of the Diboll city limits. Small Texas communities were notorious for their speed traps, she knew. The paint-flecked sign on the edge of town said

WELCOME TO DIBOLL, THE CLEANEST TOWN IN EAST TEXAS, and noted a local population of 4,870.

Am I crazy or what? she wondered. She hadn't thought twice about letting Sara do the hard work, loading up the car with most of Melissa's clothes, and toting them across town to the studio.

What a selfish thing to do, Melissa told herself, *leaving your friend to do the dirty work while you haul your dumb ass up to try and get a look inside Garth's safety deposit box.*

The bank's not going to let you see in the box, she thought. *Just because you're married to him doesn't mean they'll open up.*

None of that mattered. She had come to Diboll, she had to see. Maybe in a small town, formalities could be tossed to the wind. Maybe she could bat her eyes, or show some cleavage, or sweet-talk her way to the inside of that box.

The First National Bank of Diboll sat on a corner, one block off the highway across the street from a busy Wal-Mart. It looked like it had been built during the forties, with a faded brown facade and a single drive-in window. She parked the Harley on the edge of the parking lot, ran her hand through her dark hair and walked inside.

The interior of the bank was decrepit and musty, with only two or three elderly customers milling about. Melissa thought it looked more like a mausoleum than a bank, and it reinforced her assumption that Garth had chosen it because it was light years from Houston.

Melissa spotted a middle-aged lady with a big hairdo

sitting behind a 'Customer Service' sign. She walked over, still not sure just how she was going to do this. She sat down across from the woman and smiled while the lady finished her telephone call.

'No, the reverend said that the highway patrol had found beer cans in the back seat of the car,' the bank lady said into the telephone. 'You know, all those Langford boys are known to be drinkers. Well, listen, I've got a customer, so I'll call you later. Bye-bye.'

The bank woman hung up the phone and smiled at Melissa, showing off a mouth full of crooked teeth. 'Good morning, Miss. May I help you?' the woman asked.

Melissa opened her billfold and took out her driver's license. 'Yes, I'm Melissa Stakeman. My husband Garth and I have an account here. We're getting ready to go to Europe for two weeks and I think he may have left my passport in our safety deposit box. He flew to Dallas this morning and I can't get hold of him. I was wondering if I could just look in the box and see if he remembered to take the passport out.'

The woman used her hand to poof up her hair. 'Of course, Mrs Stakeman. You are on the signature card for the box?'

Keep smiling, Melissa thought, *and stay friendly.* 'Uh, well, you know, I don't really remember. We've had it for so long.'

'Do you have your box key?'

Melissa forced herself to remain calm, though she could feel sweat running from her underarms inside the shirt.

'Well, this is really embarrassing, but I think I may have lost the key. I've looked everywhere. It wasn't in its regular spot.'

The woman gave her a plastic smile. 'I see. Well, there's no way I can open the safety deposit box if you don't have the key. I'm sorry.'

'Oh,' Melissa said. *Now what are you going to do?*

The old lady smiled again. 'I tell you what, let me see if Mr Timmons, the manager, can help us.'

The woman slowly got up from behind the desk and disappeared behind the teller windows. A few moments later she returned, with a fiftyish bald man in tow.

Melissa repeated her story, though she thought that the bank manager, while polite, would be more of a stickler for the rules.

He spoke to the customer service woman. 'Pull Mr Stakeman's card and see if Mrs Stakeman is listed as a signatory.'

Melissa thanked him and tried to look casual. She glanced around the bank lobby and wished she had worn some nicer clothes. The bank lady came back and handed the officer a signature card.

'I'm sorry, Mrs Stakeman, but you're not listed on the card. You don't have a key, and you're not on the card. I'd like to help you, but I just don't see how I can.'

She'd known it was a long shot, and she wasn't surprised. 'That's okay, I understand. But listen, don't people have to sign in when they come to take something out of their box?'

The man nodded. 'Of course.'

'If I could just look at the sign-in sheet, then I would

know if my husband had been in to pick up the passports. Could I just check to see if he's been here?'

It was a stroke of genius. If Garth had recently been in, there would be a record of it. She knew the date that the reporter had been shot. If Garth had been in immediately before, or immediately after, then she'd know where he kept the murder weapon.

The bank officer hesitated. Melissa could see that he was weighing the request, trying to decide if it would mean breaking any rules.

'I suppose that would be okay.' He turned to the big-haired lady. 'Would you bring us the sign-in book?'

The bank manager eyed her suspiciously while the old lady disappeared again. It seemed as if she were gone forever, and Melissa just knew that at any moment, the bank manager would yell 'Ah-ha!' and call her bluff.

After what seemed like an eternity, she saw the little old lady heading their way, carrying a large, blue book. The bank manager led Melissa over to a nearby credenza. He flipped through the pages until he found the S's, then he stepped back to show the page to Melissa.

In such a small town, there wasn't that much activity in the safety deposit boxes. Six months' worth of visits from everyone with a last name that began with S was noted on a single, handwritten page.

Melissa's eyes moved down the sheet. About halfway down she saw it. There were actually two notations of interest to Melissa. The first date, October 28th, was before Joseph Farmer was killed. The second date, November 3rd, yesterday.

Right next to each of the dates were the signatures. A confident, bold stroke which read: Garth A. Stakeman.

There was just one problem. It wasn't Garth's handwriting.

29

The Quintell Campaign had rented the main ballroom at Houston's Hyatt Regency Hotel for the election night celebration. Campaign staffers were expecting a crowd of between 1,500 and 2,000, but by the time Alan Stakeman arrived, at least twice that many were on hand.

Texas Bob's party had attracted the attention of Houston's elite society. Diamonds and emeralds were the gems of choice, with low-cut evening gowns competing with high hemlines in the war for attention. There were more tuxedos than New Year's Eve, and Alan knew the event would be written up in the society columns.

Texas Bob had hired Houston's most popular (and most expensive) party organizer to handle all aspects of the affair. The food, of course, was catered by Texas Bob's Restaurants, but all other details were left in the capable hands of Jose Rodriguez. Jose, who looked no older than eighteen, preferred ruffled shirts, had a long, black ponytail which came down to the center of his back, and ran his own company, aptly called Events. He was initially cool about the idea of handling the affair for a good ole boy like Texas Bob.

Alan was in Bob's office the day Jose was hired, when the swishy Latin told Bob that he wasn't interested in the job because he thought 'all politicians are crooks'. Bob wrote out a campaign check for $50,000, and told Jose to come back for more if he needed it. Jose took the money.

The Hyatt's main ballroom was as big as a football field, and Bob had instructed the decorators to spare no expense. Looking around the massive room, Alan believed Texas Bob had gotten his money's worth. Oversized posters of a smiling Bob and Ellen Quintell were placed at varying heights around the walls. Alan guessed there were around three hundred brand new, white picnic tables scattered around the room. Each was covered by red and white checked table cloths, and every table had two large arrangements of fresh, white chrysanthemums. The flowers emerged from huge, ceramic vases made in the shape and color of Uncle Sam's tophat. Red and white striped bunting encircled the entire room, adding a touch of political tradition to what looked like a giant cookout.

Fifteen large-screen-projection televisions were positioned at strategic spots, each patched into the central campaign computer that would provide instant updates of vote totals throughout the evening.

Jesus, Alan thought, *must be nice to be this rich.* He looked across at his girlfriend Charlotte, and compared her to the other dolled-up women in the ballroom. No doubt about it – she'd stack up with the best. Charlotte was not only beautiful, she had a sensual air about her that made her easily the sexiest woman in the place. He leaned over and gave her a quick nibble on the ear.

Alan was feeling energized, not only because it was election night, but also from the knowledge that soon the world would be told that he was an innocent man.

Innocent, he thought, mumbling the word to himself. He focused on it, letting the idea ring through his psyche. It didn't even matter if he won or lost tonight; when the word got out that the police had said 'innocent', Alan would be ushered back into the smoky rooms of power. No more hushed tones when he came into a restaurant, no more snubs from stuck-up society types, or whispered judgments from politicians who thought they were too good to associate with him.

Yeah, he thought, *I'll be back on top in no time.*

He'd already won over many new admirers. Bringing a loud-talking, political neophyte like Bob Quintell to this point was, in itself, an amazing accomplishment. What was more, they had a real shot at victory. Then what would people say?

Walking through the ballroom, Alan could feel the admiration from many in the crowd. Even though these people weren't aware of Fishbein's pending announcement, Alan had earned their respect with his savvy campaign management.

Making their way across the crowded ballroom, Alan put his arm around Charlotte's slender waist and pulled her close. 'I wish we were naked right now.'

He took her face in his hands and gave her a passionate kiss. She returned his passion and discreetly pressed her leg up against his crotch. Several couples in their immediate vicinity toasted them, pointing and smiling as if they were cheering for newlyweds.

Alan bowed to the crowd, then excused himself to find the backstage area. He had to check in and make sure everything was under control before he went upstairs to the campaign headquarters. Two young guys, who looked like they had been recruited from a rock band's road crew, were frantically working with a maze of wires and controls, in the final stages of patchwork between the ballroom and the central computer system.

They reassured him that everything was on schedule, and the evening would go off without a technical snafu. He found Charlotte talking to the wife of a Houston City councilman, and took her arm. 'Pardon us, but we're wanted upstairs,' he said.

Alan and Charlotte were the last ones in a crowded elevator headed upstairs. During the elevator ride, Charlotte stood between Alan and the door, discreetly pressing her behind into his crotch. The sexual stirrings reminded Alan of the last time he'd attended one of these big political shindigs. Fifteen years ago, a few weeks before Justine's death, he'd been at a post-election party and had found himself the recipient of a sexual feast. That night, his client had won, and all manner of women were coming on to him throughout the evening. He was pulled into darkened stairways and fondled in elevators. That memory plus the proximity of Charlotte's tight buttocks gave him a full erection in his tuxedo pants, and Alan hoped he would be able to exit the elevator with decorum.

The Quintell Campaign had bought up all of the eighteenth floor, renting ten rooms and four suites for the weekend. Three of the suites were set aside as hospitality centers for various segments of the campaign. The large, three bedroom Presidential Suite was organized as campaign central. The hotel rooms were for high-ranking staffers who were from out of town or became too drunk to drive home.

As soon as the elevator doors opened on eighteen, Alan knew they were in the right place. Very loud country music was blasting from one of the suites. Alan peeked inside, then pulled Charlotte next to him in the hall.

'Honey, we're going to have to stop off at these hospitality rooms first, just to make an appearance. Once we get to Texas Bob's suite, there will be a lot of people pulling on me. I won't be able to hang with you every minute. There could be times when I'm gone for twenty or thirty minutes. But I'll try not to leave you alone any more than I have to.'

Her eyes told him she was captivated by the excitement of the evening. 'I understand. Just don't go home without me.'

He gave her a kiss that told her he wouldn't. They entered Suite 1804, where a half dozen blue collar types were sitting around the living room laughing and yelling. Alan recognized three of the men – they were volunteers who had been voices on testimonial radio commercials. Alan and Charlotte stopped off at the bar, then took their drinks over to the group. Alan shook hands with everyone and made small talk for a minute. The men looked like they had been celebrating since that morning, and once they'd all greeted Alan and Charlotte they went back to their drunken conversation.

A bald man who Alan remembered as an auto mechanic stood up and faced the group, as if it were his turn.

'Okay everybody, lithen to me!' The bald man hesitated to make sure everyone was paying attention. He held his head high and recited from memory the script lines he'd recorded for Texas Bob's commercial. His speech was slurred and it was hard to understand him. 'I'm vhothing for Tesxas Bob Quintell 'cause he knows what it means to work for a liffing.'

The other men in the room cheered and laughed, slapping the mechanic on the back before offering a toast. The next man stood up, this one an unfamiliar face to Alan, but one with a voice that had been heard on eighty radio stations across the state. 'Texhaz Bob Quindtell belivffes in fameelliy valuzzes – and evreebodez right to protecdt their hombe from crimnls.'

Alan and Charlotte laughed as the drunks continued reciting their lines. After a few minutes, they waved goodbye to the group and he and Charlotte went down to the next hospitality suite.

Outside of Suite 1806, Alan hesitated. 'This is where the money crowd is. It's going to be a very different scene in there.'

Different it was. Alan opened the door into a room that looked like a mini Las Vegas casino. In the left corner of the room, two card tables, each with seven players, sat underneath a thick haze of tobacco smoke. In the right corner, a portable crap table had been brought in, and a dozen or more tuxedoed players swilled booze and handled stacks of cash.

Bartenders and waitresses moved expertly around the crowd, keeping a constant flow of liquor to the partygoers. A giant board was on the wall on one side of the room, a big rectangle filled with small squares. Inside many of the squares were various initials, and across the top of the poster it read: GUESS WHAT TIME THE LOSER WILL CONCEDE THE RACE.

A number of the Republican advisors from Washington DC were talking among themselves in the corner. They waved Alan over to their group.

'Hey, Stakeman, great party. Are the good guys gonna win?' The man asking the questions was in his early forties, overweight with a too-small, dark suit straining against his stomach.

'It's in the bag,' Alan said. 'But it's going to be very close. It might be tomorrow before it's all said and done.'

Alan led Charlotte past the bar, nodding to several high rollers in the middle of a dice game near the balcony. 'The money guys always gamble,' Alan whispered to Charlotte. 'It's the main reason they get involved in politics. Everything about it is like shooting craps.'

Charlotte seemed fascinated.

'This is just a game to most contributors,' Alan continued. 'Some of them donate money to both sides. But the men in this room make up the nucleus of Texas Bob's fundraising effort. They deserve a night of fun, considering that they were responsible for raising over twenty million dollars.'

'Twenty million?' Charlotte repeated.

He could tell she was impressed. 'C'mon honey, it's almost nine, and I need to get down to the computer center.'

Alan and Charlotte made another pass around the room, exchanging pleasantries with several people. They went down the hall to Suite 1810, which had gold paint on double doors that read PRESIDENTIAL SUITE. Alan glanced at Charlotte just before he opened the doors. 'I wonder if Clinton is here.'

The first thing that hit them was the sound of ringing telephones. The suite came with five telephones, but the campaign had installed an extra dozen just for this evening. About thirty people milled around the room, each working on their own brand of campaign anxiety. The suite itself was large, probably around 3,000 square feet, and featured a well stocked wet bar, a huge couch and love seat, and large windows which looked out over Houston's angular skyline.

A woman walked up and handed Alan a stack of telephone messages, most from radio and television stations across the state. Flipping through the messages, Alan realized that a lot of stations go on the air live for election night coverage the moment the polls close. That meant that now, almost an hour into the count, they would be desperate to fill airtime.

'Anyone talk to Texas Bob?' Alan asked. All heads

shook no and Alan asked a secretary to locate a portable tape recorder for him. He was handed a recorder and found a quiet corner.

He spoke crisply into the microphone. 'Our polls indicate that this will be a very close election. All of us in the Quintell Campaign want to express our gratitude to the hundreds of Texas voters who have volunteered their time and money to help our campaign. We've made a lot of new friends, and been gratified to find widespread support for our views in every part of this great state. We want to thank our opponent, Senator Smart, for keeping the election clean and above board, and we wish him well in whatever field he chooses to go in to.'

Alan handed the tape recorder back to the secretary. 'The next time a media person needs a statement, just play 'em the tape.'

As he and Charlotte crossed the room, Alan was mobbed by people wanting to get the inside scoop.

'Hey, Alan, did we get all the vans up to Dallas on time? I talked to them at two o'clock, and they said there had been some mix-up . . .'

'Stakeman, what's the word? Are we gonna get any of the Hispanic vote?'

'Alan Stakeman, just the man I want to see. A good friend of mine is a reporter with KLBJ Radio in Austin. Do you think you could give her a quick call? She needs an actuality real bad . . .'

'Somebody told me Philip Smart is taking a trip to Africa next week, on some kind of fact-finding deal. Guess he's trying to get all the perks he can before he loses his job . . .'

Alan handled each request with as much aplomb as he could muster. It took him twenty minutes to find his way to the other side of the room, to the locked door behind which was the computer center manned by Lamar Suskie. Alan knocked twice rapidly, then once, then three more quick raps. It was a special code he'd worked out with his pollster.

The door opened a crack and Alan nodded to Lamar. Alan told Charlotte she was on her own for a few minutes, and he disappeared behind the door.

Alan laughed when he got in the room and got a good look at Lamar. Lamar Suskie looked like someone who hadn't slept in a week, which probably wasn't far from the truth. The beds had been removed from the room, and in their place sat three personal computers, a bank of telephones, a copy machine, a fax, and a laser printer. One entire wall was covered with printouts, and a small card table was littered with can wrappers, coffee cups, a box of Kentucky Fried Chicken, and a half-empty bottle of vodka.

Alan knew that Lamar would have the most up-to-the-minute vote totals between now and the final count. The Quintell Campaign had positioned volunteers in every one of Texas's 254 counties. Each volunteer was told to stay at their county's Registrar of Voters office, and as soon as the vote totals were tabulated, they were to be phoned into campaign central.

The metropolitan counties wouldn't be any problem, since they were all computerized and would have their final numbers within ninety minutes of the polls closing. But out in the sparsely populated rural counties, it could take hours. With Texas Bob's statewide hook-up, the Quintell

Campaign would have final but unofficial totals faster than the Texas Secretary of State's office.

Alan looked into his old friend's bleary eyes and smiled. 'How's it going, Lamar?'

Lamar seemed irritated. 'Tell those drunk sumbitches to quit knocking on the door. I've told them all a hundred times, just shove the information under the door and leave me the hell alone.'

'They're just curious, that's all. But I'll talk to them. Tell me what we've got so far.'

Lamar scratched his head and looked around the room. Alan knew what he was going through – the feeling that at any moment, your brain would explode from an information overload.

Lamar pushed a button on one of the computers and the printer sprang to life. 'Be just a second, Alan. I just finished the latest data entry.'

Alan felt adrenaline rush through his system as he waited for the printout to emerge. After a few seconds, the machine stopped and Lamar tore off the top two sheets and handed them over. Alan's eyes moved down an alphabetical list of numbers by counties.

Texas Commissioner of Elections – US Senate Race

COUNTY	QUINTELL	SMART	% REPORTING
Anderson	7,356	7,498	32
Angelina	10,955	11,004	23
Arkansas	12,354	12,210	19

Archer	22,925	23,319	76
Bowie	18,604	18,887	39

Alan flipped to the back page to find the vote totals.

TOTAL	909,088	911,239	34

Alan whistled and handed the printout over to Lamar. 'Shit, that's close. How do those numbers match up to your last poll?'

'Right on the money. I told you yesterday, the damn thing is too close to call.'

Alan nodded. 'I'm going to try and find someone to guard the door, to stop people from knocking. I'll be coming in every fifteen minutes from here on out. We appreciate your hard work.'

Lamar picked up the bottle of vodka and took a long pull. 'Tell Texas Bob I want a bonus.'

At 9:45 p.m. the double doors to the Presidential Suite opened and Texas Bob and Ellen came in. Conversations stopped, as everyone in the room got to their feet and applauded the Quintells. Bob was nervous, slowly moving through the crowd, greeting and thanking his closest supporters. Someone near the back of the room began chanting 'speech, speech', and Bob was forced to address the room.

Texas Bob felt unnaturally shy addressing the group. His mind flashed on many things he wanted to say, but his heart took over. 'In a couple of hours, this campaign will be a thing of the past. And Ellen and I want everyone to know, regardless of how things end up, that this has been a special time for us. It's been a tough six months, and many of you have given so generously of your time and your money, that we could never repay you.' He paused and looked around the room. 'So please, don't ask for your money back.'

Everyone laughed at the joke, and Texas Bob relaxed a little. 'But seriously, it's times like these that show a man who his true friends are. When good people are drawn together with a common philosophy, a common goal, friendships are formed that will last a lifetime.' Bob held up a drink in salute to the room. 'I'm a very wealthy man, and I don't mean the fleeting kind of wealth that you get from money, but rich in the priceless commodity of friendship. No matter what happens, I want you to know that Ellen and I love each and every one of you.'

Bob toasted the group and everyone joined him in a sip. 'Now,' Bob said, with a determined look on his face. 'Let's go see how bad we kicked Philip Smart's ass!'

Alan came up behind Charlotte and put his hand on the small of her back. She was listening to one of the Washington Republicans brag about a governorship he had delivered to the party.

At his touch she glanced over in his direction and winked. Alan looked at his watch and searched the room: ten thirty and still no sign of Garth. *Where the hell is he?* Alan wondered.

Alan carefully picked his way through the Presidential Suite and found Texas Bob, talking to an oil man from

Amarillo. He stood quietly at his side until Bob noticed him and could excuse himself. Alan took him over to the door to Lamar's computer room and gave the secret knock. After a couple of minutes, Lamar opened the door, handing over the latest printout without comment. Alan flipped through the first few pages of county-by-county numbers quickly. He slowed down his reading when he got to the middle of the alphabet. Texas Bob read over Alan's shoulder.

Texas Commissioner of Elections – US Senate Race

COUNTY	QUINTELL	SMART	% REPORTING
NAVARRO	31,218	31,876	89
NEWTON	42,875	43,499	82
OCHILTREE	53,283	56,207	74
PALO PINTO	30,983	31,294	100
PARKER	52,238	41,198	100
PECOS	69,847	72,295	100
PRESIDIO	40,098	40,001	98

Everywhere he looked, the numbers told the same story. This race was going to go down to the wire. Alan could see the trends, and hoped that they wouldn't have to endure a long wait. If the difference between the two candidates ended up being one per cent or less, there would automatically be a recount. If that were to happen, the official results would not be known until tomorrow, or even the next day.

VAL VERDI	33,294	33,339	100
VICTORIA	21,118	21,328	100
WARD	39,938	40,109	90
WASHINGTON	37,746	36,272	87
WHARTON	52,874	60,274	90
WILSON	34,430	34,338	100
WICHITA	63,996	63,999	100
ZAPATA	44,390	43,964	80
ZAVALA	25,482	26,463	61
TOTALS	2,999,974	3,000,197	98

Alan looked at Lamar. 'Jesus, how many—'

'Two hundred and twenty-three votes. Out of almost six million cast. It's the closest race I've ever seen.'

Alan looked at Texas Bob. 'There's definitely going to be a recount, no matter who comes out on top.'

At 2 a.m., Alan and Texas Bob decided to call it a night. For the last two hours, new numbers had trickled in, and it was clear that the official vote would have to wait until Sunday morning.

Alan found Charlotte sitting up in a chair in the Presidential Suite, asleep. He roused her gently, gave her a short kiss on the cheek, and escorted her out the door.

Texas Bob grabbed him in the hallway. 'Alan, I want you to know how much I enjoyed working with you. Win or lose, you're one helluva guy, and I'm sure you have a great future in front of you. When they get through counting, Ellen and I are going to take us a trip. A friend of mine loaned me his villa in Mexico. I'd love for you and your lady to join us down there. Garth too. Where is he, anyway? Haven't seen him all night.'

He started to tell Bob the truth, but thought better of it. 'He's not feeling good,' Alan said. 'Some kind of virus. He'll probably be okay by tomorrow. Look for both of us up here around 10 a.m. And try to get some sleep.'

30

He stopped at a convenience store on the way home and bought a cinnamon roll and a large cup of coffee. Better get some sugar and caffeine in my system, he thought. I've got to call the police when I get back to the house and discover the 'break-in'. They'll probably keep me up all night.

He had carefully worked out his story, and was confident that no amount of blue-collar cop intimidation could shake it. He'd wrapped the gun in a towel and buried it in the woods two miles from his house. Some time in the next day or so he could dig it up, drive up to the bank, and leave it in the safety deposit box he'd opened in Garth's name.

Not that he was trying to hang the murder on Garth, he told himself. If he wanted to do that, his plan would be vastly different. No – putting the safety deposit box in Garth's name merely provided an extra measure of deniability.

He finished his sweet roll and turned down the narrow street leading to his large, contemporary house. He checked his watch – a total of thirty-four minutes had passed since he'd first pulled the trigger. Four minutes behind schedule, he thought to himself.

It was a little after one o'clock in the morning, and he

knew that once he called 911, the next few days would be devoted to playing the role of the shocked, grieving husband. Play-acting isn't that hard, he knew. After all, he'd been acting as if he enjoyed being married to the Queen Bitch.

He pulled into his driveway, surprised to see two blue and white Houston Police patrol cars parked ahead. He could see a dark figure walking in the front yard, a flashlight spotting the grass.

Oh shit, the police are already here! he thought. That's not good. That's not good at all!

Fuck, he thought. I hope no one heard the gun shot. It will be hard to explain leaving the house before calling the police.

A patrol officer's face suddenly appeared outside his driver's side window. He pushed the electric window button.

'Are you Alan Stakeman?' the young officer asked.

'Yeah,' he answered. 'What's the problem, officer? Is everything all right?'

The policeman opened the car door and motioned for Alan to get out. 'No, sir, I'm afraid it's not.'

31

Alan waited patiently for the light to change, then pulled into the parking lot of the First National Bank of Diboll. He was whistling as he entered the lobby, and strolled over to the guard sitting outside the vault entrance to the safety deposit boxes. He signed the customer card and waited while the guard compared the signature to the file card.

'Garth, huh? Just like the country singer,' the guard said.

He was shown to his box and left alone. He opened the box, and inside were several letters, a couple of stock certificates, some photographs, and the .357 Magnum. He took out a white handkerchief and draped the cloth over the pistol. Glancing around to make sure no one was looking, he lifted the gun out and put it in his coat pocket. He closed the safety deposit box up and put in back in place.

Alan remembered the first time he'd been in this bank. He used one of Garth's old, discarded temporary driver's licenses to put a couple of thousand dollars in a savings account in his stepson's name. The stupid woman who opened the account didn't question the smudge mark he'd made, strategically placed where the date of birth was noted.

It had been a perfect plan, the ideal way to get rid of Justine and not have to give up half his wealth in a divorce. Originally he'd wanted to hang the whole thing on Garth, but impatience got the best of him and he killed her before a plan could be hatched.

Alan still couldn't believe that it had all blown up in his face, that the Harris County District Attorney had been able to get a conviction without ever finding the murder weapon.

Alan nodded to the guard as he left the vault, his hand inside the coat pocket where the gun rested.

'Have a nice day, Mr Stakeman.' the guard said, just as the woman from the bank's customer service desk walked by.

'Oh, so you're Mr Stakeman?' the woman said, grinning to show him all of her ugly teeth. 'I guess you remembered to come in to get that passport.'

Alan was startled that she was talking to him. 'Excuse me?'

'The passport. Your wife came by yesterday, wanting to open your box. She was worried that you'd gone out of town and forgotten them.'

Wife? he thought. He could feel the hair stand up on his arms.

'Yes,' he answered, pulling his hand out and patting his pocket, 'I got everything I needed.'

'Well good. Please tell Mrs Stakeman that we're sorry we

couldn't let her in. But, you know, she didn't have a key and she wasn't on the signature card.'

'No problem. We understand. And thank you for your concern,' Alan said.

He smiled at the guard and left the bank as quickly as he could.

Melissa has been here, he realized. A few weeks ago, Alan had sent a change of address form to the bank, so the savings account statements would stop being forwarded to his lawyer's office and start going to Garth's house. That way, whenever Fishbein got around to executing a search warrant, evidence of Garth's safety deposit box would be found.

Son of a bitch, he thought. *Melissa was in Diboll! She was trying to get a look inside the box, but the bank turned her away.*

Now what am I going to do? he wondered.

Garth pulled into the garage, happy to see that Melissa's motorcycle was gone. *Good,* he thought, *the last thing I want right now is a confrontation with my lunatic wife.*

He took a quick shower and changed clothes. He grabbed a suitcase out of the hall closet and selectively went through his chest of drawers. He picked out several shirts and slacks, neatly folding and packing several changes of underwear, a few pairs of socks and his favorite shoes. Garth wanted to get a week's worth of clothes, and took his time to make sure he selected the best stuff.

He went into his study and unlocked the drawers to his desk. Ever since he'd caught Melissa snooping around, he'd kept the desk locked, safe from her nosy eyes. He flipped through several file folders until he found the ones he wanted and placed them in his briefcase. He took all of his recent bank and credit card statements, along with an unused packet of traveler's checks, and tossed them in the briefcase.

The telephone rang. He couldn't decide whether or not to answer it. It might be Melissa. It could be Fishbein.

He waited as the answering machine picked up, then grabbed the phone when he heard his father's voice.

'Garth!' Alan said. 'Where the fuck have you been? I've been worried sick about you.'

It felt good to hear his father's voice, though he knew he was in trouble for not showing up at the election night party.

'Melissa and I had an argument,' Garth said. 'She attacked me like some kind of wild woman. As far as I'm concerned, the marriage is over.'

'I'm sorry to hear that.'

Garth continued. 'And I'm sorry about not showing up for the election night party. Have they got a final count yet?'

'It's so close that the Secretary of State's office is doing a recount, and the results won't be known until tonight or maybe tomorrow. The last word I had was that there was less than a hundred votes between them. But fuck all that, I'm more concerned about you and Melissa.'

'Thanks, but I don't think there's anything left to say,' Garth said.

'Have you talked to Melissa today?' Alan asked.

'No.'

'She's not there now?'

'No. It looks like she may have left. Her closet is pretty much cleaned out. I spent the last couple of nights in a motel. I just came by to pick up some clothes, but since she's not around, I might stay here.'

There was a long pause. 'Well, did she leave a note saying where she was, or when she would be back?'

Garth wondered why his dad cared so much about where Melissa was. 'No. Why?'

Alan's voice was low and calm. 'Nothing. I just think the two of you should get together and talk. Maybe it's not too late. Maybe the marriage can still be saved.'

'The next time we talk, it will probably be in a divorce lawyer's office. How's Texas Bob doing? I'll bet he's nervous.'

'He's going nuts, yelling and carrying on like a crazy man. He was asking about you last night. I told him you were sick. You should call him, let him know you're all right. Look, son, I'm sorry, but I've got to run. I'll call you later.'

Before Garth could say anything the phone went dead. *That's strange,* Garth thought. *I didn't even get a chance to say goodbye.*

Alan hung up the telephone and stared at the wall. He was sitting in the living room of his townhouse, wearing nothing except his boxer shorts.

Where's Melissa? he wondered. He looked at his watch: 3:30 p.m.

Where could she be? he wondered. *Does she realize what she has found? Of course she does, she's too smart not too! Well then, has she told anyone?*

He couldn't stand sitting still, not knowing what was going on. Was Melissa spilling the beans to Garth, or the police? What if she was too frightened to say anything? Maybe she was confused, terrified – maybe she hadn't yet let the cat out of the bag.

He had to make sure that she didn't open her mouth. After all these years, all this planning, he was hours away from getting everything he wanted.

He couldn't let her ruin it. He hadn't come this far to have everything unravel now!

Alan went to his clothes closet and looked for the jacket he'd worn yesterday. He jerked it off its hanger, frantically digging around in the pockets until his fingers found the piece of paper.

He spied the feminine handwriting and smiled. *Melissa, my dear,* he thought, *I guess you and I have some unfinished business.*

32

Sara O'Donnell pulled Melissa over to the pearl jewelry in the department store's display case. Melissa glanced at the jewelry but didn't comment.

After Melissa had got back from her drive, they'd taken a carload of clothes to her studio, then headed for the Galleria to try on hats and gorge on hot dogs and beer.

Melissa hadn't yet told her friend anything about the safety deposit box.

'I know – let's go get a massage,' Sara suggested.

Melissa answered by shaking her head no.

'We could go ice skating?'

Melissa wasn't enthusiastic.

They left the jewelry case and walked through the store's furniture department. A large, ornate mirror was hanging on the wall in one of the designer rooms. Melissa and Sara stopped in front of the mirror and Sara put her arm around her friend's shoulder.

'We could almost be sisters,' Sara said, noting their similar height and body shapes. 'Except your tits are a lot bigger.'

She managed to get a little smile from Melissa. They gave

up on shopping and walked out of the store to the parking lot. Melissa's motorcycle was parked near the front, and they put their helmets on and mounted the bike.

Melissa agreed to stop off and smoke a joint at Sara's apartment.

They took the long way home, heading through neighborhood streets in River Oaks, cutting across to the tree-lined avenues of the museum district near Rice University. In the cool quiet of the afternoon shadows, under the green canopy of leaves, Melissa wondered what she should do next.

You have to tell somebody, Melissa thought. *You can't just go around holding this inside. For one thing, it will eat your insides out if you don't release it. For another, you're probably breaking some law by keeping it to yourself.*

She decided to try to call Garth from Sara's place. He probably wouldn't believe her, maybe he wouldn't even listen, but she had to try.

Garth flipped on the lights in the Stakeman & Son office and closed the door behind him. After weeks of hosting almost round-the-clock political meetings, it was strange to see the suite quiet and calm.

The building's clean-up crew had yet to make their way to the 28th floor, so empty pizza boxes and crumpled paper coffee cups littered every available nook and cranny. Garth unlocked the door to his private office and stepped into its comparative tidiness. He hadn't been to work for several days, and had missed most of the last-minute beehive of activity.

He felt guilty about cutting out on the campaign, especially considering his long personal history with Bob Quintell, but events had overwhelmed him. How could they expect him to talk politics when Fishbein was accusing him of murder? What's more, he and Melissa were surely heading toward divorce, and while things hadn't been good between them for a while, the finality of a formal break-up depressed him.

But there was something else bothering him. Thoughts he'd been avoiding, realization he'd been denying.

Alan. His father. Murder. Betrayal.

The telephone on his desk gave a loud beep and startled him. He glanced toward the sound and saw that it was his private, direct number ringing. He pushed the button for the speaker phone but didn't immediately say anything.

'Garth? Garth are you there?' Melissa's voice asked.

It was dark inside the studio. There was the faint smell of clay and paint, mixed with the mustiness of old concrete. Except for the faint moonlight creeping in from the row of barred windows, and the very distant sound of freeway traffic, all was calm and quiet.

Alan turned on his flashlight and held his wrist up to check his watch: 10:45 p.m. *Jesus,* he thought, *where is she?*

A bright flash of lightning drew his eye outside the window, and like a kid, he counted, waiting for the familiar, following sound of rumbling thunder. One thousand one, one thousand two, one thousand— There it was.

He waited for another flash and repeated the game. *It's moving in fast,* he told himself. Alan remembered the weather forecast he'd seen earlier in the day. A large line of heavy thunderstorms moving in tonight, the weather man had said.

Alan had been sitting in a chair a few feet inside the front door since a little after four o'clock. He hadn't been prepared for such a long wait, and had consumed two packs of potato chips and a couple of soft drinks waiting for Melissa to return.

He really didn't need to be waiting by the door. He could have just as easily stretched out on Melissa's bed, using the video security system to keep watch. The monitor screens in the studio's apartment area gave a clear view of the basement parking lot, the main entrance, even the side of the building opposite of the door.

But he preferred waiting by the door. He wanted to get this over with, and he knew he would be able to hear the loud Harley pull in.

Alan was surprised at how calm he felt, considering this unexpected change in plans. Up to this point, the plan had been executed with military precision. *It doesn't matter about Melissa,* he told himself; *it might even make the scenario more convincing*. Once her body was found, Garth would automatically be considered the primary suspect. Alan would simply take the gun to Garth's house and hide it in the garage. The police would find it – case closed.

One more killing away and you get the big prize, he thought. Everything he had planned for and dreamed about would be his. He expected to feel more excited. To be ecstatic. *Strange,* he thought, *to come this far, successfully orchestrate this elaborate set-up and not find more joy and satisfaction in the execution of it. You ought to be jumping up and down.*

He knew what was wrong. Anticipation was always better than reality.

Yeah, life is a series of anticipations and let-downs. You're born, you learn to walk, to talk, and as soon as you get old enough to think and understand, you start anticipating. When you're a little kid, he thought, *you can't wait till your birthday. Or Halloween. Or Christmas, or for the circus to come to town.*

You dream about what it would be like to have a new bicycle, your first day of school, your first kiss, first fuck, and the first time you fall in love.

But when the reality got there, it never lived up to the anticipation. The bicycle didn't make you as cool as you thought it would. The girl wasn't the perfect, wonderful princess you had imagined her to be.

Reality couldn't compete with anticipation, he knew, because the imagination was unfettered, boundless. Things were never as good as you had hoped they would be.

He laughed out loud at his philosophizing, the giggle echoing inside the dark, cavernous studio.

How typical, he told himself. *You're about to achieve everything you wanted, and you already feel let down.*

Oh well, he thought, *at least the end is almost here. And I have Garth to thank.*

Alan had never really connected to Garth. When he and Justine first got married, Alan had tried to play the role of loving father. But once Alan discovered Justine and Garth's sick little relationship, it was all Alan could do to look at the boy.

Every now and then, Alan felt a tinge of guilt about allowing Justine to continue to use the boy. But though he found that whole affair sordid and disgusting, he wasn't sufficiently concerned to step in and try to help. Besides, Alan had his own problems. His own ambitions, and, well, he just didn't have time to play nursemaid to an immature young boy.

Later, when he was nearing his release from prison and planning his resurrection, Garth had played right into Alan's hands. Now Alan had the perfect fall guy, his son, the over-zealous enforcer, advocate and bodyguard. Garth was so good at his protector role that he had attracted the attention of Frieda Fishbein.

Which gave Alan just the opening he needed.

So you're going to reward that devotion by murdering Melissa and pinning the killing on Garth? Alan asked himself.

You're such an asshole!

He smiled.

Outside, the rain arrived, in loud, full sheets that sounded like rocks hitting the studio's old roof. Alan walked over to the window and looked outside. It was hard to see more than fifteen or twenty feet in front of him. The large drops splattered loudly against the streets, swirling into puddles and forming mini-rivers inside of minutes.

Through the noise of the rain he heard it. Faintly at first, then louder. He stepped back from the window, though he knew there was little chance he'd be spotted. He saw the single headlight of the Harley cruising toward the studio, and he moved completely back into the shadows. The motorcycle's engine was loud as it drove past the front door, the volume fading slightly as it pulled into the basement garage.

It's about fucking time you got here, Alan thought. He checked the pistol once again, making sure it was fully loaded with six shells.

Not that he would need all six shots. A gun this powerful, one bullet in the chest would leave a hole big enough to put your hand in.

Alan started to go and watch Melissa on the security monitors, then he realized that it wouldn't take her more than a few seconds to get to the front door. He cocked the pistol and rested the cool, metal barrel against the side of his face.

Outside the thunder and lightning continued. The heavy sound of rainwater pounding against the roof was deafening. He listened closely though, and could hear the beeps as she pushed the code numbers for the lock.

Taking no chances, he assumed the firing position with a two-handed grip on the gun. The door swung open and she stepped inside. A bright bolt of lightning flashed across the watery sky, giving him a perfect, silhouetted target. He fired once, hitting her squarely in the chest.

The force of the bullet knocked her backwards, back out into the rain, on the concrete entranceway. Alan waited for a moment to see if she moved. She didn't.

He stepped to the front door and stood over the body.

She had landed flat on her back. The rain pelted hard on the lifeless woman.

His eyes moved up her body and he cursed. He was looking at the face of Sara O'Donnell.

33

Melissa had just walked around the corner from the parking garage when she heard the gunshot. She was still wearing her motorcycle helmet, and watched in horror as Sara's body flew backwards, landing half-in and half-out the doorway.

Melissa froze. She thought she was hallucinating.

This isn't really happening, she thought. *It must be the rain, or stress, or something playing tricks on my eyesight.*

It was as if everything was happening in slow motion. The loud bang. Sara's body floating lazily through the air, a swirl of gun smoke. She was jolted back to reality when she saw Alan walk up and stand over her friend.

Alan was frowning. He looked up and saw Melissa watching him. Just then, Melissa spotted the gun in his hand and snapped back to reality. He raised the gun to fire and she quickly jumped to get around the corner. She leaped back as the pistol's report exploded in a terrifying boom, momentarily drowning out the sound of the thunderstorm.

She stood with her back against the wall for a split second, then turned and ran toward her motorcycle. *Oh,*

Jesus, she thought, *why did I park so far away?* She cursed herself under her breath, her neck and shoulder muscles tense, waiting for the moment when she'd hear the next gunshot.

Melissa ran as fast as she could across the empty parking lot, her cowboy boots making loud claps against the concrete floor.

These boots may be great for motorcycle riding, she thought, *but they're not worth a damn for running on rough concrete.* Twice she skidded and almost fell.

Thirty feet from the bike she started digging in her jeans pocket for the ignition key. Her hands were shaking and it was hard to stuff her fingers in her pockets while she was running. A fingernail caught on the pocket seam, ripping one of her nails off at the quick.

She finally managed to pull the key out of her jeans pocket and threw her right leg over the motorcycle. She glanced behind her, expecting to see Alan bearing down on her. Instead she saw nothing except the empty garage.

She moaned when she realized that she would have to ride past him, maybe even drive over him, to get through the only door out.

She pushed the bike off its kickstand and turned on the ignition. She'd recently done a tune-up on the bike so the Harley started instantly. Still no sign of Alan.

He knows I've got to come out the door, she thought. *He's probably hiding out of sight waiting for me to come riding up. There's nothing to do except ride like hell and hope he misses.*

She sat on the bike, revving the engine to the red line, the loud noise filling the garage. She held the throttle open, and waited for the courage to shoot through the exit.

Fuck! Alan thought. *Fuck, fuck, fuck!*

He knew he shouldn't have fired while she was in the doorway, but it was a reflex. Now he had killed some redhead and Melissa had a chance to escape.

This is not good, he told himself. *No fucking good at all!*

He started to chase her down into the parking garage, but then he realized that she'd have to come out the door to get away. Instead of chasing after her, he took off in the rain to the darkest side of the building, to his car. He knew he'd be glad he was already in the driver's seat if she somehow managed to get out of the garage.

He gunned the Lincoln Continental's big engine and fish-tailed toward the exit. The rain made it very hard to see, even with his windshield wipers on high. He thought that if he could park his car lengthwise across the exit, there'd be no room for the motorcycle to get by. She'd be blocked, trapped inside the garage, and he could take his time and make sure he killed her. He sped toward the opening, his eye watching for the moment when the Harley might come shooting out.

Alan slammed on the brakes and slid sideways several feet, coming to a stop blocking the exit space. He was pleased with his stunt driving and looked back into the garage, waiting for the Harley to come charging toward him.

Melissa cursed under her breath when she saw the black

Lincoln screech to a stop in front of the exit. She knew she had to find a way out quickly before Alan got out and came after her with the gun.

She kept racing the throttle, hoping the loud engine noise would attract someone's attention.

She stared at the Lincoln. She couldn't see him inside, her sight blocked by the tinted windows, but she knew Alan was there, waiting. She wished that she had something she could use as a weapon, something that would let her turn the tables on him.

She could drive her motorcycle into the car at full speed, of course, but the impact probably wouldn't give him much more than a jolt. The collision would surely send her flying, up over the top of the car, out into the street. If she were lucky she would die instantly. If not, she'd get to lie there in pain and wait for him to walk over and deliver the *coup de grâce*.

Melissa revved the engine even higher before letting out the clutch. The Harley shot forward, popping a wheelie as its front wheel left the concrete. Twenty feet away from where she'd started the front tire touched back down, the rubber gripping concrete as she sped toward the Lincoln. She aimed for just behind the rear tire, in the area of the car's gas tank, hoping that somehow, the force of the impact would start a fire and kill him. She shifted into third, now going at fifty miles per hour in the small garage space.

Then she saw a possible way out.

The rear of the Lincoln hadn't stopped completely flush with the left side of the exit. There was a small opening, no more than two or three feet, between the car's rear bumper and the concrete wall.

Her eyes went back to the front of the car. The passenger side window was lowering, and she could see Alan inside taking aim with his gun.

Was the opening at the rear bumper wide enough to squeeze the motorcycle through?

She took a last, quick glance toward Alan before turning the handlebars left and heading for the opening. In a split second she knew he would realize what she was doing and put the car in reverse. She had to get through before he could react.

She was still in third gear, afraid to lose momentum by shifting to fourth. She saw the car's backup lights engage and knew the car was going into reverse. Her engine was straining, screaming. She kept the bike pointed at the opening.

It's too small, she thought. *I'm going to crash!*

There was the loud sound of scraping metal as the Harley bounced between the car and the wall. Somehow, she shot through, an instant before his car's transmission kicked into gear and his rear bumper slammed into the wall.

She guided the motorcycle across the parking lot and splashed through a giant puddle, almost skidding over. She spotted a small incline leading up to a set of railroad tracks. Knowing he couldn't follow her up the hill, she took off toward the tracks, hoping they would lead her to a back street with an easy escape route.

The motorcycle shot down the railroad tracks, the cross ties jarring her front tire and handlebars as she made her escape. She couldn't see worth a damn, the rain still blowing with a north wind across Houston's deserted downtown.

He can't follow me down the tracks, she thought. *His car can't climb the hill.*

She glanced behind her to see that it was true. All clear, at least for the twenty or so feet she could see.

Oh my God, Alan's been killing all these people, she thought. *How could I be so stupid?*

Alan must have planted that stuff in Garth's office, she thought. *He wanted me to suspect Garth. He played me like a fool, and I fell for it hook, line and sinker.*

The pounding continued as she shot down the railroad tracks. Melissa realized that her left elbow was on fire, and she glanced down and saw that the sleeve of her jacket was ripped open. She tried to push the pain out of her consciousness, but each time she had to use the clutch, her grip reminded her of the injury.

She must have scraped herself pretty good on the wall, and the handlebars were bent a little sideways. She knew she was lucky to get out of the garage at all.

The rain was still pouring and she had to be careful and not drive too fast down the slick railroad tracks. She was going at almost forty miles per hour, much too fast under these extreme conditions, but she wished for even more speed. The continuous pounding on the tracks was making her arms and shoulders very tired now, and she knew she had to find a place to get off.

She drove across a short railroad trestle, probably twenty feet above the now raging Buffalo Bayou. She knew she was no more than a quarter mile from the relative safety of the downtown buildings, but she couldn't see more than a few feet around. It was impossible to tell where an escape path might be, so she concentrated on keeping the front tire straight on the track. Once she got back on the city streets, she knew she could take one of the main avenues from where she was on the northeast edge of downtown, drive a couple of miles due west and be at the headquarters of the Houston Police Department.

She cleared the trestle and immediately started looking for a possible escape route. There was a street up ahead, she remembered, as the intersection between the raised railroad tracks and a side street came into view. Melissa knew to be very careful coming off the tracks, as there was now a wide culvert visible at the bottom of the mud-covered hill.

The rain had begun to let up as she downshifted to slow the motorcycle, going from fourth to third to second as she neared the street. She leaned back and pulled up on the handlebars as her tires rolled over the rails. She slowed to a crawl, easing down the slippery embankment toward the street. Just as her tires rolled on to pavement, the black Lincoln came barreling up behind her.

Like someone suddenly turning off the shower, the rain stopped. But though the downpour had halted there was still standing water and streetwide flooding in every direction. Alan was drenched, having driven around with his head out the window, following the sound of the motorcycle's engine. He had just turned on to a narrow street between several abandoned warehouses when he saw the red flash of taillights ahead.

Gotcha, Alan thought, spotting the motorcycle sliding down the embankment. He pushed his accelerator to the floor and sped after her. The big car hit a small hill where the railroad tracks came over the street and immediately went airborne. There was a loud crunching sound when the front bumper collided with the wet street, and sparks shot up from underneath the car. He didn't see her look back, but he could tell from her reaction that she knew he was there. Melissa was working her motorcycle like a racer, leaning forward, her head low on the handlebars, the bike suddenly taking off like a rocket.

Alan knew he couldn't keep up with a motorcycle for long and hoped he had enough speed to overtake her. He aimed his hood ornament at her taillight as he pressed the accelerator against the floor.

Melissa was riding low on the bike, with no wasted movement, only her hands and foot rhythmically working the gears. Within seconds the bike's superior acceleration kicked in and he was no longer gaining on her. A couple more moments and she pulled ahead, making a sliding left turn and heading into the center of downtown.

He had to slow down to make the wide turn on the slick streets. He rounded the corner just in time to see the motorcycle nearing the far corner ahead. He knew it was useless to try to follow, realizing that his car couldn't compete on the short blocks between the tall skyscrapers. At least, from the direction they were heading, she seemed more concerned with escaping than with heading straight toward the police station. This way, if he was lucky, he'd get at least one more shot at her.

Alan pulled to a stop, Melissa's flickering taillights disappearing up ahead. *You can run but you can't hide,* he thought.

Melissa didn't know how many blocks she'd driven before she stopped zig-zagging and sneaked a look behind her. Seeing nothing, she pulled into the rear delivery area of one of the larger buildings, driving through a small, winding pathway formed by large eighteen-wheelers backed into loading docks. She had to drive slowly and pay very close attention, moving among the trucks at a greatly reduced speed.

Now that she was going more slowly, she constantly checked over her shoulder, making sure that the Lincoln didn't suddenly appear behind her. *If he follows me down here I'll be trapped,* she thought.

She found a dark corner beneath one of the ramps. She parked the motorcycle in the black shadow, turned off the engine and stepped off the bike.

Her legs were wobbly when they first touched ground and she realized that she was shaking. *Catch your breath, relax and try not to hyperventilate,* she told herself.

She took off her motorcycle helmet and let the breeze cool her sweaty forehead. Perspiration had made the hair lie flat against her head, and at once she went from hot to cold, aware of the cool, night air against her soaked clothes.

Now what do I do? she wondered. *I can't stay hidden*

forever. Eventually, he'll cruise by and find me. Should I go home? A friend's house? How about Mexico?

No, don't be stupid, she told herself. *I'm not the criminal here, he is!*

I wonder where Garth is? she thought. *I wish I had a cellular phone.*

Melissa heard the sound of splashing water, followed by the low moan of an approaching engine. It sounded like a truck but she wasn't taking any chances. She pressed herself up against the wall, so far underneath the loading ramp that she couldn't see out.

He could pull up right in front and block me in, she thought.

She forced herself to stay still and wait.

She held her breath and the sound moved away.

That's it, time to move, she realized. *You don't want to be stuck anywhere else where there's only one way out.*

She had no idea what time it was, figuring it must be some time after eleven. *This is fucking great,* she thought. *Late at night, in the dark, hiding in a deserted downtown business district with a killer on her tail.*

Her mind was racing. She knew the motorcycle could easily outrun Alan's car, but there was no way the bike could outrun a bullet. She had to be careful and not come within range of the gun. *What exactly is the range for a big pistol like that? Twenty feet? Fifty feet? Who the fuck knows?*

Get to the police station!

Though she wasn't sure exactly where in the downtown area she was, she knew she couldn't be more than five minutes or so from police headquarters. *Let's see,* she thought, *the best thing would be to take Travis to Texas Street, turn left, a couple more blocks and you'll run right into it.*

For the first time, Melissa thought about Sara, remembering the horror she had felt when the bullet knocked Sara down. *Oh, Sara, God, I'm so sorry for getting you into all this,* she thought. Was it possible Sara was still alive? Jesus, maybe she was lying there right now, alive, alone, bleeding to death outside the studio.

That does it, Melissa thought. *It's time to get this over with.*

She put her motorcycle helmet back on and climbed on the bike. *I'm going straight to the cops to get some help for Sara. And if I'm lucky, maybe they'll catch Alan with the murder weapon.*

In the silence of the empty downtown, the motorcycle's engine sounded frightfully loud. Melissa rode slowly through the parked delivery trucks, ready at any moment to gun the throttle and haul ass. She saw nothing, no movement of any kind.

A couple of hundred yards from where she'd been hiding she came to a cross street. Now that she was out of the darker alley, she turned off her motorcycle's headlight. A couple of blocks up she came to a wide, four-lane street. She read the sign. Travis Street.

She started off slowly, looking all around her for traffic of any kind. She saw a homeless man curled up on the sidewalk, sleeping against a large statue. A few blocks up a single car crossed the street, going away from her.

She pulled out on to Travis Street, with four lanes going one way, and continued to watch in all directions.

Maybe I'll come across a police car, she thought, *then I won't have to drive all the way to the station.* She moved into the center lane, keeping well clear of side streets and other possible hiding places.

Her eyes roamed the area in front of her, watching for any sign of the long, dark car.

She ran a red light at one of the intersections. *Arrest me officer; take my fat ass to jail – I'll gladly pay my fine.*

The area seemed quiet and totally deserted, the apparent calm making her senses more alert. *Six or eight more blocks, turn left and you're there,* she told herself.

Melissa noticed the throbbing in her elbow again. The further she traveled down this wide open street, the more she could feel her heart beating in her chest. A couple of blocks up ahead she noticed several construction signs, barrels blocking part of the street. She downshifted and slowed, almost coming to a stop, cautious in her approach to the intersection.

Her eyes were focused on the barrels, lined up in a V-shaped pattern that narrowed, forcing all traffic into two lanes. Melissa had a nervous feeling about the construction display, her attention glued to the spot where the barrels and the signs blocked the pathway at its narrowest point.

She slowly accelerated and held on tight to the grips.

She was concentrating so hard on the barrels that she didn't see the shadow moving toward her on her right.

One shot, Alan thought, *just give me one clear shot and I'll do the rest.* He'd been cruising the downtown district for several minutes, driving without headlights, hoping he wouldn't run up on a cop in the darkness.

He hoped that she'd eventually come this way. The obvious thing for her to do would be to head for the police station. He'd confined his patrol to an area three blocks square, in the place Melissa would most likely drive through to get to the HPD building.

She won't get away this time, he told himself. *You've come too far and got too much riding to fuck up now,* he thought.

Alan had been cruising for about ten minutes when he heard it, the unmistakable sound of the Harley. He accelerated toward Travis Street, the motorcycle's engine noise growing louder. Then he saw her.

Melissa was looking ahead and to her left. Alan was coming up at a perpendicular angle on her right. She appeared to be staring at the construction signs, as if she was expecting something to come from that spot. He stomped the accelerator and the Lincoln lurched forward.

The motorcycle and the car were on a collision course, coming up to the intersection of Travis and McKinney. He didn't think he would have time to catch up to her, turn the car around and fire, so he decided to just ram the motorcycle.

His car was traveling at least twice as fast as the motorcycle. Thirty feet from the intersection she saw him. He could see her looking around, obviously trying to decide whether to cut and run or try to accelerate past him. He had her.

It was too late for her to turn and get out of the way. All she could do was gun the bike out and try to outrun him again.

Ain't gonna happen this time, he thought.

The Lincoln had accelerated past eighty miles per hour. Alan held the steering wheel tight with both hands. He saw her twist the right hand grip, opening the throttle all the way. The motorcycle took off so quickly, she almost got by. But his right, front bumper clipped the rear tire on the motorcycle and she went into a wild spin.

He slammed on his brakes and watched the Harley make two long 360-degree circles down the middle of the rain-slicked street. For a moment he was afraid she would regain control, but then the front tire hit the curb and Melissa was thrown up over the front handlebars.

Alan's car came to a stop on the opposite side of Travis Street. He let out a whoop as Melissa's body hit the sidewalk and rolled to a stop in front of the seventy-story-tall Lone Star Tower.

34

She came down head first, on her helmet, and her body did two full cartwheels before landing sideways on the hard brick sidewalk.

When she stopped rolling, Melissa was dazed and dizzy. Every bone in her body was hurting as she struggled to sit up and take inventory of all her parts.

Her body had stopped when she hit a thirty-foot-tall, sphere-shaped abstract sculpture in the walkway in front of the bank building. For a moment she couldn't focus, as if her eyes were still rolling inside their sockets. Then her vision started to return, along with the awareness that she was in danger. She grabbed on to the base of the sculpture to pull herself up. Down the street she heard screeching tires, and looked around to see the Lincoln a half block away, turning toward her.

There was a small park-like area running down the side of the plaza in front of the Lone Star Tower. The park had been built on a raised level two feet higher than the street, and planted with a couple of dozen large shade trees. Rain water dripped from the soaked branches, and long shadows from the tall trees cast eerie shapes against the empty street.

Her first few steps brought intense, searing pain in her left leg. As she half ran, half limped across the plaza, she could feel a growing wetness moving down the inside of her jeans and she knew she was bleeding.

At least nothing is broken, she thought, *otherwise I wouldn't be able to walk.*

She had just made it into the park when the Lincoln ran over the curb and headed across the plaza. Melissa's left leg was throbbing, but she kept pushing ahead, dodging between the shadows, hoping to stay hidden in the dark spaces.

This is crazy, she told herself. *The park is much too small to use as a hiding place. I've got to get out of here now!*

At the far edge of the grassy area she jumped down off the raised wall, landing back on the sidewalk. The force of her landing sent shock waves of pain up her injured leg. Her breath was coming in loud puffs as she gritted her teeth and took off across Travis Street. She crossed the street and realized that she was heading toward the entrance to the tower's parking garage. She threw open the doors and took a couple of steps inside.

Another parking garage? she thought. *I'm not staying here.*

There was no one around. No pay phone, and not the first sign of a security guard. Her only avenue of escape was down, to the sub-level entrance to the downtown pedestrian Underground.

To her immediate right she saw an escalator, with a sign

pointing to the Underground. She glanced out the window and saw the black Lincoln burn rubber as it shot around the corner.

The escalator had been turned off for the evening, and she slid and limped down the grooved, motionless steps. At the bottom of the escalator was a large sitting area outside several closed sandwich shops. There were a couple of dozen tables and chairs that would be filled with people had it been a typical workday. In the silent darkness, the only light came from small neon beer signs inside a couple of the sandwich shops.

The pedestrian Underground itself resembled a miniature mall, with a wide, open corridor providing a common area for a variety of shops and stores inside. The entrance to the Underground was locked, blocked by two large, thick, glass doors.

Melissa limped over to the glass doors, wondering how she could get into the walkway. In the muted light she could see her reflection in the glass, and realized that she was still wearing her motorcycle helmet. *Leave it on,* she told herself. *At least that part of my body will have some protection.*

She grabbed the glass door handles and pulled with all her strength. She wasn't surprised when neither door budged an inch. She limped a few feet further down, hoping to find another, accessible entrance or perhaps some place to hide. She heard a noise above her and realized that it wouldn't be long before Alan would come down the escalator steps and shoot her.

She was not going to let that happen.

Just to the left of the glass doors she spotted a large ashtray, a three-foot-tall, heavy, ornamental thing with sand in the top. Melissa shuffled over to the ashtray and pulled it away from the wall. She wrapped both arms around it, bent at the knees and stood up, lifting the ashtray off the floor. It was heavy, but she managed to carry it over in front of the doors. Balancing on her good, right leg, she raised her hurt left leg up and propped the ashtray on her knee. The pain was horrible and almost immediately she started feeling dizzy. *Don't lose it now, girl,* she said to herself.

She slid her right hand down underneath the ashtray and gripped it tightly. Moving her left hand to the top, she lifted the heavy ashtray up off her leg and hurled it into the locked, glass doors.

Half-way down the escalator stairs, Alan heard the loud sound of glass breaking. He paused for a moment and listened. He waited, expecting to hear a loud ringing or other alarm noise. Nothing. *That doesn't mean there isn't a silent alarm,* he told himself.

Fuck it, he thought. He had to take care of Melissa before he could worry about anything else. He knew she had been injured in the motorcycle crash, and he was surprised that she'd been able to hobble this far.

He reached the bottom of the stairs and gave his eyes a minute to adjust to the dark. Alan knew this building was nothing more than a ten-story parking garage, and figured Melissa would come down here to try to get away. Alan hadn't been in the Underground more than once or twice and he had never traveled very far into the walkway. All he knew was that it connected with most of the other downtown buildings, and snaked underneath the city like roots spreading out from a giant tree.

Alan's eyes scanned the darkened area near the elevators, making sure she wasn't hiding somewhere in the shadows. His attention was drawn to a pile of broken glass on the other side of the room. He walked over to the entrance to the Underground and saw the large hole left by the heavy ashtray.

Each of the major buildings in downtown Houston was connected to the pedestrian Underground. The buildings had, in their bowels, a shopping area that included restaurants, dry cleaners, insurance companies, travel agencies, even a few retailers. Downtown workers could go underground to find all the basic services, and if they wanted to cross over to one of the other buildings, they could avoid traffic or bad weather by using one of the narrow, connecting tunnels that ran underneath the streets. The entire pedestrian Underground system covered some twenty-seven miles.

Melissa leaned against the wall and held her breath, listening for the sound of footsteps behind her. She had limped about two hundred yards into the Underground before coming to the first of the connecting tunnels. She knew she had to get out of the wide, open area she was in and try to lose her pursuer in the maze of the Underground system.

She had turned into a connecting tunnel that was no

wider than an office hallway, maybe five feet across with a ceiling about seven feet high.

If I can get up to another building, Melissa thought, *I can get back on the street and maybe head for the police station.*

There was very little light in the narrow tunnel, only a small row of dime-sized lights at ankle level along the edge of the floor. As she limped along, one shoulder was bumping against the wall, the jarring feeling working to keep her alert and help pace her movement. The enclosed space made every noise, from her breathing to the clomping and shuffling of her cowboy boots, sound much too loud.

Melissa knew that it would be very easy to get turned around in the Underground, and she vowed to pay attention and keep track of her escape route. She would spend the next ten minutes trying to alter her direction to lose Alan, she decided. After that, she would walk in one direction until she found an exit up to street level.

I can't believe this is happening to me, she thought. *Traipsing around the deserted bowels of the city, with my own father-in-law trying to kill me!*

Why didn't I see this coming? she asked herself. *Am I that naive?*

She exited out the connecting tunnel into another wide, mall-like area. There were several small restaurants, a dry cleaners and an art gallery. She stopped to catch her breath and listen for the sound of her pursuer. She let her body slide down to the floor, collapsing in a heap on the cool, beige tile.

She was sitting on the floor near the art gallery, and she

leaned her head back and looked in the display window. There was some kind of African art exhibit behind the glass. THE TRIBAL CUSTOMS OF THE WATUSI, the banner read. Large, evil-looking carved masks lined one wall of the display, while another wall formed a backdrop for a life-sized African warrior. The figure was a tall, black man dressed to the nines in colorful battle garb with an elaborate face mask. *That's some fearsome warrior,* Melissa thought, noticing the long spear the mannequin held in a rigid hand.

You have to replace your fear with determination, she told herself. *You're not going to let him catch you. You will get away!*

She knew that her best defense was to keep moving, keep twisting and turning inside the Underground where no one would be able to follow. If she stayed calm and kept moving, she'd find an escape back up to the street.

Melissa heard a loud metallic sound behind her. It sounded like it was coming from the other end of the small connecting tunnel. *Oh fuck,* she thought, *Alan's found me already!*

She knew that there wasn't enough time to make a run for it. She couldn't move fast enough to get out of sight before he exited the tunnel.

To her left was a McDonald's restaurant, all locked and gated for the night. On the outside of the restaurant was a large wooden trash can, the kind with a door marked PUSH where customers can dump their garbage into a concealed container.

She could hear footsteps getting closer, and she limped

over to the trash bin. Underneath the PUSH were two double doors. She opened them and saw a large plastic garbage container inside. She pulled the top off the container, held the top to her chest and climbed in. She pulled the outside doors closed behind her and sat quietly.

I'm sitting in a plastic trash can in the dark, she told herself. *This is not at all what I had in mind. I'm supposed to have a great marriage, a wonderful career, some kids, grandkids, the whole nine yards. I do* not *want to get shot while hiding in a trash can!*

Outside she could hear the sound of footsteps nearby. It was hard to tell but it sounded like they were coming closer. *Oh God, please no, don't let him look in here. Don't let him find me.*

She held her breath, afraid that exhaling would give away her position. The footsteps stopped just outside the trash bin. He won't look in here, she thought. He won't. Why would he look in a trash can?

Light flooded into the darkness, as the doors to the trash bin opened. She squeezed her eyes shut and waited for the sound of gunfire.

'Okay, young lady, come on out of there.'

It was a man's voice, but it was high-pitched and didn't belong to Alan Stakeman.

She opened her eyes and looked up. There was a very young, very skinny security guard standing outside, motioning to her to come out.

Alan didn't have any idea where he was. He'd walked well inside the main walkway of the Underground, careful to search out every hidden corner and shadowy hiding place along the way. He must have gone a full quarter mile down the wide, relatively bright walkway before he decided that Melissa had turned off into one of the tunnels.

He remembered passing three tunnels leading off to his right. He'd simply backtrack and search them all, one at a time. He knew that Melissa was injured, probably moving much more slowly than he was and having to stop frequently to rest.

This is a real pain in the ass, he thought, *having to chase the bitch down like this. I ought to take my time when I find her. Maybe shoot her in the stomach and let her die slowly.*

Of course, he knew he couldn't afford to hang around like that. The break-in at the Underground entrance was sure to attract attention eventually. And while he hadn't yet seen any sign of video cameras, he had to be careful not to leave other evidence that he'd been there.

He backtracked quickly, entering the first tunnel pathway that he came to, which was actually the third one he'd passed on the way in. He walked in a brisk clip, keeping a sharp eye out for any movement up ahead. He glanced back behind frequently, and stopped every thirty seconds or so to listen for the sounds of other movement.

Under different circumstances this might have been fun. *Maybe I'll take up deer hunting when this is all over with.*

Why do they hire such idiots to be security guards? Melissa thought.

She had gone through the whole story twice, making sure the young guard took note of her bloodied elbow and still-bleeding leg. She realized that she must look pretty silly, leaning against the trash bin with torn, bloodied clothing and a motorcycle helmet she refused to remove. After listening closely to her spiel, the guard's only comment was, 'You ain't supposed to be down here after closing...'

It was all she could do to keep from slapping him. 'Don't you have a gun?' she asked, not seeing one.

'We aren't allowed to carry weapons until we've been with the company for six months.'

'Jesus fucking Christ,' she muttered.

'There's no reason to take the Lord's name in vain,' the guard said.

She pointed to the walkie-talkie on the guard's belt. 'What about the radio? Can't you use your radio and call somebody? This man is trying to kill me!'

The guard shrugged. 'You know, you keep saying somebody's trying to kill you, but I ain't seen nobody down here 'cept you. And all this broken glass and stuff. You admitted that you did all that.'

She was about to grab the radio off his belt when a voice behind her interrupted.

'Ah, Melissa, there you are.'

She didn't turn around. She didn't move.

The security guard took his blue eyes off Melissa and looked back toward the voice.

'Do you know this lady?' the guard asked.

'That's him. Don't go over there,' Melissa whispered, still afraid to look behind her.

The guard glanced at her for a moment and started heading down the walkway.

Alan knew he had to ascertain whether or not the police were on their way before he took care of the guard. He had heard Melissa and the guard talking, and stuffed the pistol in his back pocket before announcing his presence.

'I'm awfully glad you found her. We've been chasing her all over this city. You see, she's my daughter-in-law and, well, she doesn't want to go back to the hospital. I hope we won't have to get the police involved in this.'

'Hospital?' the guard asked. He looked over his shoulder toward Melissa.

Alan pointed to his temple with his index finger. 'Yes, she's been in and out of the hospital for some time now.'

Alan held out his right hand and the guard took it. 'I'm Alan Stakeman, a businessman here in Houston. We've taken her all over the country for treatment, but right now she lives at a private hospital over in the Medical Center. Once a week, I take her out for the evening. You know, catch a movie, go out to eat. Ordinarily she's very sweet, and doesn't make a fuss. But for some reason this time she didn't want to go back. She ran away from me earlier, and, well, I just hope she hasn't caused any trouble.'

The guard eyed him suspiciously. 'She broke into the Underground. There's glass all over the place.'

Alan waved his hand. 'No problem. I'll be happy to pay the damages. I guess she must have set off all kinds of alarms?'

The guard shook his head. 'No. Now normally she would

have, but they're in the process of installing some new computer software, and the system has been shut off for a while. I just happened to be on patrol and spotted her running through here.'

'So,' Alan said, 'the police aren't on their way over here?'

The guard snickered and patted his walkie-talkie. 'Oh, no. Not unless I call them.'

Alan smiled. 'That's great.'

Alan reached behind him and pulled out the .357. The guard saw the gun and his mouth dropped open. Alan shot him once in the chest and watched his body fly several feet backwards.

When Alan looked up, Melissa was gone.

35

Melissa was terrified.

Alan knew almost precisely where she was inside the maze, and with her injury, she couldn't move fast enough to put any real distance between them.

You might be able to hide for a few minutes, she thought, *but it won't take him long to catch up. Stop being scared and fight back!*

Melissa made it to the nearest connecting tunnel while Alan was busy with the security guard. She was moving at her top speed, almost out of the other side of the tunnel when she heard the noise.

Boom!

The gunshot reverberated through the tunnel, so loud it made her jump. *That one was the guard – the next one's for you, girl.*

She limped through the short tunnel and exited out into another walkway. She looked around quickly for a place to hide. There was construction going on in the area, and there were building materials and some paint cans stacked near one wall.

He'll be here any second.

She looked down the long walkway and realized it was at least a hundred yards to the next connecting tunnel.

He'll get me before I can reach it, she thought.

The darkest spot in the room was in a corner, near a jut in the wall between a dry cleaners and a travel agency. She moved quickly into the corner and pressed her back flat against the wall. It was quite a bit darker there, though she would probably be visible if he looked directly at her. Her only chance was if he walked by and never looked over here.

It's not enough just to hide, Melissa thought. *You've got to slow him down, find a way to equal the odds.*

But what did she have to fight with? There was nothing of any use in the construction area. Just a few long pieces of plywood and some paint.

Christ, I've got some boards and he's got a gun!

Off in the distance, she heard footsteps heading her way. She forced herself to regulate her breathing, ensuring that no noise would be coming from her hiding place.

What if he sees me right away? she asked herself. *I'm trapped here in the corner, and he could take me out with one easy shot.*

She had to slow him down. Her hand touched the smooth, hard plastic of her motorcycle helmet, as she heard the footsteps coming closer.

She hoped he would be moving fast and would pass her on his way down the walkway. If he did that, then maybe she could sneak back out the way she came in.

The footsteps were almost upon her now and she braced

herself. The corner in which she was hiding was about ten feet back from the center of the walkway, maybe twenty feet across to the opposite wall.

The footsteps slowed as he exited the tunnel, heading into the larger room. She didn't move.

First she saw a shadow, then Alan's profile appeared around the corner. He was holding the gun in front of him in his right hand. He took a half dozen steps past her and she prayed for him to keep going.

Then he stopped.

From her point of view she could see everything his eyes were seeing. He was scanning the room, starting at the far left wall and looking in all the hiding places within his line of sight. In seconds, he would turn and be looking right at her.

Alan was almost dead center in the room, his body was turned slightly away from her.

Time to take the bull by the horns, Melissa thought.

She crouched down slightly, pressing both hands flat against the smooth wall of the Underground and took a deep breath.

She pushed herself off the wall with all her force. Her body traveled the few feet between them before he had noticed the movement and had time to spin around. She remembered how the Houston Oilers did it and when she was almost upon him, she lowered her head and plowed into his side, helmet first.

Alan let out a loud groan as her motorcycle helmet blasted him in the lower part of his rib cage. She was growling like a wild animal as all of her weight drove him down hard to the floor. She hoped she could knock the gun from his hand, grab the weapon and empty it into his body.

Melissa landed on top of Alan and immediately rolled off on to her feet. She looked back and saw that, somehow, he'd managed to hold on to the gun, though he was writhing in agony on the concrete floor.

That will slow the motherfucker down, Melissa thought.

She immediately took off and started heading back out the nearest connecting tunnel.

Garth stood inside his father's private office in the Stakeman & Son suite. He looked around the room, feeling like a stranger who had entered someone's private domain.

Garth walked over to the large window to look at the downtown Houston skyline. The rain had picked up again, blowing in from the north, with fat raindrops violently pelting the thick glass before him.

His mind was still reeling with everything Melissa had said. 'Did you know your father has a safety deposit box, in *your* name, at a bank in Diboll, Texas? That must be where he has been keeping the gun.'

As much as he didn't want to face the truth, Garth had a sick feeling that she was right. He didn't want to believe it, though if he was honest with himself, he would have to admit that for several weeks now, he too had been growing suspicious.

He came up to the offices, wanting to be close to some of his father's things, hoping that somehow, that closeness would give him some answer. Anything except the obvious conclusion.

Garth closed up the office and got on the elevator. He pushed the button for the parking garage and tried to understand what was happening.

Melissa is right, he thought. *He murdered Justine. He probably killed Farmer, and God knows who else.*

He couldn't believe he was having those thoughts. After all these years, all the emotion he had invested in that man, to find out now that it was all a big lie was more than he could stand.

The elevator doors opened into the One Shell Plaza parking garage. Garth walked over to his car and got in.

What's important now is Melissa, he thought, *and doing anything I can to make it up to her. I can't believe I've been so stupid. I can't believe she stuck with me.*

Garth pulled out into the deserted downtown streets, pointing his car in the direction of Melissa's studio.

When she'd called him at the house, Melissa had asked him to meet her and Sara over at the studio. They would talk it through, she'd said, and decide what to do.

Garth turned on the radio and the car filled with soft jazz music. He drove slowly through the rain, lost in his thoughts as he cruised on automatic pilot.

His reverie was broken a few blocks later when his car stopped at a red light at the corner of Travis Street and McKinney Street.

Through the rain a half block in front of him, he saw an old model Harley-Davidson lying on its twisted side in front of the Lone Star Tower. Twenty feet away, a black Lincoln Continental was parked at a weird angle, with two tires up on the curb.

Garth immediately recognized the vehicles, and felt the hairs stand up on the back of his neck. He gunned his Lexus through the red light and skidded to a stop in front of the Lincoln.

Pain shot through Alan's body like volts of electricity. It took him several minutes to catch his breath, and he knew it was Melissa and her goddamn motorcycle helmet that were responsible for all this pain.

Alan touched his ribs on his right side with his left hand, even the slightest pressure causing another jolt of pain to shoot across his chest.

'She broke my ribs,' he said out loud. 'She broke my fucking ribs!'

He lay on his back and looked at the ceiling. It was very painful to move, but he knew he couldn't stay there for long. Melissa was obviously one determined woman. Give her enough time and she would find her way out of here and up to the street.

Any movement which used Alan's abdominal muscles brought an immediate, intense stab of pain under his right arm. He gritted his teeth and managed to roll over on to his stomach. He used his legs and hands to push himself up off the floor, finally getting to a sitting position before stopping to catch his breath.

Off in the distance he heard the sound of glass breaking.

What is that fucking bitch doing now? he wondered.

He knew that there wasn't a street exit in the adjoining walkway. That was where Alan and the security guard had had their meeting.

Fire alarm, he thought. *Oh, fuck. What if she's breaking the glass to set off a fire alarm?*

Alan struggled to his feet, almost vomiting from the pain of his broken ribs. *Shit,* he thought, *with these ribs, I might not be able to walk any faster than she can!*

He wiped the sweat off of his gun hand and headed for the tunnel. He stopped to listen at the entrance, then shuffled along the darkened pathway, his left hand holding the tender spot on his right side, the gun held firmly out in front of him as he moved.

She could be talking to the fucking fire department right now, he told himself.

Alan remembered the radio on the security guard's belt, and wanted to kick himself for not taking it off him.

Almost at the end of the tunnel he reminded himself to be careful this time. Another blow from that fucking helmet and he might not be able to walk.

At the end of the tunnel he stopped, carefully peeking out into the large walkway. He looked to the right and saw nothing. To the left he saw the body of the security guard, a huge dark stain on the light, concrete floor underneath him. Alan walked over and pulled the walkie-talkie off the guard's belt, smashing it against the wall before moving on.

Alan's eyes moved across the businesses within his line of sight. His eyes stopped on the window of an art gallery. Huge shards of glass were scattered around the front of the store, a large hole left in the display window.

'You got a thing about breaking glass, huh Melissa?' he yelled, making his voice sound angry and frightening.

He walked over to the front of the art gallery. It wasn't a

very big store, he realized. There couldn't be very many places to hide.

His ribs were really hurting now, and he could feel an extra stab with each step. He walked down the front of the store and paused to catch his breath. He put his face up against the window, looking around inside to try to spot his prey. The interior of the store was dark, though something told him that she was hiding inside, scared and desperate.

Her attack may have given her confidence, he thought. *Be cautious, take it slow, and don't mess up again.*

He couldn't see anything from outside the store and walked back down to the display window. He used his gun barrel to tap away some of the glass around the hole, making the opening larger. He took one step up into the display window, glancing at the mannequin of the African warrior, and moved forward until he was completely inside the store.

'It's all over, Melissa,' he said. 'You don't have anywhere to go. You might as well come out.'

There was no response. Not that he expected one.

At least the store would be easy to search. An art gallery didn't have rows of clothing, or changing rooms like an apparel shop might have. Alan stepped down from the display window, moving carefully on to the floor level.

He stood still for a minute, his eyes moving very slowly down the nearest side wall. There were several pieces of sculpture and free-standing work, but nothing remotely in the shape of a woman, or large enough for her to hide behind.

Across the room he saw what looked like the sales

counter and a small desk. He could make out a dark shape on the floor next to the desk, undoubtedly Melissa crouching down. He raised the gun and pointed toward the shape.

'C'mon out. I promise I won't hurt you.'

There was no movement from the shape, and he decided to shoot now and ask questions later. He took careful aim.

'Dad – what are you doing?'

Alan whirled around and saw Garth stepping through the broken glass in the front door of the store.

'Put down the gun,' Garth said.

Alan glanced back over his shoulder toward where Melissa was hiding. He was holding the .357 in his right hand, with his left hand across his chest holding on to the broken ribs.

'What the fuck are you doing here?' Alan said.

Garth took a few steps closer. In response, Alan raised the gun and pointed it at Garth's chest.

Garth stopped. 'I don't want anyone else to get hurt. Why don't you just give me the gun and let's get out of here?'

'You shouldn't have come down here. Why are you here?'

'I want to help you.'

'You, want to help me?' Alan said. 'You couldn't help yourself out of a wet paper bag.'

'I care about you, Dad.'

Alan laughed, but the giggles caused new, sharp pains in his side. 'You *care* about me. Do you think that means something to me?'

Garth held out his hands. 'I hope it does. Can't we jus talk for a minute?'

Alan's eyes were locked on Garth. 'You want to talk What do you want to talk about? Your obsession with bein close to me? The way you pushed your wife away? Or how about your mother? You want to talk about Mommie' How Mommie used to jack you off? How she taught you to eat her pussy?'

Garth looked stunned. 'You knew about that?'

Alan nodded. 'Of course I knew. She told me.'

'And you didn't do anything to try and stop her?'

Alan shrugged. 'I killed her, didn't I? That sure as shi stopped her.'

'I want to help you. You're in trouble.'

'There's nothing going to happen to me, Garth. I'm in the driver's seat. Fishbein thinks you're the killer. And when she comes down here, she'll find Melissa's dead body, and you, over in the corner, a suicide victim.'

Garth shook his head. He started walking toward him 'Please Dad, give me the gun.'

'I wouldn't do that if I were you.'

Garth kept coming closer as Alan again raised the gun to fire.

Melissa had been hiding behind the false wall in the display in the art gallery's window. From the outside of the store she would have been completely concealed, hidden from view by a seven-foot-tall portable wall, upon which were displayed a number of African masks and artefacts.

Now! she told herself.

She jumped down and charged. She had a tight grip on the African warrior's spear she'd removed from the display. Alan, who had been looking straight at Garth, fired the gun as soon as he heard the noise behind him.

Then Alan spun around to deal with the rear attack but he was too late. Melissa lunged forward with the spear in front of her, pushed the weapon into his chest, the blade penetrating between the fourth and fifth rib, near the center of his torso.

Alan screamed and immediately dropped the gun.

The spear entered his chest near the spot already injured by her helmet attack. As he was falling, she gave the spear another hard push, driving it even deeper. She heard a whoosh of air as he collapsed on the floor.

She crawled several feet away from him across the room, not knowing if the spear would deliver a killing blow.

Alan was lying on his back, his hands pawing at the spear, its long shaft protruding three feet or more out from his chest. Blood was gushing from the wound, and she saw a small line of blood appear from the corner of his mouth.

Alan was making unintelligible animal noises, groaning and grunting as he struggled to pull free. His face was contorted in pain.

He grew weak. His hands fell away from the spear.

Melissa realized that she was crying. Alan's breathing became irregular and she heard a strange gurgling noise come from deep inside his chest.

Garth! she thought.

She unsnapped her motorcycle helmet and took it off.

She looked toward the front of the store and saw Garth lying on his stomach near the broken glass.

She ran over to Garth and looked down at him. At first she didn't think he was alive, then she saw his back moving with labored breathing.

She bent down on the floor and put her hand on his head. She gently eased him over on to his back.

A dark stain was growing across the front of his shirt, a few inches down from the center of his chest.

The gunshot wound looked serious. She ran to call an ambulance.

Epilogue

Melissa hadn't slept for much of the last forty-eight hours. It was hard to get much sleep when the nurses came into the hospital room every twenty minutes. They were monitoring Garth closely, taking his temperature, checking the many tubes coming out of his body.

It had been two days since the battle with Alan, and during that time, she had stayed in Garth's hospital room waiting, praying that he'd pull through.

The surgeon had told her that the bullet was a mere sixteenth of an inch from severing a major artery. If that had happened, he would have died of internal bleeding in less than a minute. As it was, the bullet had crashed through Garth's liver, careened off one of his kidneys, and lodged in his spinal cord. They'd have to wait to see if he was paralyzed.

Melissa was pretty banged up herself. Her left arm was bandaged for the bad scrape on her elbow. She had a fractured tibia in her left leg from the motorcycle crash and was wearing a cast from the knee down.

But she thought little of her own injuries. Garth had endured an eight-hour operation, and hadn't regained consciousness since he came out of the recovery room.

There was a knock on the door and she looked around. Bob and Ellen Quintell came into the room, each carrying a huge flower arrangement. Melissa got up from her chair and limped over to greet them. She gave Bob a big hug and Ellen a kiss on the cheek.

Texas Bob set his flowers down and looked down at Garth. 'How's our boy doing?'

Melissa felt herself tearing up. 'His vital signs are good. But he hasn't been awake since the surgery.'

Bob walked over to the bed and put his hand on Garth's shoulder and gently shook it. 'Hey, young man. You've been sleeping long enough. Time to get up.'

Melissa smiled. She knew Texas Bob really cared about Garth.

Ellen Quintell spoke. 'How are you feeling, my dear? You look pretty banged up yourself.'

Melissa nodded. 'I'm okay. Not worried—'

Bob interrupted. 'Hey, Garth. Welcome back.'

Melissa looked down and saw Garth's eyes slowly opening. She rushed back to the bed and grabbed his hand, kissing his fingers while she played with his hair.

'Hey man,' Melissa said, tears rolling out of the corners of her eyes. 'Glad you came back.'

He had to struggle to speak. He had tubes running out of his nose. 'Where am I?'

Melissa wiped the tears off her cheeks. 'You're at Hermann Hospital. Room 786. Houston, Texas. United States of America.'

He managed a small smile, though it looked crooked vith all the tubes and such.

'Where's Dad?'

Melissa leaned close and kissed his face. 'He didn't make t.'

Garth closed his eyes and nodded. For a moment Melissa hought he was going to drift back to unconsciousness.

Then he opened his eyes and looked up at Texas Bob. Hello, Bob. What happened in the election?'

Texas Bob took his hand. 'You haven't heard?'

Garth shook his head.

'Well, from now on, you can call me Senator Texas Bob.'

Garth managed another smile. 'Really? Congratulations. Vhat was the final count?'

Ellen walked over next to Bob and smiled at Garth.

'They recounted the ballots three times,' Bob said. 'In he official results, I won by forty-eight votes.'

'A landslide,' Garth said.

'Yeah, once you get up and around, you and Melissa ave to come to Washington. We'll make those lobbyists uy us the most expensive dinner in town!'

Melissa brushed back his blond hair. 'Detective Fishbein ame by. She told me to give you her condolences, and let ou know that everything's alright.'

Garth looked up at her. 'I owe you an apology.'

She pulled his hand into her lap. 'You don't owe me nything.'

'Yes, I do. I've been stupid. A jerk. I was so focused on Dad, and my own problems, that I ignored you. Can you ver forgive me?'

'I love you, Garth. I just want us to be together.'

He stared into her eyes, and began crying. A nurse cam into the room, noticed that Garth was responding, an turned to go find a doctor.

'When I get out of here, we're going to take a tri somewhere. Maybe a cruise around the world. I reall don't care where we go, as long as I'm with you.'

Melissa leaned forward and kissed his cheek. Sh carefully worked around the tubes until she could giv Garth some kind of a hug.

A doctor and several nurses came through the doo They looked down at the couple, smiled and turned aroun and left.

Texas Bob patted Melissa on the back and he and Elle slipped out of the room.

They were the only two people in the world. Nothing els existed except this moment. It wasn't the end – it was just beginning.

More Suspenseful Fiction from Headline Feature

TESTAMENT

David Morrell

'TERRORS AS INSISTENT AS A SCREAM ON A STILL NIGHT, AS A SERIES OF KICKS IN THE STOMACH . . . BRILLIANTLY TOLD' *Sunday Telegraph*

Reuben Bourne is an ordinary freelance writer in an ordinary American city. Then he publishes an article that exposes a fanatical underground network ready and able to kill anyone on command.

Suddenly Bourne becomes their target. With his family he faces a terrible vengeance of poison, fire and bullets. Their only hope is to flee the city, to take to the mountains in a headlong race for survival against all odds . . .

Since its first publication, TESTAMENT *has established itself as a contemporary thriller classic, praised as one of the most influential novels of terror, translated into numerous languages and published to critical acclaim throughout the world.*

'A GRIM AND GRIPPING NOVEL OF IMPLACABLE EVIL AND THE PURSUIT OF SURVIVAL' *Publishers Weekly*

'MORRELL STANDS HEAD AND SHOULDERS ABOVE HIS CONTEMPORARIES' *National Review*

FICTION / THRILLER 0 7472 3669 0

More Compelling Fiction from Headline Feature

JOHN T. LESCROART

HARD EVIDENCE

'A GRIPPING COURTROOM DRAMA . . . COMPELLING, CREDIBLE' *Publishers Weekly*

'Compulsively readable, a dense and involving saga of big-city crime and punishment' *San Francisco Chronicle*

Assistant D.A. Dismas Hardy has seen too much of life outside a courtroom to know that the truth isn't always as simple as it should be. Which is why some of his ultra-ambitious colleagues don't rate his prosecuting instincts as highly as their own. So when he finds himself on the trail of a murdered Silicon Valley billionaire he seizes the opportunity to emerge from beneath a mountain of minor cases and make the case his own. Before long he is prosecuting San Francisco's biggest murder trial, the accused a quiet, self-contained Japanese call girl with an impressive list of prominent clients. A woman Hardy has a sneaking, sinking suspicion might just be innocent . . .

'Turowesque, with the plot bouncing effortlessly between the courtroom and the intraoffice battle among prosecutors . . . The writing is excellent and the dialogue crackles' *Booklist*

'A blockbuster courtroom drama . . . As in *Presumed Innocent*, the courtroom battles are so keen that you almost forget there's a mystery, too. But Lescroart's laid-back, soft-shoe approach to legal intrigue is all his own' *Kirkus*

'John Lescroart is a terrific writer and this is one terrific book' Jonathan Kellerman

'An intricate plot, a great locale, wonderfully colourful characters and taut courtroom drama . . . Highly recommended' *Library Journal*

'Breathtaking' *Los Angeles Times*

FICTION / THRILLER 0 7472 4332 8

More Crime Fiction from Headline Feature

MILK AND HONEY

A PETER DECKER WHODUNNIT

FAYE KELLERMAN

'Faye Kellerman establishes herself as a unique voice in crime fiction. The central character of Peter Decker is unforgettable' James Ellroy, author of *The Black Dahlia*

Sergeant Peter Decker is driving through a modern housing estate late one night when he discovers an abandoned toddler wearing blood-stained pyjamas. No one claims the curly-headed girl and Decker and his partner, Marge Dunn, resolve to find her parents as soon as possible.

Noticing bee-stings all over the child's arm, they go on a hunt that takes them to a honey farm set in the barren scrubland surrounding Los Angeles. It's a tough landscape, the people work hard and have little time for city folk, so the two detectives aren't surprised when no welcoming party is there to receive them. Nothing, though, has prepared them for the incredible stonewalling from the locals, nor for the grisly sight that greets them in the farmhouse. But Decker and Dunn are professionals to the core and, delving deeper, find themselves stirring up a gruesome mystery far more lethal than the ordinary hornets' nest . . .

Some reviews for Faye Kellerman:

'A tour de force that shouldn't be missed . . . a stellar performance' *Publishers Weekly*

'Excellent story of rape and murder' *Time Out*

'Irresistibly plotted' *Financial Times*

FICTION / CRIME 0 7472 3430 2